THE SU1

The V

LILLY MIRREN

Black
Lab Press

Copyright © 2020 by Lilly Mirren

All rights reserved.

No part of this book may be reproduced in any form or by any electronic or mechanical means, including information storage and retrieval systems, without written permission from the author, except for the use of brief quotations in a book review.

For my family

THE WARATAH INN SERIES

The Waratah Inn
One Summer in Italy
The Summer Sisters

Christmas at the Waratah Inn
(a standalone novel)

❧ 1 ❧

OCTOBER 1943

ABRUZZI APENNINES, ITALY

His toes were cold. The rest of him was warm, although he felt some pain in his ribs. Scratch that, a lot of pain. Something was poking into him, or had bruised him, he couldn't tell. All he knew was that his tongue felt as though it was plastered to the dry roof of his mouth.

It was dark.

Maybe his eyes were shut. They seemed to be shut. There wasn't even a dot of light to be seen. He should try opening them.

With extreme effort, his eyelids lifted, and a dull ache followed in their wake. Had he drunk too much whiskey? Where was he?

With slow deliberation he let his eyes wander around the room, then blinked and tried again. His eyelids seemed to scratch dry trails on his eyeballs. It wasn't completely dark after all. A dull light emitted from a fireplace on one wall, and from a black potbellied stove in the centre of the room. There was a small, square table against one wall, along with two wooden chairs. A square frame hung above the table, and on the opposite wall, a window, shuttered by a pair of simple, pale curtains.

Another table, this one longer, was pushed up to the wall by the door. It held an array of pots, pans, bowls, a single jug, and several items of food, including a jar of olives, a piece of cheese partially wrapped in a cloth, and a brace of onions that hung above it all.

What was that smell?

A scent of something delicious, whatever was simmering on the stove, mixed with the faint aroma of animal hide and manure. His nose wrinkled, even as his stomach clenched with hunger.

A woman's voice made him turn his head, then he grimaced at the pain that shot up one side of his neck. She murmured something in a language he didn't understand. He focused on her face as best he could, his eyes taking a few moments to find their mark.

She was beautiful. Young too, though he couldn't say how young. Maybe around his age. How old was that?

His mind searched for the answer, gave up, and turned back to examining the woman.

Deep brown eyes, long, brown hair caught up in a braid of some kind with wisps falling around her tanned face. Her lips were pulled into a warm, if somewhat shy, smile. She wore a white blouse beneath a dark-coloured dress, and an apron tied around both.

"Hi..." he rasped. The sound that emitted from his mouth startled him. He'd lost his voice.

She shushed him then, stroking the side of his face with her fingertips. "Shhh..."

When he was quiet, she asked him a question, but he

didn't know what she was saying, only the inflection of her voice and the way she stopped to watch his response indicated she wanted something from him. Some kind of answer.

"Uh...I don't know what you're saying," was what he tried to say, but the words came out as a hiss and growl.

He wriggled his fingers and found they moved well enough. Beneath him was some kind of mat. It wasn't padded, simply a thin sleeping mat made of some kind of fabric. Under that appeared to be a hard, dirt floor. The room he was in was built from large stones. It was a spacious room, and there was a doorway at either end of it, but both doors were shut.

Was he a prisoner? Or did he know this woman? He couldn't tell. Though he vaguely recalled seeing her face before, as if through a kind of fog. Perhaps lying on this very mat, he'd interacted with her before. At least, the idea seemed true to him. He remembered another face as well, a man's. But that man didn't seem to be in the room now.

The woman was still talking, but he'd lost interest, unable to understand what she was saying. He should get up. Should leave. Though, where he'd go, he couldn't say.

He shifted his weight on the mat and leaned on one elbow. Pain erupted in his side, shooting down through his leg. He gasped, blinking as his vision swam.

"Shar-lee," she said.

He inhaled a slow breath.

"Shar-lee," she said again, nodding.

His eyes narrowed. What was she trying to tell him?

She smiled, pointed one finger to the ground beside him. He stared. There was something silver in the dirt, on top of a pile of folded, stained clothes. He picked it up with a groan of pain and held it close to his eyes. It was hard to see in the dull light.

A dirty string, with what looked like reddish rust

colouring it in places, held together two small, silver discs. The discs were engraved with something.

He squinted. Some sort of identification number, involving a combination of letters and numbers. And a name. "Charlie Jackson." The name had been etched by hand, at least it appeared so. It was crooked and poorly executed, but clear enough to read.

"Charlie?" he said, holding the tags up towards her.

She nodded. "*Sì*, Shar-lee! *Ben Fatto*."

The woman seemed very pleased with his efforts. He wondered what it meant. She pointed to him, her finger pressing into his chest. "Shar-lee."

Were the tags his? He tested the name in his mind. Charlie Jackson — did he recognise it? The name didn't sound familiar. Then again, he couldn't recall in that moment what his name might be. It seemed strange, it was as though his mind was straining, searching every possible synaptic pathway, yet nothing was there. He'd forgotten his own name.

Maybe he *was* Charlie Jackson.

His throat tightened. "Charlie," he repeated.

She grinned. Then, removed her finger from on top of his chest and placed it against her own. "Maria."

He nodded, finding it hard to breath. "Maria." His voice still sounded as though he'd swallowed a wasp but was returning bit by bit every time he tried using it.

Her head bobbed in approval, then she stood and hurried over to the stove. A pot bubbled on top of it, with a spoon sticking out of the top beneath a lopsided lid. She took off the lid and stirred the contents of the pot.

In that moment, Charlie didn't care what his name was, or what he'd forgotten. All he wanted was whatever he could find in that pot. His stomach tightened into a knot and he swallowed hard.

"Hungry..." he whispered. "Thirsty too."

She looked over her shoulder with a smile. He almost groaned at the look on her face. She didn't understand a word he'd said that much was clear. Still, she was making food, perhaps it was meant for him, or perhaps he was her prisoner. There was no way for him to know. He lifted a hand and studied it, no ropes or chains. Nothing bound his feet either. He glanced at the door, it was slightly ajar and didn't seem to be locked. The light in her eyes, the smile on her face — he didn't appear to be her hostage.

One hand pressed to his stomach, he pulled back a thin blanket that covered him. A pale piece of fabric was wrapped around his torso, stained with dots of blood. His blood. Not recently shed, but old, dark.

He pressed his side and winced. It hurt, but the pain was dull, not like a recent injury. Flashes of memories flitted through his thoughts. He'd woken up here before, his mind in a fog, seeing the woman's face, feeling water pressed to his lips, drinking. He'd been in this room for some time.

The woman carried a small, round bowl to him, and knelt on the floor beside him. She held up the bowl with a dip of her head, then scooped some of its contents onto a spoon and towards his mouth. It smelled delicious. Some kind of meat, with chunks of potatoes, soft vegetables, in a broth. He opened his mouth and she pushed in the spoon. Flavours exploded across his tongue as his stomach growled with hunger.

While he ate, the woman kept up a steady stream of chatter in her language. He caught a word here or there that made sense. "Charlie", "*ferito*", and "*pistola*". *Pistola* he understood. That was close enough to his own language. The rest of what she'd said sounded like utter gibberish. There'd been a battle, it seemed. She enacted some kind of scene as she spoke, pretended to fire a weapon, grasped at her side.

He'd been shot. Why? And where was he? More importantly, who was he? It seemed his name was Charlie, but the term didn't spark any recognition within him. Still, he might as well use the name for now, since he couldn't think of any other name to use.

Maria set the bowl on the ground to fetch a wooden cup with some kind of milk in it. Charlie glanced at the white liquid, then as it filled his mouth and ran down his throat, he recognised it as sheep's milk. He'd drunk it before. How did he know that? Something of his memory must be returning if he was able to recognise the milk, or maybe the woman had told him somehow during one of his previous bouts of consciousness. He shook his head, confusion making it spin.

Before his bowl of stew was empty, a man strode through the outside door and into the house. He stood framed by a rectangle of dull light that made Charlie blink as it lifted the room out of darkness. Cold air filtered into the structure, Charlie shivered and tugged his blanket up to his neck.

The man stared at Charlie, then directed his attention to Maria, speaking quick and low. She nodded, stood, and returned to the stove to dip spoonsful of the soup into another two bowls. The man shut the door behind him, disappeared through the door at the other end of the room, into what seemed to be an adjoining room, then returned without his coat, his shirt sleeves rolled up.

Maria set their bowls on a small, rough-hewn table against one wall. The two of them sat together, eating, talking. They didn't pay Charlie any more attention, so instead he focused on the silver tags and the folded clothes beneath them. He fingered the edges of the material, a pocket, a seam, the clothing looked like a military issued uniform.

Even the small amount of movement, eating the meal, drinking from a cup, watching, thinking — all of it had tired Charlie so that he seemed to have to gasp for each breath.

His eyes blinked shut, then opened again even as he struggled to focus. His hand fell away from the seam of the clothing he was studying, and onto the floor beside him. He closed his eyes again and drifted into a deep slumber.

2

OCTOBER 1996

CABARITA BEACH

The small basement smelled of dry dust and long-forgotten things. Bindi Summer sat in front of a large cupboard, both doors flung wide. Her legs crossed, she held a book in her lap, and her brow furrowed as she peered at the page. Piles of papers, notebooks, and boxes lay strewn around her.

She'd had no idea Pop was a stamp collector. She ran a fingertip over the rows of stamps, their edges curling. There were stamps from England, Portugal, Spain, the United States, and Canada. Stamps that commemorated anniversaries or celebrated the various Olympic Games. She smiled, remembering how much he'd loved to watch the games. He'd sit in his favourite armchair and shout at the television set, fists pumping with glee when his favourite team or athlete won their event.

Her sandy blonde hair was caught up in a messy ponytail on top of her head and the smattering of freckles across her nose stood out against pale skin. She sighed, slapped the stamp book shut, and pushed it onto one of the shelves in the cabinet, sending a cloud of dust into the air around her.

With a cough, she reached for another book. This time she found a collection of coins pressed into small, plastic holders. There was a thud overhead and she glanced up at the bare floorboards of the inn. The storage locker had become a refuge for all of Nan and Pop's personal collections. She and her sisters found it beneath the kitchen of the Waratah Inn right after they'd inherited the structure, when the contractor they hired to renovate the regal old building did a walk-through with them.

He'd offered to clean it up, make it larger, or turn it into a wine cellar, but they'd decided to keep it the way it was. Though Bindi wished now someone had at least run a mop over the place. She sneezed, shaking her head as her eyes smarted.

The breakfast rush was starting upstairs. The noise of footfalls on the timber floorboards grew with each minute that passed. She sighed. They didn't need her for the meal service, but she felt as though she should be up there with them. It was the busiest time of day at the inn.

She replaced the coin collection on a shelf and tugged another book free. This time it was a photograph album, standing side by side with several other albums, all covered in a fine layer of dust. The cover fell open and a thin paper page ballooned in the air, then settled against a page of black and white photographs.

Nan and Pop standing in front of a white clapboard farmhouse—most likely Nan's childhood home in Bathurst.

Nan was raised on a sheep farm just outside the country town. She and Pop had left with their son, Bindi's father, to start a new life farther north, in Cabarita Beach. That was when they'd built the Waratah Inn and embraced the role of inn keeper — something Bindi and her sisters had read about in the journals they'd discovered in an old timber box in Nan's room after her death.

The next photograph showed Nan wearing a pale top, tied around her waist, and showing off long, trim legs in a pair of hot pants. She sported large, white-rimmed sunglasses, with blonde hair curled in loops away from her pretty face and a mischievous smile on painted lips. Nan stood with one arm raised, pointing in the direction of a sign that read, "Summer Motors".

She and Pop had run a car yard in Bathurst for several years, saving enough money to start their lives over, away from the controlling influence of Nan's family, and from the spectre of memories that must've been difficult for Nan to overcome.

When Bindi read the entries in Nan's diary about her first love, Charlie Jackson, it'd made her heart ache to think of all the pain and grief her grandmother must've endured when Charlie didn't return home after the war to her and their infant son, Keith. Moving to Cabarita Beach must've been Nan and Pop's way of putting that pain behind them as they built a new family foundation of love, joy, and hope. That was the family Bindi remembered from her childhood. Whenever she'd visited her grandparents at the inn, she'd immediately warmed to their wide smiles, mischievous pranks, and ready laughter.

A knock at the door startled her, and she inhaled a quick breath before spinning to see her sister leaning on the door frame, arms crossed over her chest. Kate wore a chef's hat on her head, a white jacket buttoned down one side and black and white checked pants. Her green eyes sparkled.

"Good morning Bindi," she said.

Bindi stood up, dusting the back of her pants with one hand. "Morning. How's breakfast going?"

Kate shrugged. "Nothing to complain about. There's someone on the phone for you. A doctor... Ash or something. I couldn't quite hear, it's pretty noisy upstairs. Anything you want to tell me?"

Bindi pressed a smile to her face, her heart thudding. "No, everything's fine. He's probably calling to talk about my check up."

"You'll tell me...?" began Kate.

"Of course, if there's anything to tell, I'll let you know."

Kate left, and Bindi sagged. If the doctor was on the phone, that meant her tests had come back and he had news for her about the results. She preferred to remain downstairs, sorting through old scrap books, collections, and photographs. If she didn't know the test results, she could ignore what was going on with her health for a little longer.

She pressed fingertips to the glands beneath her throat. Still sensitive to the touch. With a sigh she glanced down at her waistline. It'd shrunk so that her shorts sagged a little and she'd had to tug them up into place more than once on the walk downstairs to the basement earlier.

With a shake of her head she climbed the narrow staircase, emerging beside the office. She shut the door behind her and sat at her desk. The phone earpiece lay on the desk. She picked it up, her stomach twisting into a knot.

"Hello, this is Bindi Summer."

"Bindi, it's Doctor Ash. How are you?"

"Fine thank you." Her stomach clenched.

"I've got the results of your tests here. I'd like to see you as soon as possible."

Her heart fell.

THE WIND HAD A NIP TO IT THAT RAISED GOOSEBUMPS UP

Bindi's arms and over her back. She tugged the tan cardigan tighter around her thin frame and hunched over bent knees. The rocky ground beneath her pressed into her rear end and she shuffled in place to find a more comfortable position.

A gull cawed nearby, higher up a hawk sailed on the updraft, wings extended, still. She watched it for a few moments, eyes squinted against the glare of the midday sun. Even through the cool wind she could feel the sun's burning rays freckling her cheeks and forehead.

Tenting a hand over her eyes she scanned the length of the beach below. She was seated on a high headland that jutted out at the end of two long, golden beaches. The grassy outcropping rose majestic above the ocean, with a sharp cliff-face tumbling to a narrow and rock-strewn shore below. A surfer duck-dived beneath a wave, and a couple strolled hand in hand along the shoreline. Otherwise, there wasn't a soul in sight in either direction.

Bindi sat, arms looped around her bent legs, chin resting on her knees, staring out into the blue expanse of water where it met the sun-bleached sky.

She'd sought out this place. Needed to be alone after her appointment with Dr Ash. It'd been bad news, as she'd thought it would be.

Lymphoma.

Non-Hodgkin lymphoma, he'd said, hands steepled together over his desk. She'd tried to pay attention while he explained the illness, what the treatment would involve. But after the word cancer, her head had buzzed and breathing became more difficult as her thoughts spun out of control.

She had cancer. Cancer.

He said they'd caught it early, it was treatable, that in all likelihood she'd be fine.

But it was cancer. People died from cancer. The thought kept running through her head — she could die.

She sucked in a deep breath and pressed her hands to her forehead then scrubbed them down over her face. Treatments. She didn't like the sound of that. She was only twenty-eight years old; she shouldn't have cancer. She was the manager at the Waratah Inn and didn't have time for treatments. She felt okay. Not wonderful, but well enough to work. No one else had suspected she was unwell, yet.

How long had she been sick? That was one of the questions she'd asked Dr Ash when finally she unstuck her dry tongue from the roof of her mouth.

"Possibly as long as six to twelve months," he'd said. She had a fever. Might've had one for that entire time. She couldn't believe she'd missed that. How had she overlooked a year-long fever? She supposed she'd gotten used to it. Low grade, still, it surprised her how out of touch with her own body she must've been not to notice a thing like that.

A wind gust pummelled her, it howled around the headland, blowing her hair in every direction, pulling strands free from her ponytail. She smoothed it back out of her eyes, finding her cheeks were moist. Tears pooled in her eyes and were whipped away by the cruel wind.

She stood with a groan. Dizziness swamped her head, and she staggered away from the cliff face, looking for the winding, narrow sandy trail that would take her back to the parking lot. She found it and navigated between two rocks, then down a steep embankment. Her head spun and thoughts swam.

Chemotherapy.

Radiotherapy.

Words she'd heard, but now that they were part of a treatment plan for her, she wondered what they involved. Why hadn't she paid more attention to what Dr Ash had said?

Could she keep working? If not, who would run the inn? What would she tell Kate, Reeda, Mima and Jack? They'd worry, or maybe they wouldn't need to worry since the doctor seemed to think she'd be okay. Perhaps she shouldn't tell them. At least not right away. A knot curled in her stomach, tightening with each question that filled her thoughts.

She tripped on a rock and fell, hands splayed out in front of her. She landed on hands and knees, skidding sideways down the steep trail, grabbed a hold of a tuft of grass with one fisted hand and stopped her descent. Then she struggled to her feet. Blood beaded and dripped down the front of her legs beneath her shorts. She swallowed, letting the tears fall.

It wasn't fair. She'd already lost so much. If only Nan were here, or Mum and Dad. She missed them all so much, now more than ever. She needed them. Needed someone to tell her everything would be okay, that she'd get through this. But there was no one.

She didn't want to worry her sister — they'd suffered as much loss as she had. If she died, they'd be the ones who would live with it. They'd be the ones hurting. She couldn't do that to them, not after all they'd been through. And they finally seemed to have grabbed a hold of some happiness in their lives. Kate was getting married, Reeda and Duncan were moving to Cabarita and had reconciled. No, she wouldn't tell them, not yet.

So, she was alone in this. No one to talk to, no one to comfort her.

She tilted her head, pushing out her chin, and limped the rest of the way down the track, tears still spilling over her cheeks.

At the bottom of the hill, the trail widened, and Bindi stopped and sat on a rock to take a better look at her injured knees. Her hair had fallen free of her ponytail and covered her face. The blood had stopped, only a few trickles down the length of her shins. She dashed away tears with the back of one hand and drew in a deep, calming breath.

"Are you okay?" The deep voice surprised her.

She pushed the hair out of her face and eyes, blinked. "Um...yes, fine thanks." The surfer she'd seen catching waves earlier stood in front of her. Drops of salt water dripped from a half-stripped wetsuit that hung around his waist. His tanned chest glistened and his blue eyes met hers with concern. One muscled arm held a worn surfboard close to his side.

His gaze flitted to her legs. "You're bleeding. I've got band-aids in the car."

Before she could say anything, he set off at a jog in the direction of the parking lot, short, bleached blond hair slicked against his head. When he returned, he had several band-aids in his hand and was wearing a shirt protruding beneath the bottom of a hoodie, and a pair of board shorts.

He knelt in front of her and dried off her knees with a beach towel, slung casually over one shoulder, then applied the band-aids to her wounds.

Bindi watched in silence, unsure of what to say. Her voice seemed to stick in her throat. His tenderness surprised her, and she sniffled one last time, wiped her cheeks dry, then stood, wincing at the pain in her ankle.

"Thanks," she said.

He shrugged, getting to his feet. His blue eyes fixed on hers. "No worries. I think you'll live." He grinned.

She whimpered. "Yeah."

"I'm Josh, by the way." He shoved his hands into the pockets of his hoodie.

Something inside her mind tweaked. *Josh*.

She studied his face. It looked a little different now, sharper angles, some blondish stubble, shorter hair than she remembered. It'd fallen to his shoulders once, but now hugged his head in what was almost a buzz cut. "Josh Owens?"

His eyes narrowed. "I thought you looked familiar. Bindi, right?"

She smiled, nodded. "That's right, Bindi Summers."

He grinned. "Yeah, Bindi Summers, the girl from the posh Sydney school. I haven't seen you in years."

She quirked an eyebrow. Is that how they'd seen her? She'd been too mired in grief at the beginning to pay much attention to what was going on in her new high school. "Ten years, to be exact."

He smiled. "That's right."

Her cheeks pinked under his gaze. Josh Owens had been the boy in high school that every girl had a crush on. The surfer with the shoulder-length golden curls, blue eyes, and shy smile. He'd been skinny then, with knobby knees and a few pimples on his cheeks. Not anymore.

She grunted as she stood to her feet. Her legs were already stiffening in the cold. Josh reached out a hand to steady her and his touch on her arm sent an even deeper flush to her cheeks.

"So, where have you been all this time?" he asked, as he helped her limp towards the parking lot.

"I've been living in Melbourne, working as a journalist."

He nodded. "Ah right. I don't pay much attention to the news, sorry."

She shrugged. "And what about you? What have you been doing for the past decade?"

"I stayed here," he said with a grunt. "Became a cop. I work at the Tweed Heads Police station."

A police officer? Now that he mentioned it, he had the air of someone in charge, someone who knew how to garner respect and was accustomed to carrying authority with him wherever he went.

"Wow, that must be an interesting job."

"That's not usually the response I get, most people don't

understand." He issued a wide grin. "But yes, it is interesting. It's hard, pretty thankless, but I love it."

They stopped beside her car and she rested a hand on the hood. "I think it's great. I've reported on crimes and events over the years and have a lot of respect for the work the police do. It's something most of us take for granted, but we'd be in trouble without you guys."

His eyes met hers. He studied her as if trying to figure her out, but there was an intensity of interest in his gaze that was unmistakable. Silence filled the space between them for a moment. It almost crackled.

He cleared his throat. "And what are you doing back on the coast, Bindi Summers?"

"My Nan died, and she left me part of the inn... I don't know if you remember the Waratah, but that's where we lived when I was a teenager."

"Oh yeah," he nodded. "I remember that place."

"Well, now it's mine...along with my two sisters. I manage it, Kate's the chef and Reeda decorated it when we did a big refurbishment recently. She's moving here from Sydney soon to help out."

He smiled. "Sounds like a good arrangement."

She inhaled a slow breath. It was a good arrangement. More than that, it'd brought her family back together — what was left of it. It was what she'd wanted for years. She'd spoken of her dreams of having her sisters in her life again many times with Nan. In the end, it'd been Nan's death that brought them back together when she left the inn to the three of them, with the stipulation they couldn't sell unless all three sisters agreed. And of course, Bindi wouldn't agree to that, much to her sisters' initial dismay. They'd come around since then, and now they loved the inn as much as she did. "It works well for us."

"It must've been hard to give up your job in Melbourne," he said.

She shrugged. "I was out of work when Nan died, it made sense to move here."

"Well, I'll have to check out the place sometime, see what you've done with it," he said.

Her heart skipped a beat. "I'd be happy to show you around."

He grinned. "Good. I look forward to it. Hope your knees feel better."

He waited until she'd pulled her car out of the lot, hands still deep in his hoodie pockets, until he tugged one out to wave over his head in her rear-vision mirror.

Her breath caught in her throat. Josh Owens from high school. She'd thought about him every now and then over the years, wondered what'd happened to him. He'd grown up, filled out, become a police officer. That was unexpected. In high school he'd been quiet and hadn't seemed interested in much other than surfing and food. She'd hoped he would ask her out, no doubt like every other girl in their year, but he hadn't.

She tried to recall who he'd taken to the formal, but the memory stubbornly refused to surface. She'd have to see if she could find Nan's photo album from that year, dig it out. Perhaps he'd been caught in a photograph or two. She'd attended the formal with friends. Jack had driven her in his truck. She'd had to hold her legs to one side, so the gear stick didn't hit her when he changed gears.

As she drove back to the inn, memories of high school flooded her thoughts. It wasn't long before the images were chased away by pictures of Doctor Ash telling her the results of her tests and describing the treatments to come. Josh Owens was handsome, kind and everything she'd always thought she'd want in a man but had never seemed able to find. Still, none of that mattered, since she was sick. She couldn't get involved with anyone, not even her high school crush. She had to focus all her energy and attention on getting well, and it wouldn't be fair to him for her to pretend everything was okay, when it wasn't. Something ached deep inside her heart and she fought back tears.

3

OCTOBER 1996

CABARITA BEACH

Bindi padded down the stairs with a yawn. Her first treatment was done. She'd been anxious about going to the hospital, but now that it was over the nervous ball of lead in her stomach had dissolved. All she felt was tired, a little light-headed, and relieved that the first procedure was out of the way.

If the treatments were always like yesterday's, she could manage it, and maybe she'd be able to keep the illness to herself for a while longer.

She glanced up at the chandelier hanging over the staircase. She'd have to make sure and remind the cleaner to dust the light fixture, it didn't look like it'd been done in a while and Bindi liked it to shine.

The breakfast service was well underway. In the kitchen, Kate buzzed about with the staff, issuing orders, flipping pancakes, and generally handling it all with ease. She was in her element. Bindi grinned to herself and slipped out the back door. She'd learned it was best for her to stay out of the way when it came to meal prep at the inn. She only frustrated her sister if she tried to get involved.

"You taking a walk?" called Kate, her hand holding tight to the frying pan.

Bindi dipped her head in assent. "Thought I might get some fresh air."

"Good idea. Wish I could come with you." Kate grinned, then turned a pancake with a spatula so that the golden underside landed smoothly face up.

"Next time?"

"Definitely. You feeling okay?" The tone of Kate's voice held a touch of concern.

Bindi swallowed. "Fine."

"Make sure you eat some breakfast."

"Of course, it smells delicious."

Bindi waved goodbye, then tucked Nan's journal beneath her arm, feeling the hard, cardboard cover press into her side. Reeda had given her Nan's journals when she returned from her trip to Italy. Bindi had been putting off reading them but had taken one with her to the first chemotherapy treatment the day before and begun to make her way through it. It was as fascinating as her sisters had said it was.

Learning about Nan through her own words scrawled in that familiar black script, on aged yellow pages, was almost addictive. She missed Nan so much, it'd been a year since Nan's death and the ache she felt inside had only seemed to grow in that time. Already she was beginning to feel more connected to Nan through the journals.

Reeda had handed her a box with the journals in it, and there'd been a few letters in there as well, pressed in beneath the books. She'd get to those later, for now she was focused on reading Nan's first journal from when she was a teenager. The mystery of what'd become of her first love, Charlie Jackson, lingered in Bindi's mind with every word that she read of their growing love affair. She and her sisters had spoken about it many times, and all three of them wanted to discover what'd happened to the man who'd turned out to be their biological grandfather. Reeda had even travelled to Italy to try to follow the trail Charlie left behind during the second world war when he disappeared, according to the authorities.

Bindi jogged along the trail towards the beach, glad she'd thought to wear a jumper. The still morning air was crisp, and she seemed to feel the cold more keenly than usual these days. Perhaps it was the weight loss, or maybe it was the lymphoma. She didn't know, and she didn't want to. She preferred not thinking about it, which she knew Nan would say was an unhealthy denial, if Nan were there.

In the cove, a pair of hooded plovers stood side by side, black heads with keen eyes over sleek white and grey bodies. They launched into the air at the sight of Bindi invading their space and circled above her, calling out their haunting cries. She watched them, squint-eyed, then strode in long steps towards the wet sand and away from their territory. One of the birds swooped her a few times, a half-hearted attempt to push her away from their nest. She waved a hand over her head and hurried along the beach without looking back.

Soon, the beach fell quiet as the plovers returned to their vigil on the sand. Bindi slowed her pace and inhaled a long, slow breath of the fresh, salty air. One of her favourite things about moving back to Cabarita Beach were the solitary walks. Feet slapping the wet sand, thoughts curling with the waves, she was able to work through problems, figure out her way forward. Her thoughts seemed to untwist and smooth out as she paced and by the time she got back to the inn, everything seemed better. She wasn't sure how she'd managed all those years in Melbourne, without those walks. She'd hurried, hunched over between meetings and appointments, through stories and business functions. She didn't miss much about those days, though she did miss having someone waiting for her at the end of the day. Even if it turned out he hadn't loved her all along the way she'd loved him.

Brendan had emailed her last month, suggesting he'd like to come to the Waratah Inn to see her. She wondered what he wanted from her. She hadn't heard from him since, but the thought of him visiting niggled at the back of her mind all the time. She chewed on one lip as she walked. What would she say to him if he did come?

After six years together, during which he'd assured her he wasn't the marrying kind, he'd broken it off abruptly and quickly become engaged to someone else. It'd hurt in a way she'd never thought possible. That, along with the loss of her job, had left her in a funk. Then, when Nan died, she'd come to Cabarita Beach for the funeral and never left. The inn was her home now, and the pain of losing Brendan, her career and her grandmother in such short order had begun to fade, until his email arrived in her inbox.

When she reached the end of the beach, Bindi sat on the sand next to the outcropping of black rocks that marked the curling ends of the cove. Castle Rock loomed high in the water in front of her. Waves crashed against it, salt spray leapt into the water with each collision, white against the deep blue of the spring sky.

She opened Nan's journal and lay it in her lap to read. The words drew her in. She felt as though she were living in pre-war Bathurst, the wind blowing through her hair as she rode her horse over the rolling hills of the Watson farm.

If only Nan had spoken to them about her childhood more often. She'd never wondered why Nan didn't talk about those times until now. The journal gave some insight as to why — there was pain in Nan's past that would've been difficult for her grandmother to face. Speaking about it might've been more than Nan could bear. She couldn't blame her for that.

It was hard enough for Bindi to tell her sisters about how life in Melbourne had fallen apart, why she'd lost her job and what'd happened between her and Brendan. And that wasn't nearly as painful an experience as what Nan had endured, losing the love of her life and her brother to a harsh and violent war. Not to mention birthing a son, out of wedlock, in wartime Australia. She couldn't imagine what Nan must've endured; the journals gave some insight but couldn't cover it all.

After a while, the sun warmed the top of Bindi's head and she looked away from the aged pages of Nan's diary to study the horizon. She'd get sunburned if she stayed on the beach much longer, besides there was a lot of work to do at the inn. She had bills to pay, supplies to order, and employees to manage.

With a sigh, she heaved to her feet, tucked the journal beneath her arm again, and ducked her head to walk back to the inn. She made it past the plovers without incident and hurried up the path, sea grasses tickling her legs and the sand warm between her toes.

She couldn't stop thinking about the letters in the box with Nan's journals. Reeda had said they were from Charlie, written to Nan during the war. She hadn't read them yet, but she'd stared at the handwriting on the envelopes that encased them. Thinking about it sparked a memory. A few weeks ago, she'd been rooting through the crawl space beneath the inn's staircase, looking for one of Nan's old files of ledger books, when she'd come across a box of letters. Some of the envelopes were addressed by the same hand, she was sure of it.

Excitement buzzed through her. Perhaps those letters were from Charlie as well, and maybe they contained some of the answers her sisters had been searching for. She picked up the pace, hurrying through the yard, past the horse stables, the chook pen, and the garden shed, then skipped up the back stairs and into the inn.

The noise in the kitchen had picked up and she scooted past the scurrying wait staff.

"You're back!" called Kate.

Bindi waved a hand over her head with a smile. "Yeah! Looks like you have your hands full."

Kate shook her head with wonder. "You'd better believe it." She grinned.

Bindi could tell her sister loved it. The inn was booked solid for the New South Wales school holidays, and Kate loved a crowd. It was her dream to build a restaurant on the property that would be open to the public, turning the Waratah Inn into a destination not only for guests but for anyone looking for a world class meal by the beach. Bindi thought it was a good idea, though it was her job to manage the books and it made her stomach clench to try to figure out how they'd pull it off.

She tugged open the doorway beneath the staircase, got down on hands and knees and crawled inside. Dusty air assailed her, and she coughed once, then sorted through the boxes. She soon found the box she was looking for, pulled off the lid, and began flicking through its contents. It was crammed with letters.

With determination, Bindi sorted the envelopes into piles based on the return addresses on their backs. There were some letters from Diana Watson, Nan's mother. Others were from Jemima Everest, or Mima as everyone knew her now. Still others were from people whose names Bindi didn't recognise. The entire box was filled with correspondence. None of the addresses were typed; all were written in neat cursive. Almost all were worn, weathered, and stained.

Some of the envelopes looked to be newer. Then, Bindi found one addressed to Edith Watson, without a postage stamp or a return address, with a date etched onto the top right corner in Nan's familiar hand. The envelope had been opened but not torn, it wasn't stained or aged in the same way as the other letters were. She set it to one side and continued sorting. By the time she'd emptied the box, there were five envelopes, addressed to Nan in the same hand, all without postage or return addresses, and all with dates added. And if she remembered rightly, the handwriting used to form Nan's name appeared to be the same as on the envelopes she had hidden away in the wooden box upstairs. Charlie's handwriting.

Bindi's heart thudded against her ribcage. She piled the rest of the envelopes back into the box, pressed the five letters into the inside cover of Nan's journal and crawled out from under the staircase. A waiter hurried by, shooting her a startled look, then recovered, a stack of dirty plates swaying between his hands.

She pushed a smile onto her face and nodded at the waiter's retreating back. She must look a fright. No doubt she had dust bunnies in her hair and dirt smudged across her face or something just as bad.

The only thing she could think of was taking a look at the letters. She climbed the stairs two at a time to her room, locked the door behind her, and hurried to the desk by the window. She sat, pulled Nan's timber box towards her, and opened the lid. Charlie's letters were beneath the rest of the journals. She took them out and lay them on the desk, then compared the newly discovered envelopes.

Yes, they were definitely written in Charlie's hand.

She slid her finger beneath the flap at the back and extracted the letter as carefully as she could manage. The letter was dated October 1952. How had Charlie gotten this letter to Nan? When had he written it, or sent it? And from where? The last she'd heard of Charlie's fate had been from Reeda's account of her meeting with an Italian man called Stefano. He'd told Reeda that he thought Charlie had been shot by the German army outside a small village in Italy after his escape from Campo 78. Had he survived? If he had, why didn't he come home to Nan and their father? Her heart in her throat, she unfolded the pages, set them on the desk and began to read.

4

SEPTEMBER 1994

MELBOURNE

The noise of the newsroom always soothed Bindi. She loved the bustle, the clack of fingers on keyboards, the hum of conversation. It spoke of excitement, adventure, the important work they did in bringing truth to the community, in making sure governments were held accountable and people were kept informed about what was going on in their communities.

It was the career she'd always dreamed of having, and now it was hers. Sometimes the realisation of that was hard for her to grasp. She was ready to admit that it wasn't everything she'd thought it would be, that sometimes the truth was harder to dig for than the sensational, and that often her bosses asked her to scrap stories in favour of others that she knew would bring a benefit to someone in power. Still, for the most part, she was proud of her work.

The lift doors whirred shut behind her and she balanced the cup of takeaway coffee in one hand more carefully as she strode forward.

It'd been four years since she'd gotten her first job at the Channel Four. Directly out of uni, she'd been an intern at first, an unpaid position that'd had her brewing jugs of tea and coffee, delivering mail through the rabbit-warren office, and cleaning up spills while she listened in on meetings, one ear pricked to catch the most important discussions.

It had taken her a full year to get promoted to fact checker, then another year to be given a chance to produce her first story. And finally, she'd become the journalist she'd always dreamed of being. The camera trained on her hadn't been the goal, telling the story was. She'd always thought she'd write for a newspaper, but she'd landed an internship at a television station instead. She still wasn't entirely comfortable having her image blasted into living rooms across Australia every night, but her producer said she'd get used to it. She wasn't sure.

As she moved through the open office, some staff greeted her, others ignored her completely, their attention firmly fixed on the screens in front of them. She found her cubicle, set down her coffee on the desk and pulled out her chair. When she sank into it, a head emerged from behind a partition.

"Good morning, Bindi."

She smiled. "Hi Debbie."

Debbie was her full-time fact checker. She'd only recently graduated from university and was keen to get ahead. Her enthusiasm made Bindi feel tired, even though Debbie was only four years younger than she was. Still, it seemed like an age since she was that bright-eyed graduate looking for a way in the door at the television station.

"Where are you going today?" asked Debbie, her eyes gleaming.

Bindi shrugged. "Don't know yet, actually."

"Did you stay late last night?"

Some of the staff from the office had gone out for drinks to celebrate a birthday for one of the more senior journalists. Bindi wished she hadn't stayed out as late as she had. There'd been karaoke involved, a new craze in Melbourne's CBD, and she'd humiliated herself with an off-key rendition of *The Sign*, by Ace of Base.

She ran a hand over her eyes with a sigh. "I stayed *too* late, I'm afraid."

Debbie giggled. "I heard about *Ace of Base*. Sounds like you had a good time."

Bindi shook her head as she logged onto her computer. "Remind me not to sing in front of a crowd again. I actually think I heard dogs howling throughout the streets of Melbourne." She chortled. "Where did you go after you left?"

Debbie's lips pursed. "I went to my boyfriend's place."

Debbie's boyfriend was a mystery over which Bindi had speculated many times. Since the fact-checker refused to tell anyone his name, Bindi could only imagine he must be someone high up at the television station, otherwise it wouldn't matter.

"Why won't you tell me who he is?" she asked, frowning as her inbox filled with email messages.

"I can't. Trust me, I want to, but he's asked me not to say anything. He's adamant about that." Debbie pouted as she wheeled her office chair into Bindi's cubicle, her feet pushing across the carpet. "Although, I really don't get why. He's an adult, so am I. We can make our own choices."

"If he's your boss, there are company rules against that," murmured Bindi, clicking through her emails one by one to see if there was anything urgent.

Debbie grunted. "I don't see why."

Bindi spun to face her with brows furrowed. "He *is* your boss?"

"I didn't say that," huffed Debbie, wheeling back to her own desk.

"Yes you did!" called Bindi at her retreating back.

"No, I didn't. And anyway, even if he was, I still don't see why it's anyone else's business."

Bindi shook her head and returned her attention to her screen. "Did you get the fact checking done for that piece on Bilton Global?"

Debbie sighed. "Yep, all done. Everything's good to go on that piece."

"Are you sure? Because I wasn't certain the quotes they gave us and attributed to Barney Caine were quite accurate. Did he confirm?"

Debbie groaned. "You mean I have to call him?"

Bindi's eyes narrowed. "Yes, you have to call him. You didn't call him?"

Her heart skipped a beat. What else hadn't Debbie checked thoroughly? Mentally she ran through all the recent stories they'd run, wondering if they'd missed anything.

"We've got the status meeting in a few minutes," reminded Debbie, clacking away at her keyboard.

Bindi sighed. The status meeting. She'd better gather her thoughts. Tim Hutchinson, her boss, would expect her to give him a full run down of her current stories and what was coming through the pipeline.

She opened the spreadsheet she used to keep track of everything she was working on, ran through it and made notes on a notepad.

Her phone rang, and she picked it up, pressed the earpiece between her shoulder and ear, and answered. "This is Bindi."

"Hey, sweetheart." Brendan's voice brought a smile to her face.

"Hi, honey, how are you this morning?"

"Better than you, I think. I didn't humiliate myself by singing and grinding in front of all my colleagues." He laughed.

Bindi feigned offence with a huff. "It was a brilliant rendition of a piece by a masterful pop icon, thank you very much."

"Hey, listen, hon, I'm not going to be able to get together tonight after all."

Bindi's lips pursed. "Oh?"

"Yeah, I've got to get this piece finished, you know how it is. Newspaper journalists never sleep, unlike you television *news-oh's*."

Her eyes narrowed. "Yeah, yeah...that's what you always say, and yet you seem to find an awful lot of time to go surfing."

He laughed. "You got me on that. So, I'll see you tomorrow instead. Okay?"

"Okay."

Just as she hung up the phone, it rang again. When she answered, Tim's distinctive voice echoed down the line. "Can you come to my office please, Summer?"

She hurried to Tim's office, which was at one end of the open space. The only office with a door, although the wall was made of glass so everyone could see through to where Tim sat behind a large, mahogany desk.

She shut the door behind her and took a seat opposite her boss. He was occupied with something on his computer screen, clicking the mouse rapidly, his brow furrowed. He tapped furiously on the keyboard, clicked again, then leaned back in his chair with a sigh, linking his hands behind his head.

His piercing brown eyes fixed on hers, making her sweat.

"Summer, you know we pride ourselves here at Channel

Four News, on making sure that we report the truth. The objective truth."

She nodded. It wasn't entirely accurate, everyone knew Tim had a thing for the Labor party, but she'd play along.

"Yes, of course."

"And what's the one thing I don't want?"

"To get sued."

"That's right, to get sued. Because if that happens, we might all be out of a job, pan handling on the streets of Melbourne by next month. Right?"

"Right," she said, her heart hammering against her ribcage. Where was this going? She didn't like the direction the conversation was taking.

He sighed, leaning forwards to steeple his hands on the desk. "I heard from Mark Romney, over at the Premier's office."

Bindi's stomach twisted into a knot. She'd run an expose on the Premier's office and their tendency to use taxpayer funding for private holidays and jets to exotic locations. The entire story had been based on statements made by former staff members. She hadn't liked the tone of the piece, but Tim had pushed her to do it. After all, it showed the Liberal state government in a bad light, and that was something he was adamant about doing and he didn't care who knew it. Still, the way he was eying her now, she knew something had gone wrong.

"Oh? Was it about that piece we did on funding personal travel with public funds?" she asked.

He nodded, one eyebrow quirking. "That's right. He says it's not true. Says he can prove you got false information from your sources, that they're slandering his staff because of a grudge, and we're slandering his office with our story."

"But Debbie called the Premier's office to confirm the facts..."

"Did she? He says no one from our office called anyone in his."

Bindi's heart fell. "But Debbie..."

"This was your responsibility, Summer. Don't blame your fact checker, she only does what you tell her to do. You're in charge, you're responsible for the story. You're the face of the piece. Everyone else does their part, but in the end, it comes down on your head."

"But I did—"

"I don't want excuses, Summer. You've left me no choice. Mark wants you fired, or he's suing the station." Tim's nostrils flared and his gaze bored into her.

Bindi's face flamed and her throat tightened. "Fired?"

He nodded. "I'm sorry, Summer, but I have to let you go. I can't risk the entire news team because of your blunder. It's a hard lesson to learn, but it's good you learn it now. You'll land on your feet again somewhere."

"No one will touch me after this, they won't trust me. You know that." Her head grew light, thoughts spun.

He shrugged, leaning back again. "You'll figure it out. You're a smart cookie."

WHEN BINDI WOKE THE NEXT MORNING, HER HEAD FELT AS though it might explode. She'd cried herself to sleep the night before. Her eyes ached, she was dehydrated, and something pounded under her scalp, like a little man wielding a hammer was trying to beat his way out. One ear was numb, as though she'd slept on it all night without moving. She knew she was tired but hadn't realised just how exhausted she'd let herself become over the past few months.

With a groan, she swung her legs over the side of the bed and cradled her head in her hands. At least she didn't have to go to work. She could spend the day in her pyjamas if she wanted to.

She still couldn't quite believe it. All those years of working towards becoming a journalist, of striving for her dreams, and she'd had the position for just over a year before being fired. She sighed, shook her head, and stood to her feet.

What would she tell Nan? Her grandmother was so proud of her, told her every time they spoke. Now... Ugh.

She inhaled a sharp breath as she filled the kettle with water from the kitchen tap. She lived in a studio unit in the middle of Melbourne. It was small, cramped, and old, but she loved it. It was hers.

One wall had the bed pressed up against it, the opposite wall had a bench with a sink and a refrigerator at the end. Everything she needed was crammed into this single open space, with only the bathroom sectioned off for a little privacy. It had everything she needed and gave her a sense of pride in having rented and decorated it entirely on her own, with the money she'd earned working hard at the station.

And now she'd probably lose her home, as well as everything else she'd already lost in her life.

Her heart squeezed at that thought. She couldn't sift through memories now, she'd end up curled in a foetal position on her bed, unable to move. So she straightened, pushed out her chin. Getting fired was not the most traumatic thing she'd experienced in the past decade. She'd survived worse, and she'd get through this too.

By the time she'd showered and tidied up the unit, it was almost lunchtime. She'd promised to meet Brendan for lunch, but that was before she'd been fired and had crawled home from work to fall into bed. With everything that'd been going on in her life, the stories she'd been covering, the meetings and research, she'd crammed her life full of activity. She hadn't taken care of herself, hadn't gotten enough rest. She'd barely seen Brendan in weeks.

She met him at a cafe down the street at noon, wearing large, black sunglasses to hide her reddened eyes. He offered her a kiss on the cheek, then sat across from her at a table outside, shaded by a round umbrella.

"Hey baby, how are you?"

She inhaled a slow breath, fingering the edge of the plastic menu. "I got fired yesterday."

"What?" His eyes widened. "You got fired? What happened?"

Bindi fought to hold back the tears that tightened her throat and made her head throb all over again. "You remember that story I ran about the Premier's office misusing public funds?"

He nodded, reached for her hand to hold in his own. "Yes, of course."

"Apparently Debbie didn't call the Premier's office to confirm some of the quotes from our sources. The Premier's calling it slander, and he's threatening to sue." She choked out the last words, still unable to believe she hadn't followed up more thoroughly. She remembered asking Debbie about the quotes, whether they'd been confirmed, and Debbie had assured her. In hindsight, she should've pressed for more — who'd confirmed it, how, what did they say?

Her head dropped into her hands.

"So, it's Debbie's fault?"

She nodded. "Yes, but I'm her boss. I should've asked more questions...made sure she'd followed through..." She groaned.

Brendan sighed, releasing her hand. "Well, don't worry about it. You'll find another job, you're a great journalist."

"Not after this," mumbled Bindi. "If it gets out that I'm the kind of journalist who produces slander, none of the other stations will want me. It's a death knell for a journo, you know that."

His lips pursed. She could tell from the way he was studying her that he understood exactly what she was saying whether he admitted it or not. Brendan was a journalist at the Melbourne Chronicle; he knew the business even better than she did, with at least five years more experience than her.

"Tell me I'm wrong," she demanded. "Would the Chronicle hire me?"

He stared at the menu, then offered her a smile. "Maybe, I could have a word with the editor...see what he says."

She shook her head. "I don't want you to risk your own career for me. No, I'll figure it out on my own."

They ordered lunch then, and the conversation moved onto other topics. Bindi ordered a chicken cob salad, and Brendan had a hamburger with every possible topping known to mankind. She never understood how he stayed as trim and fit as he did, the way he ate. Nor could she see how he managed to open his jaw wide enough to take a bite of the burger — it was stacked so high with onions, cheese, tomato, bacon, pineapple, beetroot, and lettuce that she was certain she'd never have managed it.

"So, I've got to fly to Sydney tonight," explained Brendan, after a lengthy discussion about a story he was covering. "And I'll be back in about a week. Okay?"

She nodded, her thoughts straying to their relationship and the few times they'd seen each other lately. In the past, Brendan had assured her that if they moved in together, they'd see more of each other, but she'd countered with the idea that if she moved in with him, he'd never get around to marrying her. At which he'd snorted.

"I'm not the marrying type, love," he'd said.

She couldn't count the number of times he'd said something similar to that over the six years of their relationship.

She'd met him at university, they'd both studied journalism together, and had shared their first kiss at a party in her dorm. They'd been together ever since. She loved him, but sometimes wondered if he was perhaps a little too comfortable with the arrangement. She'd always dreamed of getting married, having children, rebuilding the family she'd lost when her parents were killed in a car accident during her teen years. She was twenty-six years old, and her boyfriend didn't seem any closer to popping the question than he had been in the early days of passionate make-out sessions while they listened to Crowded House tapes in her shared dorm room.

"Do you think we'll ever get married?" she asked.

Brendan's eyebrows shot skyward. "What?" he asked around a mouthful of burger.

She sighed. "I know, you hate it when I bring it up, but I really want to understand. Where is this relationship going?"

He swallowed and dabbed his mouth with a napkin. When he smiled at her, she noticed it didn't reach his eyes. "You're only saying that because you lost your job. You're feeling a little insecure, that's no reason to start worrying about us, honey."

"No, it's not because of my job...or maybe it is, I don't know. But every time we talk about marriage, you tell me you're not the marrying type, or that marriage is an old-fashioned institution we don't need because we love each other so much...or something like that."

He reached for her hand. "That's right. We don't need it. We have each other. Who wants a bit of paper?"

She did. She wanted a bit of paper. Something that affirmed his commitment to her, his love for her. She wanted to stand up in front of her friends and family and declare that she would love him forever, that they'd be a family and raise their children together. Why couldn't he understand that?

"I want that, Brendan. I'm sorry... I know you don't get it, but that's something I want. I want us to be a family, to share our lives together, to have children."

"Whoa!" he said, leaning back in his chair. "Where is all this coming from? I've hardly seen you lately, and now you want to have kids?"

She sighed. "That's the problem, we don't see each other, and when we do, we're both tired and irritable... I want more than that."

He wiped his mouth with the napkin, pushed his chair back and stood up. Then he pulled money from his wallet and threw it on the table. "I've got to go, Bindi. I can't talk about this right now. I'm in the middle of a huge story, I've got so much going on...you have no idea."

Her brow furrowed. Yes, she did, she knew exactly what that was like. He always did that. Always minimised her career, as though it couldn't possibly measure up to his.

"I have responsibilities Bindi, and I've got a lot to get done today. We'll have to pick up this subject another time."

She slouched in her chair, crossing her arms over her chest. "Okay."

He bent to kiss her cheek. "See you later, baby. Love ya."

"Love you too."

She watched him stride away, his dark hair slicked down on his head, his unbuttoned suit coat flapping around his torso as he walked.

Sometimes she hardly recognised him anymore as the boy she'd fallen in love with all those years ago.

5

CABARITA BEACH

The morning had been so busy Bindi had barely had time to think, let alone eat anything. When the scent of something baking in the kitchen wafted into the office, she turned her head away from the computer screen and in the direction of the delicious aroma.

She didn't waste any time making her way out to the kitchen, and found Kate there, pulling trays of scones out of the oven with a pair of beach-themed oven mitts.

"That smells divine," groaned Bindi, hurrying to sit at the bench.

Kate smiled. "Would you like one?"

"Yes, please, or maybe three...no, four..."

"Okay, coming right up. Jam and cream?" Kate held a pot of strawberry jam in the air.

"Absolutely," replied Bindi, sitting straight on the stool. "I didn't have lunch...and only some fruit salad for breakfast. The sudden awareness of hunger pangs drove me out here, even though I have a million things to do."

"I hope you're taking care of yourself." Kate's brow furrowed as she peered at Bindi, pausing in her work for a moment.

"Of course," responded Bindi, swallowing hard. She hated lying to Kate, but in truth she was relieved to feel hungry. She'd lost her appetite lately and was afraid the weight loss was beginning to show. How long would she be able to keep her illness from her sisters?

Maybe she should tell them. After all, they were family. But they were happy, and she didn't want to take that away from them. Not yet anyway.

Kate filled a plate with scones, sliced them open and steam drifted towards the ceiling. She slathered them with thick, homemade strawberry jam, and cream from a local dairy that she'd whipped until it formed stiff peaks.

When Bindi bit into the first scone, she almost groaned with delight. It was soft, warm, and delicious.

She swallowed. "That is amazing. You've definitely got Nan's recipe mastered."

Kate's lips pursed. "I've been trying for a while, but I think I've managed to get the measurements just right."

"I'm happy to keep testing for you, if you want more practice," mumbled Bindi around a mouthful of the dessert.

Kate shook her head. "Good, you look like you could use a bit of fattening up. Are we working you too hard?" Concern darkened Kate's eyes as she watched Bindi eat.

Bindi chewed, biding her time to come up with a response. Just as she was about to speak, the inn's front door swung open behind her.

"Hello!" called a voice.

"Reeda!" replied Kate, wiping her hands on her apron, and hurrying to greet the eldest of the three sisters.

Bindi set down her scone with a wistful look at its creamy topping, then went to greet Reeda and her husband Duncan.

"I can't believe you're here!" she cried, throwing her arms around Reeda, and hugging her tight. "I'm so excited you're moving north. We'll be able to see you all the time."

Reeda grinned. "You might rethink that the next time I order you around."

Bindi huffed. "You're probably right about that, but for now, I'm thrilled!"

Everyone laughed. Duncan embraced her as well, and they all headed into the kitchen for more scones, with a cup of hot tea. When she'd eaten enough, Bindi leaned back in her chair to watch her sisters buzzing with conversation, her stomach full, her heart content.

"Where's all your luggage?" she asked. "Aren't you staying at the inn for a few days?"

Reeda shrugged. "We already found a place to rent. We dropped our things there before we came over."

"What? Already?" exclaimed Kate.

"Yeah, the real estate agent we were working with found us a fully furnished unit in Kingscliff. It's small, but it has everything we need," replied Duncan.

"Until we can buy our dream home," countered Reeda, with a wink.

"Yeah, until then..." Duncan leaned over to kiss Reeda on the mouth.

Bindi hid a smile. It was a relief to see Reeda and Duncan getting along so well after everything they'd been through together as a couple. There was a time she hadn't believed they'd make it, but they seemed to be doing better than ever thanks to Reeda's trip around Italy. Perhaps that was what she needed, a similar trip.

Her brow furrowed. She didn't need a trip to Italy; she needed to get well. Sometimes she forgot she was sick, and then a reminder would sound off in her head, making her stomach turn.

SHE SPENT A COUPLE OF HOURS WITH HER SISTERS AND Duncan, laughing and talking together, while guests helped themselves to the freshly made scones in the dining room. Finally, Bindi excused herself. She had paperwork to complete, along with the accounts for the previous month. There was always plenty to keep her occupied at the Waratah.

Reeda and Duncan stood to leave as well. They still had to get their things unpacked and buy a few groceries to stock their refrigerator. They'd placed most of their belongings in storage in Sydney until they were ready to buy a home, although a few of their things were arriving by truck at the end of the week.

"Do you know what you're going to do with yourselves, yet?" asked Kate, carrying the empty teacups to the sink,

Reeda sighed. "I'm going to see if I can find some design work in the area and help out here at the inn of course."

Bindi grinned. "Thank goodness, we could use the help."

"I've got an interview at Tweed Hospital on Thursday," added Duncan. "And I've been accepted into *Médecins Sans Frontières*."

"Doctor's Without Borders? That's wonderful!" declared Bindi. "Congrats."

"Well done," added Kate with a grin.

"Thanks, I'm really looking forward to it. I plan on alternating between paid work and volunteer hours. It's been a while since I was so excited about medicine. I got into it because I wanted to help people, and this will give me a chance to do even more of that. At least, I hope it will."

Bindi shook her head. "You're both amazing. Meanwhile, I have to get back into the office and crunch numbers. No rest for the weary." She headed back to the office, still marvelling at her high-achieving sister and brother-in-law. Sometimes she missed the excitement of working in journalism. But the inn was her home now, and being with her sisters, and close to Mima and Jack made it all worthwhile.

She logged onto the computer and got to work. Before she knew it, another hour had passed, and the sounds of dinner preparations echoed through the closed door from the kitchen.

Bindi's stomach complained. She should grab an apple Since her appetite had been almost non-existent for months now, if she felt a pang of hunger, she knew she should take the opportunity to eat. But she wanted to finish the invoices first, then she'd go in search of something to eat. She blinked hard a few times, her eyes aching from staring at the computer screen for too long, then flicked through the pile of invoices on the desk in front of her.

Just as she was typing up a new payment to their laundry service, she heard a bang in the kitchen, quickly followed by a shout and a loud clatter, as though a pan had been flung across the kitchen floor.

Her heart skipped a beat and she rushed from the office to find out what'd happened.

"Kate, are you okay?"

Kate leaned on the bench, her brow furrowed and one hand held high in front of her face. Staff scurried in every direction, working hard to prepare the meal. A few had stopped to watch Kate with sympathetic expressions, seeming unsure what to do to help. Bindi hid a smile; her sister could be intimidating to the younger members of staff. She couldn't blame their reluctance to step forward. Kate was quite the force of nature when she chose to be.

"I burned myself," she said through gritted teeth, her face twisted in pain. "Ugh. It hurts."

One of the staff moved to help Kate, but Bindi waved

them off. "I'll take care of her, thanks." She hurried to Kate's side, to study the burn more closely. "Let me see."

Kate lowered her hand. An angry red welt appeared on the inside of one of Kate's wrists, and along the palm of her hand.

"Okay, it's not too bad. I don't think we have to go to the hospital. I'll get the first aid kit," said Bindi. "For now, hold it under the cold tap."

Kate complied, her lips pursed and face pale, while Bindi went in search of medical supplies. She kept the first aid kit in the office cupboard, since it was close to the kitchen and wouldn't be in Kate's way. Her sister had gotten militant about what could be stored in the kitchen since they'd extended the inn's restaurant to include lunch and dinner menus. She said they didn't have enough space to store what they needed, so anything else would have to find another home.

By the time she returned with the kit, Kate's colour had returned. She was still running water over the burn and at the same time was calling out orders to the staff who bustled about the kitchen filling platters, bowls and tureens with succulent roast meats, a colourful array of roast vegetables and gravy, and ferrying them post haste towards the dining room.

Bindi reached for Kate's hand, but her sister raised it in the air to wave at a waitress. She tried to grasp it again and Kate ducked away to taste the gravy, then shouted a few more orders.

"Kate," hissed Bindi, with a tight smile. "Come here so I can take care of that burn."

Kate's nostrils flared. "I don't have time."

"It'll only take a minute."

She sighed, returned to where Bindi stood, and stretched

out her hand. "This is ridiculous. The kitchen is too small for what we're trying to achieve here. We're getting busier all the time, at least it feels that way. I'm working with what is essentially a large domestic kitchen, and I'm trying to make it work as a commercial space."

Bindi dried Kate's hand gently with a clean cloth, then set about applying paw-paw salve, before wrapping it with a bandage. "I didn't realise things had gotten so bad."

Kate huffed. "It's been like this for a while, I haven't wanted to say anything. I know it feels like we only just finished renovating the place, but if we're serious about opening the restaurant to the public—"

"Which we are. Right?" interrupted Bindi, as she finished up and packed everything back into the first aid kit.

Kate nodded. "I am... If you and Reeda are on board."

"I think it's a great idea. You're a wonderful chef, Kate, and it would be a shame not to share your talents. But only if it's what you want to do. If you'd rather, we can go back to only serving breakfast."

"I really think the restaurant is a big draw card for guests," replied Kate. She ran a hand over the bandana that was tied around her head, holding her hair out of the way, and suddenly looked more tired than Bindi had seen her in a long time.

"The guests love the restaurant, and honestly there isn't much available locally. If they didn't eat here, there are a few places to go in Kingscliff and Tweed Heads, but nothing with food like we're offering." Bindi smiled, patted Kate's arm. "I think it's time to build your big kitchen."

"Can we afford it?" asked Kate, one eyebrow quirked.

Bindi nodded. "We still had a little money left from Nan's account, and I've been putting some aside every month since we opened. Still, I'd like to know if this is what you want,

Kate. I know guests will love it, and I'm sure we'll get plenty of interest from the public, but what about you? Is this what you want?"

Kate sighed, and a soft smile drifted across her full lips. "It's always been my dream to have my own restaurant."

"Then, we'll do it," replied Bindi with a nod of her head.

"Are you sure?"

"Certain. I'll call Reeda to check what she has to say on the matter, but last time we talked about it she seemed open to it."

Kate grinned. "So, we're building a commercial kitchen and restaurant?"

"Yep, I suppose we are."

The two sisters hugged. Tears welled in Bindi's eyes. It warmed her heart to see the excitement on her sister's face. From the beginning she'd worried that the Waratah Inn wouldn't be enough of a challenge for Kate, that in the end she'd head back to the city to find a prestigious chef's job, not satisfied by working in the inn's small kitchen. But she could see now that Kate was as invested in the business as she was herself. This restaurant would be a good thing for the inn and for Kate.

Bindi returned to the office and put away the medical supplies, as Kate got back to serving the evening meal to their guests. Just as she was about to sit at her desk, she heard the bell at the reception counter ting. She sighed, rubbed her hands down the sides of her pants and hurried out to meet the visitor. She hadn't been expecting any late check-ins, though one of the guests on the list hadn't showed earlier. Maybe they'd been held up along the way. She didn't understand the name, scrawled in the guest book, though she often couldn't read Kate's writing.

When she reached the foyer, she had to work hard not to

let her mouth fall open. Instead, she pushed a smile onto her lips.

"Brendan, what a surprise..."

BRENDAN, STOOD AT THE INN'S RECEPTION COUNTER, HIS hands pushed deep into his jeans' pockets, a backpack on the floor beside him. His brown hair was mussed, and his dark eyes fixed on her, losing her in their depth.

He grinned and enveloped her in a warm embrace, his arms holding her close. She could feel his heartbeat through the thin shirt against her ear. He cradled her head in his hands the way he used to when they were dating. Something inside of her melted; it was all so familiar. She missed him. But he was engaged to someone else, hadn't wanted to marry her. She squirmed out of his grasp.

"Hi Bindi," he said, taking a step backwards.

"What...what are you doing here?" She didn't want to sound rude but couldn't think of anything else to say.

"I told you I was coming." His brow furrowed.

"I know, but I didn't realise... Never mind, it's good to see you."

She bustled behind the reception counter, determined to be a good hostess even if her heart was thudding against her rib cage and nausea had welled in her gut.

"Let's see, you're in room eight," she began, running her finger down the booking sheet. "I'll help you get your things to your room. Normally, Jack would do that but he's out with the horses now. You'll love this room, Reeda decorated it... actually she decorated the entire inn when we renovated recently."

She was rambling, she knew it and he did too — she could

tell by the amused look on his face. Still, she wasn't sure how to stop. If she stopped talking, he'd talk, and she didn't want to hear what he had to say. Why was he here? He'd said he wanted to talk to her, to get some closure on their relationship, but he could've done that over the telephone. The way he was looking at her now brought a warmth to her cheeks. She recognised that look. He was flirting with her.

He studied her with a bemused look. "Are you nervous, Bindi?"

She sighed. "I guess. It's been a while since I saw you."

She stepped out from behind the counter and reached for his backpack. He waved her off and picked it up himself, then followed her up the inn's wide staircase to the third floor.

He didn't say anything until they reached his room. She handed him the key with a brief smile, then set her hands on her hips. "Breakfast starts at seven," she began.

He interrupted by reaching for her hand and tugging it away from her waist, to hold between his. He threaded his fingers through hers. Heat flooded her body.

"I had to see you, Bindi." He ran a thumb around the palm of her hand, stepped closer. "I missed you."

She was confused. Why was he here? Was it really because he missed her? "But you broke up with me," she objected. "You got engaged to someone else after telling me you didn't want to marry me because you weren't the marrying type."

Brief irritation flashed across his face, then his eyes softened. "I know, I was horrible to you. But now... I don't know if I've made the right decision."

Her eyes narrowed. "You don't know?"

"I'm not sure. I do know one thing; I miss having you in my life. And Amy, that's my fiancée's name, she's not like you. She's different, and I thought that was a good thing. She's a hairdresser, she isn't so invested in her career, she wants a family..."

Bindi's gut churned. "I wanted a family."

He nodded, stepping closer again. She had to look up to see his face. He was tall and his lithe body loomed over her, his lips hovered above hers. "I know you did, and I didn't appreciate that. I thought we were too similar, that it couldn't work between us."

He closed the gap between them, his breath hot on her mouth as he moved to kiss her.

That he'd had doubts about them was news to her. He'd never shared those kinds of doubts with her, always assuring her that he loved her, wanted to be with her.

"Where does your fiancée think you are right now, Brendan?" Her words halted his progress towards her lips.

"She knows I travel for work. She's used to it, I'm hardly home."

"Home? Do you live together?"

He nodded, his cheeks colouring.

Bindi took a step back, shaking her head. "I can't believe this... I've got to go."

She left him standing in front of the door with the brass number eight in its centre and fled down the staircase and back to the office. She hadn't been seated behind her desk long when a wave of nausea hit her. She ran to the small bathroom attached to the kitchen and reached a stall just in time to throw up.

When she was done, she slumped against the wall and wiped her mouth with a paper towel. Exhaustion swamped her body. She stared at her reflection in the narrow bathroom mirror. Dark shadows clung beneath her eyes her skin was pallid. She'd always been thin, but now she looked unwell. She wouldn't be able to hide it much longer — it was time to tell her sisters what was going on.

She didn't have the time or energy to deal with Brendan right now. The fact that he was questioning his decision to leave her, to move in with another woman and ask that woman to marry him, didn't give her the comfort she once might've felt. Right now, all she needed to do was to get through each day and beat this illness. There wasn't room in her life for anything else.

6

CABARITA BEACH

The pile of dishes in the sink teetered. Where was Mima? And that girl, the one they'd hired to clear tables and wash dishes, she seemed to have disappeared along with everyone else.

Edie Summer sighed and wiped the sweat from her forehead with the back of one hand. She adjusted the fit of the bandana that was wrapped around her head, pulling her blonde hair away from her face. Two pigtails bobbed against her shoulders.

She should leave the dirty dishes as they were. It was what she'd hired people to do, take over these kinds of chores. There'd been too much balanced on her shoulders for too long, at least that's what Paul had said one night hunched over the books.

"We've got enough to cover hiring someone to help in the kitchen, and we should do it," he'd mused, glasses perched on the end of his nose. "You work too hard."

"So do you," she'd pointed out.

He'd laughed at that. "Fair point. Perhaps we should get a handyman as well, while we're at it."

They hadn't found a handyman, no one local who had the time or the capability. That was one of the pitfalls of opening an inn in the middle of nowhere. But a girl from a local farm had taken the kitchen hand job, and so far, she'd done well. If only Edie knew where she was at that moment.

"Breathe," said a voice behind her, warm against her neck.

Two hands pressed to her waist and spun her around. "You look like you're about to burst a blood vessel," said Paul.

He kissed the tip of her nose, then her forehead, before he moved to her lips and planted a warm, sweet kiss there as well.

She smiled, the tension shifting from her head to her neck. "These dishes won't do themselves."

"Lucy will be back shortly. She'll do them. Why don't you take a break?"

They'd opened the inn almost twenty years earlier, and over most of that time they hadn't hired much in the way of help. It'd been mostly her and Paul doing everything around the place, and she'd become accustomed to things being that way. It'd meant that as the inn's popularity grew, so did her workload. At first, running the Waratah had been fun, every now and then they'd receive a guest and she'd take care of them like they were the Sultan of Brunei. But then, word had spread of the rustic boutique inn nestled on the shores of an untouched cove, and they'd slowly found themselves buried in guests.

Since Keith left home to attend university in Sydney six years earlier, it seemed Edie had done little more than work, night and day. Partly because of the popularity of their inn, but secretly, she knew she was using the activity to mask the loneliness she felt at not having her son close by any longer.

Sydney was so far away. They hardly heard from him, and

she was accustomed to having him around, to talk to, to embrace, to massage her shoulders or hear about her day. He'd grown into a responsible, thoughtful, kind — if somewhat neurotic — young man. She loved him more than she'd thought it possible, and now he was gone.

If only they'd been able to have more children, their home wouldn't be empty now. Of course, they had their guests, and often the guests brought children with them, but it wasn't the same. She'd get down on the floor with them, play dolls or trains, even had a box of toys that she'd pull out from the living room cupboards for that purpose. But what she really wanted was to see her granddaughter.

Edie set a kettle on the gas stove to boil, then crossed her arms to keep from washing the dirty dishes. She eyed them with a quick intake of breath, even as Lucy barrelled into the room, red-cheeked.

She offered Lucy a smile, and the girl grinned, then set about tying an apron around her waist and running hot water into the sink.

Paul caught her eye and cocked his head as if to show her he'd been right, and she couldn't help chuckling beneath her breath. Even after all these years, he was still so cute at times. He sat at the dining table, the accounting book open in front of him, pen poised above the page. His clothes were dirty and sweat-stained, his hair lank against his head — he'd spent the morning fixing the northern fence line. He must've been exhausted but didn't show it. Nothing seemed to faze her tall, strong husband. He rarely complained, instead focusing on whatever had to be done with a smile.

What had she done to deserve having someone so wonderful in her life? He'd helped her raise Keith, was a kind, patient, and generous father in her son's life. They'd never spoken to Keith about the adoption, and she'd assumed he'd remember that Paul wasn't his birth father, but he didn't seem to. From what she could tell, Keith was convinced Paul was his father, and she didn't have the heart to tell him otherwise. It would've hurt Paul to hear her say the words, she was sure of that. He'd devoted every day of the past twenty years to being the kind of husband and father that she and Keith needed, and she couldn't take that away from him.

Besides, Charlie had never returned from the war and his parents had died years ago. There was really no reason for Keith to know the truth, not when the truth could hurt the man sitting across from her, the man who'd dedicated his life to making their little family happy.

The truth, such as it was, would serve only to hurt the two men who made her heart whole. So, she kept it to herself, hidden down inside her, and would take out the memories every now and then to turn them over, examine them, sift through the fading pictures in her mind, then file them back away again, careful not to let any escape into the world.

The only person, other than Paul, who knew the truth about Keith's father, was Mima. And she'd agreed not to say anything.

Perhaps one day she would open that wound and bring Charlie's story to light, but not yet. Not with Keith living in Sydney with his one-year old daughter and pretty young wife. Not when she rarely saw him as it was. She didn't want to give him any excuse not to visit more often.

The kettle whistled on the stove top and she poured two cups of tea into large, china mugs. Then, added milk and handed one to Paul. As she carried her own to the table to sit with him, she tripped on the edge of a floor tile and a wave of tea spilled over the side of her cup, wetting the floor.

She cried out, set the almost empty cup on the table, and peered at the wet floor, anger boiling over.

"Perfect! Just what I need! Another mess to clean up."

Paul leapt to his feet and hurried to wrap his arms around

her. He tilted her head with a finger pressed to her chin, until her gaze met his. Tears spilled into her eyes, and frustration churned in her gut.

"It's fine, don't worry about it. Lucy and I will clean it up."

She stamped her foot, conscious that she was a forty-one-year-old woman acting like a child, but not caring. "I can't believe I did that. I spend all day, every day, cleaning, wiping, scrubbing, and washing, and now I've got to mop the kitchen floor again."

He shook his head, a smile tickling his lips. "Don't worry about it, we'll take care of it. Sweetheart, this business is getting too big for the two of us to handle on our own. You're gonna have to get used to the idea of having people help, and you're going to have to rest."

"I rest," she countered.

"I mean more than when you fall into bed at night. I think the two of us should take a break every afternoon. We should switch off, no matter what's going on, and sit down, put our feet up, go for a swim...something to relax and recharge before the dinner rush. What do you say?"

It wasn't a bad idea. In fact, the more she thought about it, the more appealing it became. She gave a quick nod. "Okay. I think it might work. Of course, I'm not sure how everything will get done..."

He stroked a wisp of hair away from her face. "We'll cross that bridge when we come to it."

It was one of his favourite sayings; he said it to her often. Whenever she worried about something that could happen, or should happen but might not, he'd bring comfort to her, calm her with those words. It was a saying his mother used. That was what he'd told her. She'd been quiet then, pensive, thinking through what it must be like for a mother to lose her son to a country on the other side of the world. Sydney seemed far enough for her. She couldn't imagine having Keith disappear around the globe to build his family.

She shivered. "I think I'll go out to the garden, do some digging. It always helps me feel better."

The garden was her happy place. It stretched from near the chook pen almost all the way to the stables. A rectangular swathe of land that was hers, only hers, to do with as she liked. Paul had built it for her years ago, and she'd tended it lovingly ever since. It held the precious Waratah bushes she'd brought as seeds from Bathurst when they first moved to Cabarita. It also held the vegetables, salads, and some of the fruit Mima served to the inn's guests. Edie took pride in the fact that their menu was filled with fresh garden produce. She loved digging in the dirt, pulling weeds, and patiently tending to plants until they burst through the soil, reached skyward, and blossomed.

Edie carried her small bag of garden tools over one shoulder, a rake balanced beneath her arm, through the neat garden gate. She set everything on the ground, then squinted through the glare of the sun to where Mima lay, on a banana lounge, in her red and white polka dot bikini. A tent-like round hat balanced on top of her head, large white rimmed sunglasses peering out from beneath its brim.

"Hey, hon."

Mima worked hard in the kitchen, but never seemed to have trouble taking time off to rest when her job was done, unlike Edie.

Mima stirred, yawned. "Oh, hi Edie. Time for some gardening?"

Edie nodded and raised a small shovel in one gloved hand as a kind of salute.

She set to work, loosening the soil around a newly planted set of snap pea vines. They'd burst through the dirt a week earlier, and she was concerned it might be too early in the season. Thankfully, the cool nights were growing warmer each day and there was no chance of a frost this far north.

Her thoughts returned to her granddaughter. Nyreeda Summer had been born a year earlier, though Paul and his wife Mary called her Reeda, and Edie liked the name right away. She'd immediately convinced Paul to drive them both to Sydney, leaving the inn entirely in Mima's care for a full two weeks. Mima had insisted she could take care of things, and Edie had to admit she'd managed it — in fact she'd done better than Edie could've hoped. As Paul pointed out, it was high time Edie gave her friend credit for pulling her life back together.

The sight of Reeda's little fists pumping in the air, hearing her mewling cry, all of it had brought tears to Edie's eyes. She was a beautiful child. Edie had spent the two weeks of their visit cradling little Reeda in her arms and helping Mary around the house. She was conscious of not wanting to get in her daughter-in-law's way, but Mary was loving, patient and made Edie and Paul feel right at home in their rented, three-bedroom brick home.

If only they lived closer. Edie longed to be able to see Reeda's sweet face every day. She'd be so much bigger now. It was time for her and Paul to plan another visit south. Perhaps they'd go for Christmas.

"Everything okay, hon?" Mima's voice broke through her reverie.

Her friend leaned against the rickety garden fence her curves hugged by the fashionable bikini.

Edie glanced up at her with a half-smile. "Thinking about Reeda, how much I miss her. That's all."

"I can't wait to see her," replied Mima with a wistful smile.

"I feel like I'm always missing people," huffed Edie, digging the shovel harder into the dirt.

"That's life, my love."

Mima's flippant remark only stirred anger in her veins. What did she mean? Of course it was part of life, as though Edie didn't know it. She knew it better than anyone.

"I know that," she hissed.

"Don't get pissy with me," replied Mima.

Edie sighed. "I'm sorry, only I feel as though I've lost everyone I've loved. If they haven't passed, they live so far away I hardly get to see them..." She sighed, stopped digging, and settled back on her haunches.

"Thinking about Charlie again?" asked Mima, chewing on her lower lip.

"Always," replied Edie.

It was true, he was never far from her thoughts. How long had it been since she'd seen his face? Too long. She barely remembered what he looked like. His face used to be etched in her brain, now it was nothing but a whisper. Had he even been real?

Mima sighed. "Sweetheart, I say this with love...you have a wonderful life here. Is it perfect? No, of course not because nothing is. But from the outside looking in, it's pretty darned close."

Edie's heart contracted. She knew how Mima longed to have a family of her own. Back when they were younger it was all she'd wanted. When she lost her fiancé in the war, she'd never fully recovered from it, and had given up on the idea of love. Edie was blessed: she had Paul, Keith and his family, her parents — even if they did live so far away. She should be grateful, she knew that. Sometimes it was hard to keep things in the right perspective though, especially during the everyday slog of life.

"I know...you're right."

Mima shook her head. "Your husband adores you, sometimes I think you take that for granted. I wish...I wish Ollie were here, looking at me the way Paul looks at you. You don't know how lucky you are." Mima's voice wavered and she cleared her throat. "I'm not trying to razz you, only pointing out what you're clearly missing."

Edie swallowed, dipped her head. "I miss Keith and Mary, little Reeda, my parents...Charlie." The last was said in a whisper, almost as though she were ashamed to admit it, but it was true. She missed him. Oh, she loved Paul, there was no doubt about that, but the love she'd lost in the war always lingered in the recesses of her mind. What might have been, what couldn't be, the life she'd lost the day he was captured.

Mima pushed through the garden gate, took Edie's hand, and tugged her to her feet. Edie stood with a groan.

"Sweetheart, you know how much I care about you. You're my family, you're my best friend, but I have to tell you something..."

Edie held her breath, waiting for the words she knew were coming.

"You've got to let go of the past. It's time to bury those memories. They've got a hold on you, and you're not living your life the way it should be lived — fully vested, fully committed. You're stuck in the past, and it's holding you back. There's nothing any of us can do to fix what's been done, or to take back the lives that were ripped from our hands all those years ago. But what we can do is choose to put it all behind us and live in this moment. Paul deserves that, and so do you."

When Edie was finished working in the garden, she put her tools away, Mima's words still ringing in her ears. Had she lived too long in the past? She felt the truth of it yet hadn't realised it until the moment Mima spoke it out loud.

She hurried inside to wash her hands, then strode into the owner's suite. The queen-sized bed was neatly made, a bunch of fresh flowers sat in a vase on a side table, their sweet scent filling the room. Colourful swirling wallpaper lined the walls, giving the room a vibrant look, and bright orange curtains peeled back from a square window that looked out across the yard towards the sound of the waves sighing in the cove.

She sat on the bed, careful not to wrinkle the bedspread too badly, and pulled a wooden box out from beneath it. She straightened, then flipped open the lid. Her fingers traced the carvings, the head of the horse she'd loved so well for so long, the lines of flowers and vines that blended away from it. A smile tugged at her lips, even as tears blurred her vision.

So many memories, so much loss.

She sighed as she turned the small, silver ring around and around on her pinky finger. She pulled it free, and set it in the box, her heart aching with a pain she hadn't felt in years. Grief wracked her body with sobs.

The ring sat in the middle of the box, small, alone. She stared at it, as tears wound their way down her cheeks. She pulled her gaze away and opened her bedside drawer. A stack of journals was piled in there, along with some knitting and the latest Agatha Christie novel. She took the journals out of the drawer, patted around inside it to make sure she'd retrieved them all, then stacked them inside the box as well.

Edie said a prayer for Charlie, for the love she'd lost so long ago, and for the wound that still ached in her heart.

"Goodbye," she whispered. "Farewell, my love."

A groan issued from the depths of her gut and she covered her mouth with one hand. It was time to move on, to put the past behind her. More than time. She'd married another, raised a family, she was a grandmother. How could this wound still carry on its wings so much raw pain?

The lid flipped shut with a dull thud. Edie knelt beside the bed and pushed the box beneath it. She couldn't bear to get rid of it entirely, but for now it could lay hidden in the darkness. Forgotten.

She stood to her feet, smoothed the front of her bright yellow culottes, and inhaled a long slow breath. Then, she wiped the tears from her cheeks with the back of her hand and strode from the room, pulling the door shut with a solid click behind her.

❦ 7 ❧

CABARITA BEACH

Bindi lay on her bed staring at the ceiling. She'd retreated upstairs to take a nap and had slept for a good two hours. Her eyes were leaden, her thoughts disoriented. She rolled onto her side to look at the clock on the bedside table. It was eight o'clock at night, which meant the tea service would be almost over. The rush would be past, and her stomach cramped with hunger.

She swung her legs over the side of the bed with a yawn and sat up, then clamped her hands to either side of her head to stave off the dizziness that enveloped her. She waited, breathing deep. Finally ready, she headed downstairs. She hadn't even taken a moment to glance in the mirror. She must look a fright, but she didn't care. She was tired, sick, and hungry. She couldn't pretend everything was okay any longer.

On her way to the dining room, she passed the sitting room. The glow of a lamp caught her eye and she glanced inside to see Brendan, seated in an armchair with a book open in his lap.

He looked up at her, smiled and shut the book, then strode towards her. "There you are. I was wondering when you'd show. Kate told me you usually come downstairs for some tea, then take it up to your room. I thought we could eat together...if that's okay with you?"

Bindi gave a mute nod. Brendan fell into step beside her. "You okay, honey? You look a little tired."

She wanted to laugh, but that might seem rude, or a bit unhinged. Instead, she offered him a tight smile. "Yes, I am tired actually. I had a nap, and I'm not really awake yet."

He nodded. "Ah, right. That's why the hair thing..." He waved a hand at her hair with a wry smile.

"Bad?"

"No, not bad. Cute...actually, this trend might catch on. The bed-head look is in at the moment, right?"

He'd always had a way of disarming her when she was feeling tense, or when things between them got too heated.

"That's right. It's called bed-head chic. I really think we'll see it on the runways in Paris soon."

They laughed together as the seating hostess found them a table. Bindi wasn't used to eating in the dining room with the guests, usually preferring instead to eat with her sisters on the verandah when they were around, or otherwise by herself in her room in front of an episode of *Neighbours*. Thinking about it made her wonder if perhaps she'd invested in building enough of a life for herself in Cabarita. She'd been living there for over a year and yet hadn't really made any friendships outside the inn.

They ordered their meals and Bindi took a sip of the sparkling water their waitress brought them while they waited. Brendan talked to her about everything going on in Melbourne, and she found she didn't miss it at all. Hearing about their friends' lives and what was happening in the community of journalists she'd been part of made her grateful she'd walked away from it all. She loved her quiet life in Cabarita. She should've made the move much sooner and might have if she hadn't been waiting for Brendan to be ready to get serious about their relationship. How many years had she wasted on him?

When their meals arrived, they each fell silent for a few moments. Kate's steak pie with mashed potatoes and fresh vegetables was one of Bindi's favourites. She sliced off a piece of the pie and savoured the taste as the flavours of steak, onion, mushrooms, and gravy exploded in her mouth.

"This is delicious," said Brendan around a mouthful of pastry.

Bindi nodded. "Kate makes delicious food."

"That's right, I forgot Kate was cooking here. The whole place is really impressive, Bindi." He glanced around the dining room. "It's a beautiful inn, the food is amazing, the ambience is perfect. Well done."

She glowed beneath his praise. It felt good to have Brendan compliment what they'd built, even if he wasn't in her life anymore. She was proud of herself and her sisters and loved hearing the confirmation of the work they'd done from other people as well.

"Thank you, we're really happy with how it turned out."

"I still can't believe that twit at Channel Four fired you," he said, leading into a subject that was still a little raw for Bindi.

She flinched. "Yeah, it was hard walking away, knowing that it was my fault, that I'd destroyed the career I'd dreamed of having for so long."

He shook his head, chewed, and swallowed. "But it wasn't your fault at all. It was your fact checker. I asked around after you left, and apparently Debbie and Tim were having an affair. He threw you under the bus for her, because of their relationship."

Bindi's breath caught in her throat. She knew Debbie was messing around with someone in the office but hadn't known for sure it was their boss. It made sense though, given the way Debbie wouldn't say who she was seeing. She'd even wondered about it a few times.

"Wow. I didn't know that."

"Yeah, he shouldn't have done it."

Bindi sighed. "I see what you're saying, but it doesn't matter — Debbie was working for me, I was responsible. I should've checked up on her work. It was my mistake."

Brendan sighed, reached for her hand, and squeezed it. "You're always so good."

She grunted. "Am I?"

He nodded. "Yeah, you always do the right thing. You're really too good, actually." His eyes sparkled. "Sometimes I wish you'd just forget about being good for a little while and call them names or something."

"That would make you feel better?"

"A little," he admitted.

She took another bite of pie, still thinking about what he'd said. Most of the time she'd worked with Debbie, she'd had no idea Debbie was dating Tim. And the worst of it was, Tim was married and had two children. Had he left his wife? Bindi didn't think so, which meant he'd been having an affair with her fact checker. No wonder he hadn't wanted to discipline Debbie for her shoddy work.

"You've got a good thing going here, Bindi," said Brendan, interrupting her thoughts. "I wish I had something like this to go to."

She frowned. "But you love your job."

He shrugged, digging through the pile of carrots and peas on his plate with his fork. "Yeah, but I don't think it's going to work out. My boss has it in for me."

"Why, what happened?" Her eyes narrowed. This was a

pattern with Brendan. He seemed hardly able to stay in any job for more than a couple of years.

"Oh you know, the usual stuff. Anyway, I told you I'd ask around for you, and Pete was really interested when I told him about your work and that you were available."

Bindi set down her fork to listen.

Brendan studied her face a moment, then continued. "He's pretty upset with me right now about an argument we had. He threatened to fire me, but he said that if you come back to Melbourne with me, we could work together, and he'd forget the whole thing. He's a fan of your work, apparently. Wants to get together to talk about it, about opportunities at the newspaper. Says he knows Tim, thinks he's a self-serving bottom feeder — his words, not mine."

"I don't have any experience as a newspaper journalist," she countered.

"He knows that, but he thinks you'd be perfect for this column he's been wanting to launch, all about Generation X."

"Generation X?"

"Yeah, that's what they're calling us, you know, our generation."

She inhaled a slow breath. Was this the real reason he'd come to Cabarita to see her? To save his own job? He didn't miss her at all, just wanted her to come back to Melbourne so his boss wouldn't fire him.

"That's why you're here?" she asked.

He shook his head. "No, it's one of the reasons, but like I told you — I miss you. We were good together. I'm confused... I don't know what I want. But I had to see you. Give me another chance...that's all I ask."

Bindi's head spun. He missed her. He needed her. Wanted her to come back to Melbourne with him. But she'd moved on with her life. Still, journalism had been her dream. If she could get a job at a newspaper in Melbourne, would that be enough? Would that mean more to her than running the inn?

"I don't know..." she said. "I need some time to think about all of this. It's a lot."

He cocked his head. "I know, I've landed it on you all at once. Sorry about that." He wiped his lips with a napkin. "Take your time to think it through, I'll be here."

He stood, kissed her cheek, and strode from the dining room, leaving her seated at the table alone.

❦

WHEN BINDI HAD CLEANED HER PLATE OF PIE AND MASHED potatoes, she wandered into the kitchen. A cup of tea sounded enticing. She heard voices on the verandah and peered out through the window on tiptoe. Kate and Reeda sat in rocking chairs, feet resting on the top railing as they talked and laughed together.

She smiled, set the kettle to boil and scooped tea leaves into a tea pot. By the time the tea was ready, she'd filled a plate with melting moment biscuits, and added it all to a tray along with cups and saucers. She carried the tray out through the back door, and along the verandah to where her sisters were seated.

A cool breeze lifted the hair from her neck. Waves pounded against the shore in the cove, a steady rhythm that brought comfort to her troubled thoughts. She wasn't ready for this, but it was time.

Kate faced her with a smile.

Reeda laughed. "There you are. We'd wondered what had become of you. Your hair has a weird...kind of untamed look tonight."

Bindi chuckled, set the tray on a table between her sisters.

"Thanks, I'm fashion forward. Didn't you know? This is the new trend."

"You always look beautiful. Grab a seat." Kate waved a hand at an empty rocking chair.

She joined them, sighing as she leaned back in the chair, her feet pumping softly to rock back and forth.

"It's so lovely out here at this time of night," she said.

"Mmm," agreed Reeda.

Kate leaned forwards in her chair. "So, that guy in there... is that Brendan? As in your ex-boyfriend?"

Bindi stopped rocking and sighed. "Yep. Oh, and thanks for booking him in without telling me, by the way."

"What? Did I?" Kate's incredulous voice told Bindi she hadn't known who Brendan was when she filled in the booking at the reception counter.

"Never mind." It didn't make much difference. Whether she'd known he was coming or not, she could never have guessed his reasons. She still couldn't wrap her head around his proposal — he wanted her to give him another chance, to move back to Melbourne and to take a job as a columnist at his newspaper. It was overwhelming.

"So, what does he want?" asked Reeda.

Bindi shrugged. "To get back together, I think."

"What?" Kate stared at Bindi, wide-eyed. "That's not what you want, is it?"

"I don't think so... I mean, no. I don't know." Bindi scrubbed her face with both hands. "He wants me to move back, and his boss is interested in hiring me at his newspaper."

Kate blinked. "Are you going to do it?"

Bindi sighed. "I don't know."

Reeda reached for Bindi's hand and squeezed it. "You should do whatever is best for you, honey. We support you whatever you decide."

"Yes, definitely," added Kate. "We'd miss you, of course, but if that's what you want to do, go for it."

Bindi blinked back tears. Her sisters were so good to her, she loved them in a way she hadn't believed she could again after everything that'd pushed them apart as teenagers. Losing their parents in a car accident had put a rift between the three of them that they hadn't truly been able to overcome until Nan died.

"I don't think I want any of that...not anymore," replied Bindi. "Thanks for the support though."

"Are you sure?" prodded Reeda. "I don't want you to have any regrets."

"I'm not sure, but there's something else going on in my life that I need to talk to you about. And the stuff with Brendan really isn't my priority at the moment. I'm going to tell him no, for now at least, because I have to focus on myself."

Kate's brow furrowed. "Okay. What's going on?"

Bindi shifted in her seat. This was harder than she'd thought it would be. She stood, strode to the verandah rail, clenched her hands around it, then turned to face her sisters. "As you've both noticed, lately I've looked a bit tired."

Kate and Reeda both nodded.

"I haven't been feeling well, either. So, I went to see a doctor. Doctor Ash in Kingscliff. He ran some tests, and it turns out I'm sick."

Reeda frowned. "How sick?"

"I have Non-Hodgkin lymphoma."

Kate covered her mouth with a hand. "Cancer?"

Bindi nodded.

Kate's eyes filled with tears. "No." She shook her head. "No!"

Reeda crossed her arms over her chest, her face hardening. Her nostrils flared.

"Doctor Ash says the prognosis is good. I've already begun chemo, and apparently, we caught it early. It's very likely I'll beat this thing and get back to living my life in no time." Bindi tried to brighten the words with a smile.

"This isn't fair," snapped Reeda. She turned away, facing into the darkness.

Kate reached Bindi in two strides, wrapped her arms around her sister and squeezed tight. She sobbed into Bindi's shoulder. "We'll fight this. We will. You're going to be okay."

Bindi curled her own hands around Kate's thin waist. "I know, I'm young and strong."

"I can't lose you," whispered Kate against Bindi's hair.

"I know...you won't. I'm not going anywhere."

Reeda stood and joined them, silently enveloping both sisters with her arms. She didn't speak, her face pinched. Bindi smiled at her through a veil of tears. Reeda nodded, bit down on her lips.

"It's not fair," she repeated, her teeth clenching down on the words. "We've been through enough. You've been through enough."

"I'll need you both..." began Bindi.

"We're here," replied Reeda firmly.

"Yes, whatever you need," added Kate. "We're a family. We'll beat this thing together."

8

ABRUZZI APENNINES, ITALY

The mountainside was rugged, steep with jagged rocky outcroppings that pushed through the white blanket of snow. The narrow dirt track he was following was mostly clear, but on either side of the trail, snow piled high where the sheep's hooves hadn't trampled it. Charlie stopped walking a moment to catch his breath. He leaned on his walking stick, the tip of it pressed into the palm of his leather glove.

Ahead of him, the small herd of sheep trotted as one, all headed in the direction of a cosy stone cottage in the distance. A trail of smoke curled from a stout chimney, dark windows peered like eyes surveilling the mountain range beyond and the valley, almost hidden from view below.

There weren't any trees this far up the mountain, only the occasional squat bush, or straggling shrubbery. Grass poked through in places where a sharp hoof had dug it up, but otherwise everywhere he looked was white or the slate grey of protruding rock.

A maremma trotted around the outside of the herd, first this way, and then that. Charlie studied the large, cream-coloured dog, a smile curling the corners of his mouth. She was an intelligent beast. He'd shouted her name, Aldo, only once that day. Otherwise, she followed his whistled commands without complaint, eager to please. She'd earned the bowl of warm gruel that awaited her at the cottage.

It was his first time taking the herd lower on the mountain to graze alone. Bruno had given him that freedom when they'd awoken before dawn that morning. Charlie had accompanied him many times over the past few weeks, ever since he'd managed to leave his sleeping mat and wander around the cabin without experiencing too much discomfort.

Bruno had grunted when he saw him, then handed him a coat and indicated he should follow. They'd skirted the mountain that day, and it'd taken every ounce of strength and determination Charlie had to make it back to the cabin, puffing and heaving for breath.

Even though he still didn't remember anything about himself, who he was, where he was from, or how he'd ended up on this mountain, Charlie enjoyed getting outside and inhaling the crisp, fresh air into his lungs. Ever since that day he'd felt his strength returning bit by bit, his muscles rebuilding piece by piece. He could climb the mountain now without pain in his side, though he still relied on a walking stick for support.

Maria had removed his bandage for the last time two weeks ago. He'd examined the wound and discovered it was completely healed with only a pink scar to show anything had happened. He pressed the place now with gloved fingers through his thick coat, and it felt good, strong.

He smiled, whistled to the dog, and watched as she drove the sheep towards their pen. Something about this felt familiar. Perhaps he'd herded sheep this way before or whistled to a dog in a similar manner. He couldn't be sure, only knew that it stirred something within him, something he couldn't quite place.

He'd begun working on the language. Learning words, bit by bit, sound by sound. Building a way to communicate with the man and woman who hosted him in their house. That much he'd figured within a short while of waking — he was their guest, they'd cared for him, nursed him back to health after being shot. Why he'd been shot and by whom, he still couldn't say. So far, he hadn't seen anyone other than Bruno and Maria in the months he'd slept on the floor of their stone cottage, even though he could communicate better with them now, neither one of his hosts liked to talk much about what went on outside their own insular world. No sign of another chimney spewing smoke on his mountainside walks either. No evidence of a nearby village, nothing to suggest that anyone else lived in the vicinity. And no one who spoke his language.

Every now and then he'd see something, like the dog rounding in on the sheep, and it'd spark a distant memory. Only the memory would be nothing more than a vapour, and no matter how quickly his mind grasped at its edges it never fully materialised. He felt it hover there, but it didn't reveal itself to him, didn't break through the haze that blanketed his mind still.

He shut the sheep into their pen and fed the dog in the small, timber stable set into the hillside. Then, he trudged along the winding, snow-covered path to the house. Snow had begun to fall while he was in the stable. Silent and white, it drifted in swirls to rest on the ground. It settled on his whiskers, his shoulders, and teased his numb nose.

Behind the cottage, Bruno's axe thudded into a log, hewing it in two. Charlie raised a hand in greeting and Bruno nodded in his direction, the swing of his axe never pausing in its descent. Keeping a cottage warm in this mountain range was a full-time job. Bruno settled the pieces of firewood on top of a pile that lined one entire outside wall of the cottage. Surely there was enough firewood to keep the fire burning until spring. Charlie didn't think he'd ever seen so much stacked in one place, though he couldn't be sure. Regardless, Bruno spent a portion of every day splitting more wood.

Inside the cabin, warmth quickly chased away the cold. A fire roared in the hearth and glowed in the pot-bellied stove. Maria stood by the stove, peering beneath the lid of a large, black pot. The scent filled his nostrils and his stomach clenched with hunger.

"*Spezzatino?*" he asked.

She nodded, smiled. "*Sì spezzatino...*" Mutton stew, one of his favourite meals.

He tugged the knit cap from his head and hung it on the wall, followed by his jacket. A few flakes of snow fell to the ground and he stared at them in dismay, thinking he should've brushed them off outside, now they'd leave a wet patch on the floor.

In the other small room, adjoining the main living area, he washed his hands and face in a bowl of water, then dried them on a towel. The room belonged to Maria and Bruno. There were two beds, one against each wall, with a curtain strung between them. It was a strange way for father and daughter to live, at least he assumed that's what they were from the way they interacted with one another. There was a photograph in a frame on one wall of a woman, dressed in black, he assumed had been Maria's mother. Though with his limited understanding of their language, he couldn't be certain of anything.

Since he'd woken that first time on his sleeping mat to discover himself in the cabin, Bruno had hewn an extra chair. Now there were three, crowded around the small square table. Charlie sat in his, arms crossed over his chest, and watched as Maria finished preparing the meal. She dished out three servings of the stew and set them each on the table just as Bruno pushed through the door and stamped the cold from his feet with a grunt.

Bruno and Maria conversed in their strange tongue for several minutes while Bruno washed up, calling to each other across the cabin.

When Maria laughed at something her father said, it lit up her face. Charlie smiled, unable to resist mirroring her joy. She caught his eye and her cheeks flushed red.

"*Stai bene?*" she asked.

He nodded, guessing that she'd enquired about his day, or his health. "Yes, I feel much better today. Thank you. *Grazie*."

Her flush deepened. She leaned across him to pour water from a jug into the three cups on the table. Her scent filled his nostrils, stirring something deep within him.

After the meal, he sat on his sleeping mat, his back pressed to the wall. Bruno lounged in a rocking chair by the fire, a pipe nestled between his lips and puffs of smoke issuing from his mouth every now and then. Maria busied herself cleaning up after their meal.

Charlie held the silver discs in his hands, the ones that'd told him what his name might be. He studied them again, as he had many times. On the other side from his name, was stamped an insignia, and written beneath it was "Royal Australian Airforce". So he was a soldier, perhaps even a pilot.

Though he couldn't remember the details of his life, he somehow knew that Australia wasn't anywhere near where he now found himself living. So what was he doing there?

When he looked up, he found Bruno studying him with interest. The man stood to his feet and lumbered into the other room, soon returning with what looked to be a folded newspaper. Charlie had wondered what Bruno was doing while he was out on the mountainside all day with the herd. He must've travelled to a nearby town.

Bruno handed the newspaper to Charlie and pointed to the headline with a grunt.

"Aerei tedeschi bombardarono le navi alleate nel porto di Bari."

What did it mean? Charlie glanced at Bruno, who nodded in encouragement, puffing again on his pipe. Then, he turned on his heel and headed back to his rocking chair.

Charlie returned his attention to the newspaper, unfolded it, and began attempting to read it. Seeing the foreign words on paper seemed easier to understand than hearing them, and before long he'd managed to translate enough of them to work out a little of their meaning.

In the centre of the page was a photograph of a port, with ships burning, black smoke billowing from their hulls. The word *Bari* stood out beneath the image. He'd seen Italian words before, but he wasn't sure how he recognised them. He knew somehow that the words on the page were written in that language and that he must be in Italy. He was a soldier in a war. It was the only likely explanation given the uniform he'd discovered by his makeshift bed. But if that were true, where was the rest of his battalion? Perhaps he was an escaped prisoner. Or maybe they'd all been killed or captured, and he was the only one left.

Charlie let the newspaper fall into his lap. He stared at the wall, the words he'd read swirling in his mind. None of it making much sense. One word stood out, *Germania*. Germany. They were the enemy, he felt it somehow.

He was a soldier in a war in Italy; he'd been separated from his battalion. A soldier who was far from home in a foreign land where he didn't speak the language. If he ventured from this small mountainside farm, he might be captured, possibly killed. The Germans could be anywhere, could stumble across him at any moment. He'd have to be more careful, make sure they didn't find him.

Maria met his gaze, her cheeks pink, her smile hesitant. His heart skipped a beat. He'd have to make sure this family who'd taken him in weren't in danger either, and to do that he'd have to stay hidden, at least until he figured out where the Germans were stationed and how he could escape.

❧ 9 ❧

CABARITA BEACH

The night before Kate and Alex's wedding, Bindi sat at a long table in a crowded restaurant. She couldn't believe Kate was getting married. After tomorrow, Bindi would be the only single Summer sister left. The din of conversation muffled the words being spoken throughout the restaurant. Bindi leaned back in her chair, sipping a glass of water as she scanned the room. Friends and family leaned together around small tables to talk, laugh, and share a meal together after the wedding rehearsal.

She sat next to Kate, who was deep in conversation with Alex and Reeda over the state of the beaches. Sand erosion was causing some distress among locals, and conversations about how to best address it oscillated between the various options, like dune care, sand dredging, and leaving nature to resolve the issue itself.

Bindi wasn't interested in joining the discussion. She preferred to listen, to watch, to enjoy being with her loved ones. How many more opportunities like this would she get?

She knew she shouldn't be morbid. If Kate or Reeda could overhear her thoughts, they'd tell her to stop thinking that way, that she was going to make it through this cancer scare and be well on her way to an amazing life on the other side of it.

They'd be right, of course. She had to stay positive. Still, today she didn't feel like it. In fact, she felt awful. A wave of nausea swamped her, and she clamped a hand over her mouth, swallowing it down. She'd been to the hospital for a treatment the day before and was feeling the effects of it now. Her head throbbed with pain, her body was weak, and she couldn't keep down any of the delicious food that crowded the plate in front of her.

They'd run through the wedding rehearsal that afternoon. She and Reeda were bridesmaids, opposite Alex's younger brother, Matt, and Reeda's husband, Duncan. The rehearsal had been awkward and stilted, and Bindi hoped the wedding would run smoother, as the pastor officiating the service had assured them all it would.

"I think I've still got sand in my teeth," said Matt, beside her.

She faced him with a grin. "Really?" He'd taken a dive in the sand while attempting to speed walk her down the aisle. "Let's try moving a little slower tomorrow, okay?"

He nodded, his pimply face flushing red. "I was nervous."

"Nothing to be nervous about, just hold onto my arm and I'll even count for you under my breath if you like."

"Thanks." He fidgeted with his knife and fork. His plate had been wiped clean of the roast they'd been served half an hour earlier. Bindi's plate had barely been touched.

"You're not hungry?" he asked.

She shook her head. "Nope."

"I'll eat your roast beef...if you don't want it."

"Be my guest." She pushed her plate towards him and

watched in amusement as he tucked into it with gusto. He was nineteen years old, and his stomach never seemed to reach full capacity. He was always eating something.

Bindi rested her chin in her hands and scanned the room. Mima's eyes found hers. Mima arched her eyebrows, as if to ask a question.

Bindi swallowed the swirling nausea. She shook her head in Mima's direction. Mima pushed out her chair and lumbered over to where Bindi sat.

"You okay, love?"

"I don't feel great."

"Want to get some fresh air?"

She nodded.

Mima held out a hand and Bindi took it, her own soon enfolded in Mima's larger one. Together they walked through the crowded restaurant, skirting around tables, and smiling and nodding at guests who called out a greeting.

Outside, a cool breeze lifted over Greenmount Beach and soothed Bindi's clammy forehead. They walked a few paces until they found a park bench, and both sagged into it at the same time.

"Thanks, Mima."

"Anytime, my love. I hate that you're sick."

"I know." When she'd told Mima about the lymphoma, she'd worried the older woman might faint. Mima's lips had clenched tight together, and her face had turned a shade of pale she'd never seen before.

Mima patted her hand. "Is there anything I can do to help?"

"You being here is help enough."

"You know, Edie would've been great at this — taking care of you, helping you get through it...she was always great at looking after people," sighed Mima.

"She was good at that. I miss her." The familiar clenching

of her heart at the pricking of memories passed quickly. Each time she felt it, the grief moved on faster than the time before. It was fading most days. Sometimes it felt heavy, other times she could think of her grandmother and smile. "But I'm glad you're here, Mima."

She smiled at Mima and squeezed her hand. Mima looked at her with glistening eyes. "Me too, honey."

The dull roar of waves hummed nearby — the ocean inky black from where they sat. Overhead, rainbow lorikeets squawked and tittered, settling to sleep in the tall, green fir trees that lined the edge of the road. People ambled by in twos and threes. A shout followed by raucous laughter. The noise came from a local hotel where the murmur of conversation ebbed and flowed through the cool night air.

"I never had children of my own..." mused Mima, her voice soft.

"Did you want to?"

Mima huffed. "Of course. I would've loved to be surrounded by little cherub faces...in a way. Though, after Ollie died, I couldn't face the idea of finding someone else. When I finally pulled my life back together, I was living with your grandparents and the days ticked by. I never met anyone else I wanted to spend my life with and before I knew it, those days were gone. You only get a window of opportunity to build a family, and it's gone faster than you can imagine."

Bindi studied Mima's profile, her throat tightening. "I'm sorry, Mima."

Mima sighed. "Don't be sorry for me, I wouldn't change a thing. I ended up with all of you in my life, didn't I?"

Bindi nodded, unable to speak around the lump in her throat.

"That's what I'm trying to say — I never had my own children, or grandchildren, but I always felt as though Keith, and now you girls, were my family. And if anything happens..."

Her voice broke, and she inhaled a long, slow breath, her gaze meeting Bindi's.

Bindi smiled through a blur of tears. "Nothing's going to happen Mima. I'm going to be fine."

"I know, honey. You're strong, you'll get through this." Mima patted her hand. "It's just...you get to my age and you assume you'll die first. That's how it's meant to be. You're not supposed to outlive..." She hesitated, shook her head. "I love ya, kiddo. You may not know it, but you're the one who held all this together after Edie died."

Bindi rested a head on Mima's shoulder. "I love you too, Mima."

❦

THEY'D BEEN SEATED OUTSIDE FOR A WHILE BEFORE KATE came to find them. She encouraged them back inside and Bindi was feeling well enough to manage it, so she followed Kate and Mima back to the restaurant's door. Before she stepped inside, someone called her name from the street.

She spun around with narrowed eyes. Brendan.

"Oh, hi. What are you doing here?"

He grinned, shrugged. "You told me where you were eating, I thought I'd come and see if you wanted a lift home. It'd be good to talk and we haven't really had a chance yet. I've been staying at the inn a week, and you're always busy..."

Behind her, Kate called out. "Bindi, everything okay?"

She nodded. "Brendan's here, he's going to take me home."

Kate hurried to her side. "Brendan's here? Oh, hi Brendan." She waved a hand in his direction and he offered a brief nod. "You want to go back to the inn?"

Bindi shrugged. "Only if it's okay with you. I'm not feeling great, and I wouldn't mind getting to bed early."

"Of course." Kate embraced her, kissed her cheek. "Thanks for coming, I know it was hard for you to manage. I really wanted you to be here, though. So, thank you."

"Of course, I wouldn't have missed it for the world."

"I'm going to check on you when I get home...okay?" Kate stepped back, studying Bindi's face. She did that a lot these days, looking for any sign of the illness hidden away inside Bindi's body, no doubt. She worried and Bindi knew that. Though Kate didn't say it, instead adopting a cheerful tone and wide smile.

"Thanks," replied Bindi.

"I'll get your purse." Kate rushed into the restaurant, soon returning with Bindi's small, back purse.

Bindi slung the strap over one shoulder. She smoothed both hands down the skirt of her black halter-top dress. She'd bought the dress weeks earlier on sale at Tweed City. Already it was too big for her, loose around her stomach, hips, and breasts.

Bindi walked beside Brendan to his hire-car. He opened the door for her, and she slid into the leather seat with a sigh of relief. Even if it was unexpected to see Brendan, and she was dreading the conversation they were about to have, she was also relieved to be headed back to the inn. She pictured her bed and a rush of fatigue washed over her.

Bindi leaned her head against the car door, peering out the window as they drove.

When they reached the inn, she was struggling to keep her eyes open. Brendan had kept up a steady stream of chatter all the way there, talking about Melbourne, their friends, what was going on in people's lives she hadn't thought about in over a year. It surprised her how quickly she'd let go of that life. How little she thought about her friends, her job, her colleagues. It'd been easier to walk away and start again than she'd expected it to be. Part of that was the fact that Brendan was inextricably wound up in every part of her old life, and he'd caused her so much hurt and pain that walking away and not looking back had been the only way to cope.

Inside the inn, guests milled about. Wait staff were clearing the last of the evening meal from the dining room. Some carried cups of coffee into the dining and sitting rooms, or glasses of port and wine. Others were tidying, wiping, cleaning. The inn buzzed with activity and fairly hummed with life.

It was more than Bindi cared to face.

"Should we sit on the verandah?" she asked.

Brendan nodded, offered her a hand. She took it and they walked together out through the back door to where it was quiet. They found some rocking chairs at one end where they could be alone and sat, side-by-side, facing the darkness. He still held her hand. Her palm felt clammy.

"Have you thought about what we discussed?" he asked suddenly.

Bindi swallowed. She'd known he would ask her about it but had been putting off this conversation all week. "I have..."

"And?"

"And, I think it's best I stay here for now."

"What does that mean?" he faced her, releasing her hand, the crease between his eyes deepening.

She sighed. "I'm happy here."

"But what about us?"

"There is no us, Bren. You left me for another woman, or did you forget that?"

He scrubbed both hands over his face. "I told you, I'm confused about it all. I think it might've been a mistake... I miss you."

"You think?"

"I don't know." He slumped down in the chair, set his feet

on the verandah railing and began pumping, rocking the chair back and forth.

"But you're engaged to be married, Bren. You told me you weren't the marrying type, we were together for six years and you never once considered asking me to be your wife," she said, her voice rising steadily. "And here you are, newly engaged to someone else." She sat forwards in her seat, then stood and paced to the railing and back again.

He stood as well, faced her, both hands pressed to his hips. "You were always there... I took you for granted. I'm sorry. We got together so young, and I was focused on my career. Then Amy came along, and she was mysterious, exciting... I don't know. I guess I wasn't thinking clearly or something."

"What do you mean, Amy came along? Did you have an affair with her while we were still together?"

His nostrils flared.

"I knew it! I knew it," she cried.

"I'm sorry."

Bindi started pacing again. "And what's the matter now, the mystery is gone?"

He shrugged. "Something like that. I realise what I gave up. You and I, we have a history together. I don't know how to live without you."

He reached for her, but she pulled away. "You broke my heart. Did you know that?"

He inhaled a sharp breath. "I'm sorry."

"I thought we'd spend our lives together, and you..." She shook her head, slumped. "You were right."

"What?" he asked, his brow furrowed.

"You were right to break things off. We weren't good together. I wish you hadn't done it the way you did, and it hurt for a long time, but I've moved on."

He shook his head. "I can't believe you moved on so quickly."

"Don't go down that path... You know I had to. You left, you got engaged, did you think I should hang around pining for you?"

He grunted. "I thought maybe you'd give me another chance...after everything we've been through together."

She leaned on the verandah railing, staring out in the direction of the beach. The thunder of waves in the distance drew her in. Brendan joined her, sliding closer until their shoulders brushed together.

"You look beautiful tonight," he whispered, his eyes dark.

She smiled. "Thank you."

"Don't give up on us so soon. And you should think about that job offer...it's a good job, you'd like it."

"And if I go back with you, your boss will keep you on?"

His face reddened. "Something like that."

She sighed. "I'm sorry, Bren. I can't do it."

A plover called in the distance. He sighed. "I wish you'd —"

"There's something else," she interrupted.

He frowned. "Okay."

"I'm sick."

"Sick?"

"It's cancer."

His eyes darkened. "What?"

She nodded. "So, that's another reason I want to stay in Cabarita Beach. I need to be with my family right now. And I couldn't deal with starting a new, challenging job. I have to focus on getting well."

He took a step back, his hands clenched at his sides. "You have cancer? I mean, I could tell you'd lost some weight, but I thought it was the stress of everything — us, your grandmother, the inn... Does this mean...?"

"I'm not dying, if that's what you're asking. It's treatable, and I'm doing chemo at the moment. I'm going to be well again, it might take a little while, but I'll be fine." She felt like she was saying that a lot these days. *I'll be fine*. It's what everyone in her life wanted to hear, needed to hear. And she needed to believe it as well. So, she said it, over and over. Maybe if she said it often enough, emphatically enough, it would be true.

Brendan stepped forward, kissed her forehead, then pulled away. "I'm so sorry, Bindi. I hope you'll get through it. I can't... I can't do this though."

He spun on his heel and fled along the length of the verandah, jumped down the stairs and disappeared into the darkness, headed in the direction of the beach. She knew him well enough to know he needed time alone now to process what she'd said. She wasn't surprised he couldn't face her illness. She'd had six years to learn everything about him and one thing that'd always bothered her was his tendency to run from the hard stuff.

She sighed, straightened, and wandered back into the inn and upstairs to her room. She stood inside the room, glancing around at the few knick-knacks she'd gathered since she moved there. Most of her belongings were in storage in Kingscliff, since she only had this room at the inn. When Kate and Alex were married tomorrow, Kate was moving into Alex's house and she would move downstairs to the suite. She'd finally have enough space to move in all the things she'd shipped up from the unit in Melbourne. She'd miss this room though; it was cosy and had been her home for over a year.

She sighed, headed for the bathroom, and washed her face with warm water. It seemed to help with the nausea, although what she really needed now was sleep. Would it be this way for all of the chemotherapy treatments? She hoped not, but it was likely she guessed. The doctor had said there would be side effects. At least she only had another half dozen treatments to get through. After that, they'd decide whether she needed radiation or not. Something new to face. She couldn't think about that now. A gigantic yawn almost split her face in two.

She changed into pyjamas, climbed into bed, and rested her grateful head on her soft pillow. Brendan's words rang in her head, and she couldn't help running through the conversation over again in her mind. Had she made the right choice? Part of her longed to return to the life she'd left behind, but she knew it wouldn't make her happy. No, she was happy in Cabarita, at the Waratah Inn. It was her home now, she had family here, and a job that gave her more satisfaction than journalism ever had. She had a fight ahead of her that needed all the support she could get, and that support was here, not back in Melbourne with a group of people who'd barely called or emailed more than once or twice since she left. Her home was at the inn. And it was here she'd stay.

CABARITA BEACH

K ate Summer sat on the verandah at the Waratah Inn, her feet tucked up beneath her, a cup of steaming hot coffee nestled between her hands. The collar of her white dressing gown tickled her neck, and she inhaled a long slow breath.

She was getting married today.

At twenty-nine years of age she was marrying the man of her dreams. Alex had done it all before, of course. He'd married his late wife right out of university. Then, he'd lost her to cancer four years earlier, and moved to Kingscliff to escape the pain. She hated that he'd had to experience that, to go through the trauma of losing his wife and leaving behind everything and everyone he loved in Coffs Harbour, but she was grateful they met. Grateful he'd chosen to work part-time at the inn, taking care of the horses for Nan. Grateful for all the time they'd spent together since, getting to know one another, falling deeper in love with each day that passed.

And today, they'd finally be husband and wife. She would move out of the downstairs suite at the inn, where Nan and Pop had lived together for years, and join Alex in his house in Kingscliff. She'd already moved most of her possessions out earlier in the week. All she had left in the suite were the things she needed for the wedding and her honeymoon luggage.

Butterflies skittered in her stomach as she crossed her legs beneath her gown and let her eyes drift shut. A shout made her jump, and her eyes blinked open, taking in the winding sunlit path through the garden that led to the cove beyond. Alex jogged along the path, dripping wet with a surfboard beneath his arm.

He raised a hand in salute, and she waved back, a smile curling her lips. If nothing else, she was grateful for such a handsome soon-to-be husband who looked amazing in a pair of board shorts.

She laughed to herself, her face warming as he climbed the stairs and set down his surfboard against the verandah railing. He kissed her lips. Wet and salty, his lips pressed gently to hers, then he took a step back.

"Want a hug?"

She shook her head with a chuckle. "No thanks, I'm fine."

"Sure?" He cocked his head to one side, his hazel eyes sparking with mischief.

"Definitely." She tugged her dressing gown tighter around her body.

"Why are you sitting out here and not doing...I don't know...makeup or something with your sisters?"

"You have no idea what we're going to be doing all day today, do you?"

He shook his head and droplets of water fell from the dark hair slicked against his scalp. "I don't know...girly things, I guess."

"We're picking up the flowers, taking them to Mima's house, then we'll collect the cake and take it to the reception venue, where we'll check on the catering. After that we'll go to a cafe for brunch, then the hairdressers and finally we'll get our makeup done before the photographer arrives."

"Great...have fun." His eyebrows arched in disbelief.

"What about you and the boys? What are you up to?"

"We'll play a round of golf, shower and then show up on the beach in our suits, I guess."

She shook her head. "You definitely have the easy part."

He shrugged. "We can't help our natural beauty. Don't be jealous."

She slapped his arm playfully.

When she sighed, he arched an eyebrow. "What's up sweetheart?" He caressed her arm with one hand.

"I'm worried about Bindi."

He nodded. "Right. Me too."

"You are?"

"Of course. She's looking a bit thin and more pale than usual, don't you think?"

Kate's heart skipped a beat and her stomach tightened. She hated to admit it. Part of her wanted to stay upbeat, to only think positive thoughts. Not to let the worry, the anxiety, the dread seep in. She couldn't do it, had to be strong — for Bindi's sake. She was the big sister, Bindi had no one else to lean on but her, Reeda and Mima.

With their parents gone, Kate felt the weight of parental responsibility landed in large part on her shoulders. Since Bindi told them about her illness, Reeda had retreated into herself, the way she always did with anything emotional or confronting. Mima didn't live at the inn, and had other things occupying her time and attention. It was Kate who watched Bindi suffering, drove her to treatments at the hospital, and held her hair back when she threw up her breakfast.

She shivered, set her coffee mug on the floor, and embraced herself. Blinded by tears, she whispered. "I'm not ready to lose her."

Alex squatted beside her, took her hands in his and squeezed them. "You're not going to lose her. And whatever happens, I'm here for you. We'll get through this together."

She nodded and her throat was tight. "I know this must be hard for you, seeing it happen again..."

His jaw clenched. "I hate it." His eyes flashed.

"I'm sorry."

"Don't be. This isn't the same thing as what happened with Anna. She had a different type of cancer and she didn't have a chance. Doctor Ash says that Bindi's going to make it through this, that they've caught it early, it's not aggressive, she'll be okay."

She nodded, sniffled. "You're right. I was thinking about you, about how you lost your wife, and it reminded me of Bindi..."

He smiled. "You can't think about this today, honey. This is our wedding day. I'm so excited to marry you and start our lives together. This thing with Bindi will pass, she'll recover, and we'll all live a long time together. You and Bindi will take after Edie and Mima, puttering around in the garden, riding horses along the beach, arguing, and getting up to mischief together for many, long years to come."

She laughed, her throat aching. "I hope so."

He kissed her forehead.

"Did you have a nice surf?"

He nodded. "It's perfect out there. The waves are a little small but curling nicely. You should head out — if you have time between all the flowers and cakes and stuff."

Her eyes narrowed. "I remember a time when you said you didn't surf, but you've been going out a lot more lately."

"Yeah, I stopped surfing for a while after Anna died. It

was something we used to do together all the time. How we met, actually, out beyond the break down off the main beach. When she died, I couldn't face going out into the surf alone. It hurt too much. But now, since I met you... I can face it. And not only that, I've begun to enjoy surfing again. It's something I look forward to, and that's all because of you."

Kate stroked the side of his face, cupped his cheek in her hand and moved closer to kiss his soft lips. "Today is a day for new beginnings."

He smiled, filling her heart with joy. "New beginnings."

THE SCENT OF FLORAL PERFUME DRIFTED OUT OF THE bathroom into Kate's suite at the inn. She smiled as she pulled on her wedding dress. It was a simple sheath dress, that almost reached the floor. It featured a plunging neckline with an even deeper plunge in the back, with capped sleeves and a matching veil that the hairdresser had fixed into her hair with pins alongside several fresh, pink rosebuds.

She studied her reflection in the full-length mirror as Reeda zipped up the side of her dress. Reeda squeezed Kate, with a smile aimed over her shoulder at the mirror. "You look stunning."

Kate smiled, working hard not to cry. She couldn't believe it was all coming together so well. They'd picked up and delivered everything, had a delicious brunch together with some of her friends, and were only waiting on the photographer to arrive before they headed to Coolangatta. She and Alex had decided to get married at Rainbow Bay, on the beach. The weather was perfect, the sun shone, there was a hint of a breeze, and no sign of rain. And in two hours' time, she'd be Mrs. Cannon.

Bindi joined them in the bedroom, her sandy blonde hair

piled into a bun on top of her head, with strands woven together and held in place by more pink rosebuds. The pink contrasted with the green of her eyes. Her blush highlighted the rise of her cheeks.

"Bindi, you're beautiful." Kate reached for her sisters' hands and held them between her own, as a lump formed in her throat. "And you too, Reeda. Wow. I'm so grateful for both of you. Thank you for being here. You've helped to make this the most special day of my life."

Bindi nodded, her eyes gleaming. "I love you, sis."

"You too," replied Kate.

Reeda sighed. "Well, I guess I'd better say it too... I love you, Katie. You know I do."

"Did that hurt?" asked Kate.

"A little bit." Reeda's eyes narrowed. "Moving on, let's get this veil sorted, and I'll find your shoes." Reeda was the sister least comfortable with expressing her emotions, but it was clear to Kate how much her sister cared about her. She'd never doubt that again. After so many years estranged from each other, her heart overflowed with love for the two women she'd spent so much time running from. They'd all suffered when they lost their parents and their relationships had never really recovered. Not until Nan brought them back together by bequeathing them the Waratah Inn.

There was a knock at the door, and Mima poked her head inside.

"Well, look at the three of you." She wiped a stray tear from one eye. "Just letting you know the photographer is here, and ready to start snapping photos."

The three of them gathered their shoes and purses and headed outside to pose in the gardens surrounding the inn while the photographer took snapshots. Kate's heart raced, as the time on her watch ticked by.

When they were done, they wandered out to the front of

the inn to wait for the limousine that would take them all to Coolangatta. Mima was seated on a chair in the shade by the driveway, knitting in her lap, needles clacking. She wore a lilac coloured dress, with a cream wrap around her arms and matching cream pumps. Jack was there as well, standing beside her, his hands clenched together in front of his grey suit. His silver hair was combed neatly against his scalp and his tie knotted tight beneath his chin. He looked uncomfortable and handsome all at the same time.

"Jack, you look amazing," declared Bindi, standing on tiptoe to kiss his cheek.

His face flushed red and he mumbled something about being unable to breathe in this thing.

Kate kissed his cheek next. "Thank you for all your help in putting this together," she said. "And for giving me away at the wedding."

He smiled, his eyes gleaming. "It's one of the greatest honours of my life, sweetheart." He embraced her, and her chest ached with memories of Nan, Mum, and Dad, who couldn't be there with her and who she wished with all her heart could see her marry Alex, and how happy he made her.

As if he could read her thoughts, Jack said. "Edie would be really proud of you, today."

Kate smiled, unable to reply. Reeda embraced Jack as well, just as the long, white limousine pulled into the driveway, tyres crackling on the gravel as it circled around to where they were waiting.

They climbed in, and Kate peered out at the inn, its pale-yellow walls and white trim gleaming in the bright, spring sunshine.

"I can't believe you're not going to live here anymore," whispered Bindi.

Kate squeezed her hand. "I know, me too."

"I'm going to miss having you around at night. It'll just be me...that's so strange."

"You and two dozen guests, plus a night manager."

Bindi shrugged. "True, I guess I won't really be alone. Not while I'm living at the Waratah."

"And besides, I'm only a few minutes away if you ever need me. I still want to drink those hot chocolates together, sitting on the verandah, and don't forget our sunset walks on the beach."

"Good," replied Bindi, leaning her head on Kate's shoulder. "Just as long as you don't forget about me."

"That could never happen." Kate stroked Bindi's hair.

◈

THE WIND PICKED UP AND COOLED THE FILM OF SWEAT that coated Kate's body. She stared down at the beach, through the sea grass and undulating dunes. Guests sat in white chairs or stood, talking together. She inhaled a sharp breath. This was it. She was getting married. She'd begun to wonder if this day would ever come. Her engagement to Davis had dragged on for months without them ever setting a date, and she'd been fine with that. When she and Alex became engaged though, she couldn't wait to mark the day in the calendar when she'd become his wife.

Kate glanced down at her dress, smoothed it against her legs. She held a bouquet of pink roses in one hand. Ahead of her, in a line of sorts, stood Reeda and Bindi. They wore pale pink sheath dresses and held white roses in bouquets accented with sprigs of baby's breath. She shot them a smile. Reeda reached out a hand to squeeze her arm.

"Show time," she whispered with a smile.

Kate nodded, blinked once, then again. Her stomach squeezed as nerves fluttered. Bindi blew her a kiss.

She smiled at Jack who stepped forwards and offered her his arm. She took it. It comforted her to feel his warmth and strength beside her. The breeze riffled his grey hair.

He grinned. "You look beautiful, love."

"Thanks, Jack."

"I guess this is it." He patted her hand.

"I guess so."

"You know, I was married." His sentence hung in the air between them.

Kate's brow furrowed. She couldn't imagine Jack married, or with a family. But of course, it made sense. She'd never thought of Jack as a man with a past. He was Jack. Always there, in the background, quiet and solitary.

"You were?"

He nodded. "Twice, actually."

"Really? Wow. How is it possible I didn't know this about you?"

He chuckled. "I don't talk about it much."

"Understatement of the century," she mumbled.

"It's wonderful," he continued, ignoring her gripe. "This thing you're doing, it's good. Alex is right for you, and I know the two of you will build a great life together."

"Any tips?" she asked, as nerves battled in her stomach.

"Don't stay angry, always apologise, and never say anything you'll regret because you can say sorry, but you can't ever take back those words."

She considered his statement. "Thanks, Jack, that's good advice."

"Oh, and remember — when you love each other, sometimes things can feel extra dramatic, you'll have high highs and low lows, and it might seem as though it's the end of the world, but there's always a new day, a chance to start again."

He studied her, a smile tickling the corner of his mouth,

the wrinkles around his eyes deepening. "And a kiss makes everything better."

"I'll remember that." She stood on tiptoe and kissed his weathered cheek. "I'm glad you're here."

Her throat tightened. It should've been Dad giving her away at her wedding. He and Mum had missed so many of the important events in her life — her graduation from high school, the cap and gown at the end of university, and now her wedding.

As though he could read her thoughts, Jack sighed. "I know your Dad would've loved this, kiddo."

She nodded, her eyes blurring with tears.

He leaned closer, cupped her cheek with his free hand. "But don't get caught up in that now, because this is a good day. We're celebrating, and your parents would want you to be happy today."

She blinked the tears away, inhaled a slow breath. "You're right. It's a happy day. Mum always loved weddings."

They began the slow walk together down the path that led through the dunes to the beach, following in the hollows in the sand left by Reeda and Bindi's feet.

"I wish you were here," Kate whispered, as images of her parents, smiling, laughing, and teasing her flashed through her mind. "I love you."

The lump in her throat swelled. She swallowed it down, shook her head and gazed at the wedding party ahead of them. When she saw Alex, the lump shrank away. His smile lit her up from the inside. He wore a white button-down shirt and charcoal pants with bare feet. His tanned skin contrasted with the white of the sand, and his curls blew free in the breeze.

The sound of music swelled from a cassette tape on a nearby table. Bindi reached the end of the makeshift aisle and stood to one side, her hands clasping her bouquet, eyes glistening. Reeda soon joined her. Then, Kate was there. Alex stood in front of her, his eyes fixed on hers.

"You're beautiful," he said.

She smiled, her heart full. This was where she was meant to be — standing beside Alex. She couldn't imagine living her life without him. He was the smile in her day, the warmth in the night, and the one she wanted to tell all her news. Excitement buzzed in her gut.

Jack shook Alex's hand, then passed her hand to him. Alex nodded in response. Kate fought back the urge to cry. She slid her hand into Alex's and squeezed. Then they faced the pastor together as a flock of gulls cawed overhead, and soon became husband and wife.

❧ 11 ❧

JUNE 1944

ABRUZZI APENNINES, ITALY

Charlie splashed a handful of water onto his face and swallowed a mouthful with a smile. The mountain stream tasted fresh, still cold as ice, even in summer. He cupped his hands again beneath the flow, watching them fill quickly with the clear liquid, then drank his fill and scrubbed his empty hands over his face. As his fingers combed his damp hair, he leaned back and rested on his haunches to look out across the valley below.

The mountain was covered in shoots of green grasses. Soft purple soapwort, navy blue helmets of the grape hyacinth, buttercups and forget-me-nots were scattered throughout the brilliant deep grasses. Pops of colour sprung up amidst the green, nestling beneath rocky outcroppings and shouldering the edges of the winding stream as it made its way over rocks and around hillocks towards the base of the mountain.

Kestrels and snow finches called and chirruped as they soared and dived overhead, snapping up insects and revelling in the beauty of the warm, summer's day. The sky was so blue

Charlie wondered if it might reach down to envelope him in its depths.

With a grunt, he stood, wiped his face with the back of his sleeve and headed for the cabin. He'd been counting the months by making marks in the dirt floor beside his bed. Footprints had blurred some of the lines, but he figured he'd been living with Maria and Bruno for at least seven months now, maybe longer.

His stride lengthened and he clipped along at a steady pace, his lungs welcoming the exertion. After so many months of herding the sheep on the mountainside, his strength had built, along with his stamina. He no longer puffed after a brisk walk along one of the many trails that meandered away from the farm towards the valley, or through the peaks. His wound was nothing more than a vague memory and a red spot on his side, with spider web tracks that ran away from it in several places.

The sheep were already locked in their pen for the night. A few bleated, most were already nodding. Behind the cottage, Maria stood by a sagging clothesline, pegging wet clothes to one end. Beyond her, a flourishing vegetable garden crawled up the incline. She'd taken to wearing men's pants in recent months, instead of the full skirts she'd donned each day when he'd first arrived, and Charlie thought it suited her. Her hair billowed around her head, brown lengths escaping her bun.

He broke into a jog, careful not to let his footfalls make a sound, threw his arms around her, and lifted her into the air. She squealed with delight, her arms flapping, until he spun her to face him. Her brown eyes flashed, her lips curling into a grin.

"Charlie..." she began.

He shushed her with a kiss, pressing his warm lips to hers, his eyes drifting shut as the familiar taste of her washed over him, wakening his body all the way to the soles of his feet.

When his eyes blinked open, she smiled at him. No longer shy, her face reflected a boldness that stole away his breath.

"You are finished early," she said, her words awash in a thick accent.

He'd been teaching her English, and she was picking it up more quickly than he'd believed possible. She'd helped him learn Italian when he'd first had the idea to reciprocate. Why not each learn the other's language? She'd been excited, explained in simple Italian that she'd never had the chance to finish high school, since when her mother died, she'd had to return to the mountains to help her father run the farm.

"I wanted to see you," he explained. "And besides, the herd ate their fill, the grass is so long and thick now."

Her cheeks flushed pink. "I'm glad to see you too."

He grinned. "You're getting so good at English, my darling."

She ducked her head, her dark lashes fanning her cheeks. "I have a good teacher."

When she met his gaze again, her eyes widened then focused on something over his shoulder. "Father!" she whispered.

She leapt away from him as though he were a hot coal, and continued pegging clothes to the line, her back to Charlie.

He shoved his hands deep into his pants pockets and studied her a moment, amusement tickling the corners of his lips. He was well enough to leave now. Well enough to find the rest of his troop, wherever they might be. Only, he didn't want to. He loved Maria. If he left her, would he ever see her again? He still didn't remember anything about his old life, but Maria and Bruno felt like family to him. Perhaps he didn't have a family of his own — if he did, wouldn't he remember them? Wouldn't something draw him back to them? Instead, he felt a compulsion to stay here with Maria.

"Charlie!" barked Bruno behind him.

Charlie strode to meet the man, and they walked side by side towards the sheep pen. Bruno marched in silence and Charlie waited for the admonishment. Had he seen Charlie and Maria embracing? Maria had been afraid of this moment, perhaps with good reason.

When they reached the pen, Bruno raised a foot to rest on the lower railing and set his hands on the top to peer at the animals in silence.

"I'm sorry... I don't know what you saw or what you think but—"

Bruno raised a hand to silence him, then spoke in Italian. Charlie understood most of what he said, with only a word here or there still unfamiliar to him.

He explained to Charlie that their food supplies were lower than expected due to carrying three, rather than two, people through a long winter. That, given the food shortages in the villages and towns in the area, it wasn't likely they'd be able to purchase enough flour or other essentials to supplement their vegetable garden and mutton for the winter to come. There were too many mouths that needed feeding in the mountains and not enough food to go around.

Charlie inhaled a sharp breath. He'd expected this conversation for months now. It was time for him to leave. He was too much of a burden on the small family. Bruno wasn't a man to show emotion, but he seemed sincerely sorry to speak the words, unable even to meet Charlie's gaze.

"It's okay," replied Charlie in halting Italian. "I understand. Only, where should I go?"

Bruno sighed. "I don't know...back to Pacentro. The Germans are still in the area, but perhaps you could head north?"

Charlie pressed both hands to his hips. That didn't sound like much of a plan to him.

"I don't want to leave," he said.

Bruno nodded, finally meeting his gaze. "I wish you did not have to."

"I want to marry Maria," added Charlie.

He watched Bruno's reaction carefully, unsure of what the man would think of his boldness. Slowly a smile built in Bruno's lips. He slapped a hand onto Charlie's shoulder.

"I know," he simply said.

Charlie's throat tightened.

"My brother has a farm, a much bigger farm than this, outside Casoli. You and Maria can marry and go there to live and work for him. He needs the help and can feed you both."

Charlie grinned. "You will give us your blessing?"

Bruno nodded. "You have my blessing, son. I will arrange it for you. You will marry in quiet when you reach Casoli."

Charlie reached out a hand and Bruno shook it hard, both men beaming.

"You've been so good to me, Bruno. Thank you."

Bruno nodded. "And you to us, Charlie. We are grateful God brought you to our home."

"But I'm concerned about you... how will you manage alone?"

"Signor Barese has a son, he has offered to help. I will be fine. You and Maria should take care of yourselves, don't worry about me."

It was the most Bruno had ever said to him that didn't involve the sheep, the dog, or splitting firewood. Charlie blinked as excitement built within him. He watched Bruno walk away.

He and Maria would be married soon. It hardly seemed real. Only, she hadn't agreed to it yet.

Charlie broke into a run, and found Maria still pinning

clothes to the now almost full clothesline. He grabbed her, spun her around, and dropped to one knee.

Her eyes darkened with confusion even as a smile teased her lips.

"Charlie, what are you doing?" she laughed over the words.

"Maria, I love you. You're like the sunshine on a cold day, the way you warm my heart. I want us to spend the rest of our lives together. Will you marry me?"

Her smile faded. "What? Marry? What did Father say?"

Charlie stood slowly, caressing Maria's hand with his fingers. "Your father gave us his blessing."

Maria's face split with a wide grin. She jumped into Charlie's arms, threw her own around his neck. Her kisses peppered his neck until he laughed and set her feet back on the ground.

"Is that a yes?" he asked.

"Yes," she nodded, her eyes gleaming.

He kissed her then and forgot all else, but for the love of the woman in his arms. For a single moment, there was no war, he knew who he was, and he wasn't lost. No longer was he alone in the world, Maria would be with him, would stand by him, holding his hands. They'd face it all together.

❦ 12 ❦

CABARITA BEACH

Bindi crossed her arms over her chest and glanced up at the morning sky. A flock of seagulls cawed as they circled overhead, then aimed for the cove. White clouds clumped and hung, unmoving, seeming as soft as cotton wool to be jumped into and slid down like a children's theme park ride.

The taxi's boot slammed shut and Brendan's face peered at her over the top of it. He rubbed his hands together.

"That's all of it. I guess I'm ready to go."

She nodded, rubbing at trails of goosebumps down the sides of her arms, dispelling them with the warmth of friction.

"Have a good trip."

He walked to her and smiled. "Thanks, I will. I hope you feel better soon."

Ever since she broke the news that she was sick, he'd been awkward, standoffish and hadn't said another thing about her returning to Melbourne with him. She'd expected it, this rapid turnaround, she knew him well enough for that. Still, it annoyed her more than she'd thought it would.

He hesitated, leaned forward, and gave her a hug. When he patted her back, she almost shook her head but resisted the urge. He'd been so certain she should give him another chance. But she knew it was only that he was having second thoughts about his new relationship and his default was to return to her. It was how he'd always been. Something wrong? Bindi would know what to do. Feeling insecure? Bindi will make it right again.

Only now, things had changed. She had a new home, a new life and not only that, but she was sick. She knew that was all he saw when he looked at her now — the illness. How had she not seen this about him all along? He was selfish. He didn't care so much about her, as about what she would do for him.

He'd hoped that by bringing her back to his newspaper, his boss would give him another chance. That by bringing her back into his life, he wouldn't feel so empty. But that wasn't up to her — she couldn't fix that gaping hole inside of him. He'd have to do that without her. She had to focus on one thing — getting well.

She was glad he was returning to Melbourne. And with the wedding out of the way, now she could give all her attention to her health.

"I'll miss you," he whispered before ducking into the cab.

He waved goodbye through the window. She raised a hand in a kind of salute as the vehicle passed from the driveway onto the road, then sighed as it accelerated away. It was the end of something. She'd let him go, finally. Not only from her life but from her heart. In fact, his visit had her second guessing how she'd managed to love him and overlook so many of his flaws for so long.

With a yawn, Bindi wandered back into the inn. It was

Sunday morning, most of the guests had checked out, and only a few would be checking in later that day. She was glad of the reprieve after a busy weekend.

Mima was in the kitchen, seated at the kitchen table with Kate. They were talking about menus and food, and Mima was smiling a lot. She missed working at the inn, Bindi could tell, but Kate made sure to include Mima in whatever was going on at the inn as often as she wanted. They had regular meetings about the menu, involving slices of cake, cups of tea and a lot of conversations that had nothing whatsoever to do with food.

Bindi smiled and headed for the kettle. She poured herself a cup of tea as well and joined them at the table.

Kate smiled at her. "He's gone?"

Bindi nodded, grimaced. "Why did I love him again?"

Mima chuckled. "The heart is a mystery, my dear. I'm only glad you figured it out now and didn't marry the guy."

"You didn't like him?" asked Bindi, her brow furrowed.

Mima's lips pursed. "I know never to speak ill of a recently deceased relationship...it can backfire on a well-meaning friend." Her belly shook as she chortled. "I've learned that lesson the hard way. But...I think there's a greater passion in you that will find its true match someday, my darling."

Bindi took a sip of tea, nodded. "Thanks, Mima. I think you're right. I don't know how I overlooked the one-sidedness of our relationship all these years. I suppose I was too busy with work to notice it, or maybe he wasn't always like that and it crept up on me while I wasn't looking."

"Oh no, he was," murmured Kate. She shot Bindi a smile.

Bindi gaped. "You didn't like him either?"

Kate shrugged. "He was okay. I liked him because my little sister adored him. But..." She cocked her head. "I didn't think he was good enough for you. Of course, no one is, so..." Kate put an arm around Bindi's shoulders and squeezed. "I want you to be happy, and he didn't seem to do that — didn't seem to make you happy. When you were around him, you were always kind of tense, distracted, worried."

Bindi shook her head. "You're right. I was. I don't think I realised it until now, since I've had some time away from him. It thought it was my personality, but honestly, I haven't felt that way since I left Melbourne."

"That calls for a celebration," said Mima, raising her teacup high. "Cheers to freedom and starting again."

"Cheers," replied Kate and Bindi together.

They clinked teacups together, laughing and chatting with the noise of the kitchen staff cleaning up after breakfast as their backdrop.

"We have to talk about my honeymoon," Kate said, her voice taking on a more serious tone.

"When are you leaving?" asked Bindi.

"In a few weeks."

"You're going to have such a lovely time," added Mima, with a wink.

"Thanks, Mima. I'm really looking forward to seeing Thailand."

"Thailand, yes...that's what I was talking about. Not the gorgeous man you're travelling with for a whole month."

"Him too." Kate chortled. "Anyway, what I was going to say is, I've narrowed down the search for a replacement cook while I'm gone."

Mima's mouth puckered. "Uh huh."

Bindi frowned. "That's good, isn't it, Mima?"

Mima shrugged.

Kate sighed. "Is there something you want to tell me, Mima?"

Mima shook her head. "No, of course not, love." She

gulped a mouthful of tea. "Except that you have a cook right in front of you."

"But I don't want to put that pressure on you, Mima. It's December, the inn is going to be so busy. It's a lot for you to take on, and you've been so relaxed and happy lately..."

Mima's eyes narrowed. "I've run this inn through December for more years than you've been alive, missy."

"Okay, okay...so you're going to take over the kitchen while I'm gone."

Mima gave an abrupt nod of the head. "Perfect. I think that's a great idea."

Bindi shook her head slowly, smiling. Mima certainly knew how to get her way. "I think it's perfect. I've got a lot on my plate as well, and now I don't have to worry about training or watching over the shoulder of someone new."

"I hadn't thought of that," replied Kate, as she chewed the inside of her cheek. "That works out well then. Thank you Mima."

Mima beamed. "I'm happy to help, my dear."

"Hello!" called Reeda's voice from the foyer.

"In here," replied Kate.

Reeda strode into the kitchen smiling. "There you are. Good morning everyone."

She went around the table kissing cheeks. Then sat with a loud sigh. "Phew. I went for a long run this morning and I think I might have overdone it a bit. But Duncan and I are loving this lifestyle. Morning run on the beach, then we had a lazy breakfast and he headed to the hospital. So, I thought I'd come over here to see what needs doing."

"I've got a few things on, I could use some help," replied Bindi.

"Great," said Reeda. "Oh, and before I forget, there's a police officer asking for you at the door."

Bindi jumped to her feet her eyes wide. "What?"

"He's cute, too." Reeda winked.

"A police officer? Did he say what this is about?"

Reeda shrugged. "He seemed to know you...and he looked really familiar. He said his name was Josh."

"Josh Owens?"

Recognition flitted across Reeda's face. "Oh yeah, Josh Owens — from high school, right?"

Bindi nodded, pushed a finger into her mouth and chewed the fingernail.

"I knew I recognised him. Boy, he grew up well." Reeda grinned. "What are you waiting for? Go and see what he wants."

Bindi found Josh standing on the verandah dressed in his blue police uniform. The dark blue, buttoned shirt was tucked into a pair of long, blue pants. His arms were crossed over his thick chest as he stared out at the curving driveway to the highway.

"Hi Josh."

He faced her with a wide smile, white teeth stark against his darkly tanned skin. "Hello Bindi, good to see you again."

She nodded. "How have you been?"

He shrugged. "Good, and you?"

"Fine. Are you headed to work?"

He shook his head. "I just finished my shift and was going to get some lunch. I hoped you might join me."

Bindi glanced at the police cruiser parked in the driveway. Her heart skipped a beat. She hadn't planned on going out with him, had almost forgotten about him with everything that'd been going on. He'd caught her off guard. "That sounds lovely. I'll get my purse."

She hurried inside, ducked through the kitchen to the office and grabbed her purse. "I'm going out for lunch," she called over her shoulder as she scurried by Kate and Reeda. She didn't stop to see the looks on their faces. In all honesty, after she'd eaten breakfast that morning she'd felt nothing but nausea. Still, perhaps she'd be hungry by the time they got to the restaurant. They could have lunch together, as friends, and talk about their school days. It didn't have to mean anything more than that.

Josh drove them to Kingscliff and pulled into a parking space opposite the beach. They walked across the road to a small cafe and grabbed seats on the footpath, where they could see the ocean and smell the salt in the air.

"Have you eaten here before?" Bindi asked.

"All the time. It's one of my favourite haunts."

"What's good here?"

"Everything," he replied. "They do breakfast all day and I probably like the poached eggs with hollandaise best."

They ordered from the waitress, dressed in shorts and a crop top. Then, Bindi sipped a cup of coffee while they talked about the old days, who still lived in the area, what they were doing and who had married someone from high school. Bindi was surprised how many of her fellow graduates had remained in the area, had married each other, and already had a brood of children. She owned a car. That was about as much as she'd managed as an adult, apart from getting fired. It was strange to think of school friends who were married and raising children at her age.

"Wow, I feel as though I've really underachieved." Her lips pursed.

The waitress set their plates of food in front of them. Two perfectly poached eggs perched on top of a thick slice of sourdough toast. She prodded one with her fork, and yellow yolk oozed out to cover the bread.

"I saw you on tv a few times," replied Josh. "I don't think that's underachieving. You're pretty amazing, actually."

Her face flushed with warmth. "Thanks. I thought you didn't watch the news."

He shrugged. "That wasn't entirely true."

She laughed. "You're impressive yourself — you're actually out there every day making the world a safer place to live. Now, that's amazing."

He shrugged. "I don't know...sometimes I feel like all I do is crowd control. Last night, every call-out we had was to do with drunks or domestics."

She chewed on a bite of eggs and swallowed. "That must be really hard."

He nodded. "It's rewarding too, but definitely not what I thought it'd be when I signed up."

"Do you think you'll stick with it?"

"Yeah, I can't imagine doing anything else. I'm going to sit my Detective's exam next year, hopefully move up the ladder a bit."

"That sounds great." She smiled.

The conversation between them flowed smoothly, easily, as they ate. Bindi found she didn't have to pretend when she was with him. Something about the fact that he'd known her when they were teenagers made her relax. She hadn't dressed up, wasn't wearing makeup, her hair was pulled into a messy ponytail, and she didn't care. She felt at home — in Kingscliff, and with Josh.

After both plates were clean, and they'd finished a second cup of coffee each, Josh yawned. He covered his mouth with a fist, but Bindi smiled. "You should get some sleep."

"I'm sorry. I'm really enjoying spending time with you, but I haven't slept in a while."

"It's fine, of course. I can't even imagine doing night shifts, I'm so hopeless at missing sleep. If I don't get enough sleep, I'm like a bear with a sore head."

He chuckled. "Good to know. I'll make a note of that: get Bindi to bed on time."

Intense blue eyes fixed on hers, and a delicious shiver ran

up her spine. He was flirting with her, and she couldn't help liking it. He was the most attractive man she'd ever been on a date with, and something about the uniform took it to a new level.

Still, she had to stay strong. She'd already made a decision about dating — she might feel good in that moment, but she wasn't well. She needed all her energy and attention to fight the illness. And besides, it wouldn't be fair on Josh to start a relationship with the words, "I have cancer" on her lips. If he walked away, he'd be a jerk. And if he didn't, he'd be stuck with her through the treatments...and what if she didn't make it? What if it all went wrong? No, it wouldn't be right to put him in that situation.

Josh drove her home and they chatted and flirted the whole way. By the time they reached the inn, Bindi was wishing they could keep driving, keep talking. She'd had such a nice time with him, she didn't want it to end.

He climbed out and opened her door, then took her hand and walked with her up the stairs. They stood on the verandah together in silence a moment. He wove his fingers through hers, met her gaze with a look that sucked the air from her lungs and set her heart racing.

"Bindi..." he began, his voice low.

"I have to talk to you about something," she interrupted, her words coming out all breathy and broken.

He arched an eyebrow. "Okay? What is it?"

She tugged her hand free of his and stood with both hands pressed firmly to the top railing. If she kept them there, she'd be safe from the tingles that ran up and down the length of her arms when he held her hands. She inhaled a slow breath. "You're a really great guy..."

"Uh huh."

"But I'm not looking for a relationship right now. It's not

personal, I like you a lot, but I have some things going on in my life that need my complete attention. I'm sorry."

She faced him, steeling herself to keep her resolve in spite of the way he was looking at her.

He smiled. "I understand. Don't worry about it." He kissed her cheek, lingering several long moments, his breath warming her skin and sending sparks of heat through her body. "Let me know when you're ready for more," he whispered against her hair.

Then he was gone. His car pulled out of the driveway with a six-cylinder growl, and soon disappeared.

Bindi leaned against the wall of the inn with a groan and covered her face with both hands. She slapped her forehead once with the palm of her hand, her entire body alive with warmth, longing for him to hold her, kiss her. But he was gone, and it was her own doing. She groaned again, pushed off the wall and walked into the inn.

Of course she had to find the most perfect guy in the world now. Now, when she was sick and fighting for her life, and couldn't go out with him. She'd pushed him away; he wouldn't understand why. She might never see him again, although living in a small community like Cabarita Beach, that didn't seem likely. Still, he probably wouldn't ask her out again. He seemed perfect, most likely was perfect, and now he was gone.

❊ 13 ❊

ABRUZZI APENNINES, ITALY

The truck crawled along the narrow double-track dirt road away from the farm. Charlie pulled back the canvas that covered the rear entrance to the truck bed and peered out. Bruno stood with one hand raised, in front of the cottage. Sheep milled about him, and the dog sat regal by his side. Behind him, the cottage stood dark against the mountainside, no light shone within, no smoke breathed from its stout chimney.

Something inside Charlie shifted, grew heavy. What were they doing? They were leaving the only home he knew, the only place he was safe. It felt as though they were moving directly into the path of a wolf. The Wehrmacht was everywhere, according to Bruno. He'd heard rumours from neighbours who'd visited town more recently that the Germans had been scooping up all the prisoners who'd escaped from a prison they called Campo 78. Bruno figured Charlie must've come from there, since he had no weapon or supplies, only the clothes on his back, when they found him lying prone, bleeding into the earth.

Charlie had asked if anyone had been with him, and Bruno had given a sad nod. There were bodies, no one living. Even Charlie had seemed dead at first, until he'd groaned. They'd buried the rest of the men and had almost thrown Charlie in with them but for that single noise uttered from a parched throat. It'd given him a fright Bruno had said with a chuckle. Made him almost jump out of his skin, a dead man groaning that way.

The truck bumped and jolted along the rock-strewn trail, jostling Charlie where he sat on a barrel in the back. It turned a corner and Bruno was lost from view. Would he be lonely up there on the mountain with only the dog for company?

Charlie scanned the back of the truck, his gaze roving over the various cartons, boxes and barrels stacked all around him. Maria sat up front with their neighbour, Signor Barese. She was visiting her uncle outside Casoli, it made sense. The Australian soldier didn't have any good reason to be there, so he was hidden away behind barrels and crates of produce, on their way to be sold at market in Casoli.

The canvas had swung back into place now and all he could see was the dark insides of the truck's bed. The vehicle rolled to one side, then another as it crept over rocks, up hill-sides, and down slopes. Finally, when he felt as though his teeth couldn't take any more of the jerking, rolling climb, the truck settled into a steady pace. They'd reached the road.

The roar of the engine grew as the vehicle accelerated, and Charlie relaxed against a bag of dried beans, grateful for smooth, sweeping road. He must've fallen asleep, because the next thing he realised, he was jolted awake by the truck coming to a stop.

He straightened in place and listened intently. Had they reached Maria's uncle's place already? Just then, someone shouted in German, and the hairs on the back of his neck stood to attention. He couldn't say how, but for some reason he understood the words. He must've learned German in the life he no longer recalled.

"Attention!" the voice shouted again. "Step out of your vehicle."

His pulse raced and his breath caught in his throat as he squirmed down low behind a barrel of olives. He glanced around himself frantically and rested on an old blanket Barese had given him for warmth during the journey. He tugged on the worn woollen fabric and pulled it to cover every part of himself with the scratchy and stiff blanket.

The front door of the truck slammed shut and footsteps echoed on the tarmac beside the vehicle. Charlie raised himself to his haunches, slow and steady, careful not to make a sound. He blinked in the pitch black, his entire body bristled, ready to leap from his hiding place, to fight.

Voices came close, speaking to each other in German. One laughed, another followed it. Then, he could hear Barese's voice asking if the soldiers were having a good day, and did they like strawberries, because he had some that were delicious.

The soldiers seemed to warm to that idea and the tone of their voices changed, became more jovial, conversational. They moved towards the back of the truck and Charlie tensed as light flooded through the open canvas flaps.

"Here they are," said Barese in German.

There was silence for a few moments, but for the occasional murmur of pleasure and smacking of lips.

Then, a booming voice. "What else do you have here?"

"Some olives, grains, vegetables and cured meats."

"Where are you going?" asked the soldier.

"There's a market in Casoli."

The soldiers joked together about the last time they'd

eaten a strawberry or even had a decent meal, and Charlie waited while Barese pulled boxes and bags of food from the back of the truck and handed them to the soldiers.

"We have to search the vehicle," said a voice.

Charlie's heart dropped.

Another voice interrupted the first. "But we can see that you're hiding nothing. Carry on. *Heil Hitler*."

Barese murmured his thanks even as the back of the truck was thrown once again into darkness. A door slammed again, then the truck's engine roared to life and the vehicle swayed as it pulled away from the checkpoint.

Charlie dropped onto his rear, his heart hammering. The breath he'd been holding tight in his throat released and he covered his face with both hands. That'd been close.

***

WHEN THEY REACHED THE FARM, IT WAS GROWING DARK. The air was cool, and the wind whistled through a crack in the truck bed making Charlie shiver. He'd kept the blanket wrapped around himself ever since they passed through the checkpoint and was grateful for it now.

The truck's engine switched off after a brief sojourn down a winding track of some kind and the quiet of a countryside evening enveloped him. A cock crowed, and in the distance a few sheep bleated in a kind of harmony.

The truck doors creaked open, slammed shut. Someone banged a hand on the side.

"Out you get," said Barese's voice in Italian.

Charlie climbed slowly from his hiding place, working the kinks out of his back and legs. He stumbled forwards with legs almost numb from being folded in the cold for so long and climbed out through the canvas flaps.

Maria was there. She smiled and took his hand in hers to

squeeze it for a moment. Then, the family was there. Maria embraced her uncle Angelo, and his wife, Catriona. A throng of children, ranging in age from two years old to about twelve, surrounded her, all talking at once, all wanting to know everything that'd happened in her life since the last time they saw her.

Charlie smiled as she kissed each one, exclaiming over a homespun garment or a rag doll as she gave every child her undivided attention for a few moments. He stood in the background, unsure of what to say. He didn't understand much of what was being said, they were talking fast and over top of each other, using colloquialisms he didn't know.

Finally, the conversation slowed, and Maria stepped back to stand beside him. "This is Charlie," she said.

Angelo held out a hand and shook Charlie's firmly, a smile crinkling the corners of his eyes. He looked so much like Bruno it warmed Charlie to him immediately, though he was much younger.

"Welcome," he said. "We are glad to have you here."

"Thank you so much for allowing us to stay with you," Charlie said.

Then Catriona welcomed him with kisses to each cheek, and the children stood in a solemn line to shake his hand. When each had taken their turn, they ran off towards the house squealing and laughing.

Charlie thanked their neighbour, who deposited their single small suitcase at Charlie's feet, shook his hand with a nod and was gone.

They fell into the bustling life of early mornings, hard work, and more plentiful food quickly at the farm. It wasn't as quiet as it'd been living in the mountain cottage, but Charlie enjoyed the interactions with Maria's family, especially the children whose noise filled the air and brought warmth to the farmhouse.

He ate everything he could get his hands on, his appetite seemed unending, now that there was enough food for everyone.

Charlie helped Angelo with the chores and Maria stayed mostly inside the house with her aunt. After a few days, a priest showed up at the house unannounced and married them in a quiet ceremony in the quaint farmhouse's small, dark living room. The priest looked tired, with dark smudges beneath his eyes. He finished the vows in Italian, said a few more words Charlie didn't comprehend, shook hands quietly all around and left.

When Charlie's gaze met Maria's, she grinned, her eyes gleaming.

"We are married," she said, in halting English.

He laughed. "Well, how about that."

Charlie found he liked married life even more than he'd expected he would. He whistled about his work, thinking of Maria more than what he was doing, so that Angelo often had to reprimand him. But he did so with a grin on his face.

"Love," Angelo said. "I remember what it is like to be so young and in love. It is the thing that holds all the world together." Then, he'd slap Charlie on the shoulder and tell him to concentrate on what he was doing.

Sometimes when he was lying next to Maria in their narrow, hard bed at night, he thought about his old life. Wondered what it must've been like, who his family was, if perhaps he should've tried to find his unit after all instead of building a new life for himself.

He comforted himself with the knowledge that at least there was no wife or children waiting for him, since there was no ring on his finger and from a glimpse of his face in a mirror on the wall of the farmhouse, he guessed his age to be around twenty. Surely, he couldn't have married by such a young age? No, he was bound to have some kind of recollection of such an event. It seemed to him this was the first time he'd said the vows that tied him to Maria for life. It wasn't the kind of thing a person could easily forget. Though of course, he didn't remember anything about his former life.

A few days later, Maria coloured his blonde hair with something her aunt gave her that stained the water and turned his hair a dusky shade of brown. Maria laughed when she'd towelled it dry, and said he looked like a stranger to her now. He'd grabbed her up in his arms, tickled her until tears streaked her cheeks and then kissed them all away.

Whatever his life had been, this was his life now. Dwelling on things he couldn't remember or control wouldn't help him. He was happy. Content in his new life. He pushed the concerns of what he might've left behind out of his mind and focused on the present, the future with his new family. How could he return to a life he didn't know? To a role in an army he didn't remember, to a family who might or might not exist? He couldn't do that, not when Maria was here by his side, warm and inviting. Not when he had a place, a home, a hearth, and a family who'd welcomed him in with open arms.

They stayed at the farm. Maria often went to town with her aunt, and Angelo took produce to the market. But Charlie stayed out of sight. They didn't need people talking, Angelo had said. So Charlie hid in the barn whenever guests called at the farmhouse and spent the rest of his days working with the sheep, or in the barn or fields. It was a good life, hard work and lonely at times when the family was all at mass without him or visiting a neighbour. Those were the moments when he couldn't keep thoughts of his past from returning. But when the house was full, with children laughing, playing, and arguing, and with Maria smiling up at him, he was happy.

❧ 14 ❧

DECEMBER 1996

CABARITA BEACH

The words on the page blurred as Bindi's mind wandered. She couldn't get into her book, no matter how long she sat there in the hospital waiting room trying. She wondered if Duncan was working. Of course, she wasn't exactly sure what part of the hospital he worked in, and even if she knew, he might be in surgery. There wasn't much point in looking for him. Still, she could do with a walk. Anything to take her attention away from the fact that she was waiting for a treatment.

The hospital was running behind schedule today, and she'd arrived early for her appointment as well. All which meant she'd been sitting in the waiting room for ten minutes so far and might be there for a lot longer yet if the line of patients waiting with her was any indication.

With a sigh she glanced around the room. The walls were lined with blue, plastic cushioned chairs. Each white wall held a nondescript painting of some kind. Everything smelled of disinfectant.

The waiting room was next to the emergency room. So at least there was a steady stream of injured patients coming in through the large double doors to keep her occupied. So far, they'd had a kid with a broken leg, an elderly woman who'd had a fall and was pushed through the doors in a wheelchair, and a teenager who'd gotten something in his eye. The boy sat now, hand over his eye, staring at something in his lap.

In another room, the girl with the broken leg screamed, then sobbed.

Bindi's heart ached and her eyes smarted with tears. She didn't know how emergency staff managed to deal with all the pain and suffering they handled on a daily basis. She was too tender hearted to be able to hear a kid shout in pain without crying too.

She opened the book again, stared at the black words typed on the page. They blurred, and she sighed. It'd been three weeks since her lunch date with Josh Owens. Every time she slowed down her thoughts returned to him. Had she made the right choice by putting distance between them? She hadn't heard from him since and was more disappointed than she should've been by that. After all, it'd been her choice. Had she hoped maybe he would ignore what she'd said? She squeezed her eyes shut and pinched the bridge of her nose. No, this time in her life was for healing, not for beginning a new relationship.

The emergency room doors banged open again, and she looked up. Who was it this time?

Two police officers walked through the doors, flanking a man with blood streaming down one arm. A nurse rushed to greet them and took the man into a small room with the officers close behind. One of them had blonde hair, tanned skin.

Josh.

Bindi gasped and ducked her head. Then, peered up at him through narrowed eyes. If he turned right now, he'd see her. She shook her head. What did it matter? She was an adult. She could manage an awkward conversation as well as the next person. Although...perhaps she should move, sit on the other side of the room where she'd be hidden from view by the wall.

Before she could do anything, he glanced up at her, as if he'd felt her eyes on him. His gaze met hers, the corners of his mouth lifting in a smile. He said something to his partner, then headed in her direction.

She stood to her feet, smoothed the front of her shorts with nervous hands.

"Hi, Bindi," he said, leaning forwards to kiss her cheek. "What are you doing here?" He glanced around, as though looking for someone.

"Hi Josh, just hanging out in the hospital. You know... good place to read a book." She held up the book in her hand with a wry smile.

His eyes narrowed. "Okay." His gaze travelled around the room, landing on a sign above a nearby doorway. It read, "Oncology outpatients". His eyes widened and found her face. "Bindi, what's going on?"

She sighed, set the book down on a chair beside her, then wrung her hands together. Having him there, with her, brought a lump into her throat. She'd missed him. How was that possible after only one date?

"I'm sick. I wanted to tell you, but..." She shrugged.

"Sick?"

"Cancer," she replied, her tone matter of fact. It was out in the open now, and she was relieved. She hated having to hide it from him, to pretend that everything was fine. Hated him not knowing why she'd ended things between them before they'd even started.

He sucked in a quick breath. "What?"

"I'm sorry I didn't tell you."

"No, it's fine. We only had one date. I wouldn't expect you to tell me..." He combed fingers through his hair. "I'm so sorry, Bindi."

"Thanks."

"Is this..." he began, then hesitated, seeming unsure of what to say next. "Is this why you told me you didn't want to go out with me?"

She nodded. "Sorry."

"Is there any other reason? Or was that it?"

His partner called his name from the other room. Josh waved him off with one hand, his attention fixed on Bindi's face.

"No other reason. I really like you, Josh. I love spending time with you, but I'm sick. I have to give my attention to getting well, and it wouldn't be fair to you..."

His brow furrowed. "All this time I thought you didn't want to..." He shook his head. "I can't get you out of my head, Bindi. I want to see you again."

"But Josh, I'm sick. I have treatments, work, my sisters... I'm busy with all of that. I feel unwell a lot of the time, I throw up, I might even lose my hair. I mean, so far so good, but you never know."

His eyes narrowed. "So, you don't want to date me?"

"No, that's not it. I don't want to put you in this position. We've only been on one date, and you shouldn't be stuck with someone who has cancer. It wouldn't be fair on you."

He sighed, took her hand in his and cupped it close to his chest. "Why don't you let me decide what I want to be stuck with?"

She sighed. "I guess I can do that."

"I don't want you going through this alone."

"I'm not alone," she replied.

He glanced around the waiting room. "Where is everyone?"

Her cheeks flushed red. "They're busy."

"So, let me help. I'll be here for you, and we can take things as slow as you like. I want to spend time with you, that's all."

Bindi's heart thudded against her ribs. "Okay."

He kissed her cheek, squeezed her hand, and sat.

They chatted while she waited, until finally a nurse came out of a closed door to call her name. She'd almost forgotten why she was there until the sound of her name jolted her back to reality. She stood with a sharp intake of breath, running her hands down the front of her shorts.

"I guess I'm next," she said.

He smiled. "You'll be fine."

"I know..." Her stomach clenched.

"I'll call you," he said. Then leaned in to kiss her cheek, his breath caressing her skin.

She watched him go, her pulse racing, her head light. Had that really happened? Somehow, he'd convinced her to date him, even though she'd been adamantly against the idea only minutes earlier.

He was confident, almost cocky in a way. Definitely not the type of man she'd usually go for. He had no guile. Was simply himself and expected people to take him as he was. And he was cute. So cute, she'd been surprised when he asked her out the first time, and equally as surprised now. She'd figured he'd forgotten all about her after their date. No doubt women threw themselves at him all day long. What was it about her mousy hair, freckled cheeks, and bony figure that attracted him to her? She shook her head. Whatever it was, she was glad of it — couldn't wait to see him again. Still, Josh Owens was a mystery. And his timing couldn't have been worse.

❧ 15 ❧

MAY 1945

CASOLI, ITALY

The markets buzzed with activity. People came and went, a few with baskets swinging from their arms. They stared at Charlie as they passed — who was he? What was he doing there? He hadn't seen any other young men his age since they'd arrived that morning to sell produce at the markets.

At some point in the past year, Angelo had come up with the idea that they could tell people he was a cousin, visiting from Milan, to help out during the war on Angelo's farm. That he'd been injured as a boy and wasn't able to fight. Besides, the Germans had left Italy a month earlier when Mussolini fell. He didn't have to pretend to be Italian anymore, not if he didn't want to. Still, they'd chosen to be cautious. The war was still raging, and it was anyone's guess what might happen next. Stuck on the farm, Charlie felt out of touch with what was going on in the world, but they heard news every now and then from one of the neighbours who had a wireless radio.

"We sold out of almost everything," said Maria, bumping his elbow with hers. "Uncle Angelo will be happy."

"There wasn't much chance we wouldn't," replied Charlie. His Italian was almost flawless now, at least that was what Maria told him. He never spoke in English anymore, unless she asked him to. "There's so little food and everyone is hungry."

She nodded. "Yes, but not much money either." A sigh. "Still, we've done well I think."

"Why are there so many people in the square today? They don't seem to be shopping."

Over the past few hours, the square that held the market-place had begun to fill. A trickle of people filtered in at first, then slowly that trickle had built until there was barely room to move. People smiled, talked amongst themselves. Some carried streamers they threw into the air, others drank out of bottles they'd brought with them.

Maria shook her head. She waved at a woman passing by. "Excuse me, signora, what is happening?"

The woman shrugged. "There is an announcement," she said, before hurrying on.

Maria frowned. "An announcement? Do you think this is it?"

"The end of the war?" asked Charlie. "Maybe." They knew it was coming. Everyone said it was only a matter of time. The Germans had retreated, were being chased out of Italy by the Allies. Since moving to Casoli, Charlie had read everything he could get his hands on, most of it propaganda put out by the Germans or the pro-German government. Then, when he learned the language, he'd struck up conversations with friends and neighbours.

He knew all about the war now, the details of who was fighting on either side, what they were fighting for. He just didn't know who he was, and still couldn't recall the details of his life from before he was shot and woke up in Bruno and Maria's mountain cabin.

They packed their things into the baskets they'd brought with them to town, mostly empty now, and joined the crowd. The momentum hurried them along, until they found themselves standing in a throng of people, waiting. Around them, several people held wireless radios in their hands. One man turned his up and held it aloft, several others followed his lead. A man's voice echoed over the crowd's heads.

"Who is that?" asked Charlie, as a man's voice crackled over the airwaves.

Maria shrugged. "Winston Churchill, I think."

MY DEAR FRIENDS, THIS IS YOUR HOUR. THIS IS NOT VICTORY of a party or of any class. It's a victory of the great British nation as a whole. We were the first, in this ancient island, to draw the sword against tyranny.

AS THE MAN'S VOICE CONTINUED, THE CROWD AROUND them erupted into shouting, catcalls, and whistles. Everyone surged forward, embracing each other and dancing in the street. Some leaned against stone walls or slumped to the cobblestones below and cried. Still others kissed the closest lips.

Charlie stood frozen in place. The war was over? He didn't know anything but living in fear, hiding away, hoping and praying for peace. He couldn't remember a life before it. What now? What would he do now?

Maria faced him with her own troubled thoughts written clearly across her pretty face. "The war is over."

He forced a smile to his face. Joy filled his heart, but fear pushed it down, making him tremble. "I know."

"It's wonderful," she said, standing on tiptoe to wrap one arm around his neck, the other still clutching her basket.

"Yes, it is." He lifted her up and twirled her around.

When he set her feet on the ground, she stared up at him, her doe-eyes searching his. "Does this mean...are you going to leave us?" she patted her swollen belly, stroking one hand around its growing girth in a circular movement.

He stared at the place where his child grew within her. "Of course not," he said, shaking his head. "This is my home now, it's where I belong. You're my family. Where would I go? I don't even know who I am. I might know my name, but that's not enough. I can't bear the idea of returning to a family I don't remember. And what if they're all dead? No, I want to stay here, with you."

She set her basket on the ground by her feet and encircled him with both arms, tears glimmering in her eyes. "The war is over!" she cried.

He kissed her. The war was over. They could rebuild their lives, do what they wanted. No more hiding, no more fear. No one to take him away from his family. They were free.

❧ 16 ❧

CABARITA BEACH

The letter drifted from Bindi's hand to the bed covers below. She let it fall, staring up at the ceiling with tears in her eyes. The past few days she'd taken to reading the letters Charlie had written to Nan, doing her best to try and find something between the lines that might help her discover what'd happened to him.

That he'd lost his memory and married an Italian woman almost broke her heart. Poor Nan, to receive this letter finally after so many years had passed. Obviously, Charlie must've figured out eventually who he was, remembered his name and what he'd left behind, or he couldn't have written to his "Darling Edie," as the letter was addressed.

Bindi wiped the tears from her cheeks, folded the letter and pushed it back into the wooden box. Her fingers travelled over its surface, tracing the outline of the horse's head, and wondering how long it'd taken the teenaged boy to carve all those years ago. His heart had been full of love and hope when he'd marked the wood with his pocket-knife. How sad it was for her to know all that would be gone from his life soon after.

If Charlie had survived in Italy long enough to write these letters to Nan, what had become of him? Was he there still? If so, it was a shame they hadn't discovered his whereabouts before Reeda's trip. She could've met him, if he was still alive.

Bindi got out of bed with a grunt. The treatment the day before had knocked the wind right out of her. She was worn out and planned on spending the day doing paperwork in the office. Maybe she'd even finish work early and watch movies in her bedroom.

After a hot shower and change of clothes, she felt a little better. She found Mima in the kitchen, arguing with Kate over the best way to stew strawberries to make strawberry jam.

"You don't need to add anything but sugar and lemon juice. Trust me," she said.

Bindi smiled as Kate did her best to argue for a more complex jam, to no avail. Kate kissed Bindi on the cheek with a shake of her head. "Sometimes, Mima is impossible."

Bindi huffed. "I think you've met your match."

"Hey, I'm easy going and carefree."

"Sure you are."

Kate snorted as she headed towards the dining room. "I'm going to check on breakfast, make sure everyone's finished and the staff are doing their jobs."

Bindi waved her goodbye, as she poured herself a cup of tea and looked around the kitchen for something to eat. "Have I missed breakfast entirely?"

Mima shook her head. "Of course not, love. There's some left over bircher muesli, yoghurt, and fruit in the fridge if you're interested."

Bindi made herself a bowl of bircher muesli and sat at the

table with it. Mima grabbed a cup of tea as well and joined her.

"Sorry I couldn't go to the hospital with you yesterday," she said. "How are you feeling, honey?"

Bindi waved a hand back and forth. "So, so. I think I'll be okay once I get some of this food into me."

She took a bite of the muesli and chewed, still thinking about Charlie's letters. She hadn't yet told Mima, Kate or Reeda about Josh and their encounter at the hospital. She wasn't sure of what to tell them and didn't know if it would come to anything. He'd said he would call her, but there were no guarantees. She preferred to think about something else. Nan and Charlie's letters were just the thing to distract her from the silent telephone hanging on the kitchen wall.

"Everything okay, love?" asked Mima.

"Yes, I'm fine. Tired, but not too bad considering. I was reading one of Charlie's letters to Nan."

Mima arched an eyebrow. "Oh?"

"I wish we knew where he was. It's so heartbreaking to read all they went through, knowing that he never made it back, that they both married other people. Did they ever stop loving each other? Was Nan happy with Pop? My heart hurts thinking about it." Bindi shook her head slowly, swallowing around the lump building in her throat.

Mima sighed. "She was very happy with your grandfather, my dear. Yes, she went through a period of mourning, as so many of us did after the war. But she didn't hear from Charlie for so many years..."

Bindi's eyes narrowed. She was certain Mima knew more than she was letting on. "When? When did she get the letters? They're not time stamped — well some of them are, and others aren't. Where did they come from?"

Mima raised both hands as if in surrender. "Whoa. Slow

down, honey. Slow down. I don't know all that. Edie didn't tell me everything, you know."

Bindi wasn't sure she believed Mima entirely. "I thought the two of you were thick as thieves."

"We were, but even best friends keep some secrets from each other."

A rumble outside caught Bindi's ear. Tyres crunched on the driveway.

"That'll be Betty," said Mima. "She's taking me lawn bowling. Can you believe it? I'm officially joining the retirement community now. And maybe we'll even meet some handsome men in white." She kissed Bindi on the cheek, her eyes sparking with laughter, then hurried to meet her friend.

Bindi listened as Mima and Betty talked and giggled together all the way back to Betty's car. She finished her muesli in silence, thinking about what Mima had said. Had Mima really been in the dark about Charlie's letters? Did she know where he ended up, when he sent the letters to Nan? She had to know more than she was letting on. She and Nan talked about everything — at least that was the way Bindi remembered it.

She rinsed out her plate and did a lap of the inn's ground floor, as she always did first thing in the morning. She'd slept late, breakfast was well and truly over and most of the guests had rushed back to their rooms to pack and check out or had headed out to begin their day at the beach. The inn was quiet, but for the murmur of a few voices in the sitting room.

With curiosity spurring her forward, she poked her head through the doorway to see who was there. Kate, Reeda, and two men sat across from each other in armchairs. Large plans were laid out, sprawling white sheets of paper, on the coffee table between them. Kate was leaning over the table, her shoulders hunched, her eyes fixed on something as she discussed it with the others.

"'Morning," said Bindi, her eyes narrowing. What was going on? It looked like a business meeting, but if it was, why hadn't she been included, given she was the manager of the inn?

Reeda smiled at her.

Kate glanced up and scooted back into her chair, straightening with, Bindi was satisfied to see, a flash of guilt in her eyes. "Hi Bindi, there you are. I was about to come and get you..."

"I apologise for my lateness." Bindi held out a hand to the two men. "Pleased to meet you, I'm Bindi Summer."

The men each shook hands, introducing themselves as Kurt and Kevin from *Prestige Architects*.

Bindi's nostrils flared. "You're discussing the restaurant and kitchen?"

Kate nodded. "We're meeting to talk about the initial plans. Kevin put together this draft sketch and we're going over it together."

Bindi found a chair against the back wall and dragged it over to join their circle. They returned to their discussions, almost as if she wasn't there. She watched and listened in silence, and when the men left, rolling their plans, and dropping them into long cylindrical boxes to carry beneath their arms, she watched them go without a smile.

Kate and Reeda showed the men out, then returned.

Kate pushed a smile onto her face. "I think that went well. How about you, Bindi?"

Bindi glowered at her. "When did you know about this meeting?"

"What?"

"Come on, Bindi," Reeda tried. "Don't be angry with us, we're trying to get things moving on the restaurant."

Bindi pressed her lips together. "I understand that, I only wonder why you didn't feel the need to include me. I'm a part of this team, I run the inn. Don't you think I should be part of any meetings?"

Kate and Reeda exchanged a worried glance that only further incensed Bindi.

"We didn't want to tire you out," replied Reeda, resting a hand on Bindi's arm. "We're worried about you."

"I understand that." Bindi sighed. "But I'm not dead yet."

Kate gasped. "Bindi, don't talk that way!"

"Well, you're excluding me from business meetings...are you trying to set things up to run without me?" As the words poured from her mouth, she could hear how irrational she was becoming, how much she was overreacting, yet couldn't seem to stop herself.

She sobbed, unable to check the heaving in her chest. "I'm still here. I'm a part of this business and this family."

Kate enveloped Bindi in a warm embrace. "Of course you are, that's not what we're doing. We're trying to take care of you, not give you too many things to worry about. We don't want you to overdo it."

"Look, Bindi, I know you're frustrated, but we can handle this," added Reeda, her arms crossed over her chest.

Bindi sobbed even more loudly. "I know you can. I'm tired, and I'm scared, and I don't want you to replace me. Not yet."

Reeda joined them, adding her arms around both Kate and Bindi. She squeezed, and Bindi felt warm and loved in the middle of all of it all.

"We could never replace you, honey. You know that. What is this all about?"

"I don't know," wailed Bindi.

Kate smiled. "Okay, well, if you'd like to sit down together, we can grab a cup of tea and talk through everything the architects suggested to get your input. Does that sound like a good idea?"

Bindi nodded.

Reeda fetched three cups of tea on a tray from the kitchen, and Kate hurried to the office to get some paper and pencils. Then, she laid the paper out on the table and did her best to sketch out the design they'd discussed with the architects. Even seeing the rough outline on a piece of printer paper set Bindi's heart racing. It was exciting to see the inn expanding, becoming something more than even Nan and Pop had envisioned. Would it be worth it? Would it work out? She hoped so, they were gambling a lot on making the Waratah Inn a destination worth visiting.

"I can't believe we'll be living in a construction zone again so soon," she mumbled.

Reeda grunted. "I know, it feels like we finished the renovation last week."

"This won't disrupt the entire place, though," replied Kate. "We've decided to set up a makeshift kitchen in the storage room off the dining area. We can fit the refrigerator and dishwasher in there, and it already has a powder room with a sink. But while the construction is underway, we'll have to reduce our offerings to a cold breakfast, and that's about it."

"I think guests will understand," added Bindi.

"I hope so." Kate sighed, and ran fingers through her hair. "Anything you'd like to add?"

Bindi studied the rough drawing, glanced around the inn, her mind running over all the things a guest might want to find at a destination like the Waratah. It was a boutique inn, which mean luxury. Once they had a restaurant and commercial kitchen, they'd be able to bring in the public, which would mean more foot traffic. However, they couldn't house additional guests, they'd still have the same number of bedrooms.

"I think we should consider something that might make

the inn feel more luxurious. I mean, the decor is beautiful, the bedrooms are stunning, especially now they each have their own bathrooms and walk in robes. We'll have a world class restaurant... Our guests will expect luxury. What if we offered spa services?"

"Where would we put a spa?" asked Reeda, her brow furrowed. "And I'm sure there are laws about how to run something like that. I'm not saying no, it's a good idea, but let's think about it."

"Or, what about a swimming pool?" added Bindi.

The more she thought about it, the more she liked the idea.

"A swimming pool?" asked Kate. "But we're right next to the beach."

"I know, but sometimes people don't want to swim at the beach."

"Maybe..." Kate wasn't convinced, Bindi could see it in her eyes.

"Look around," replied Bindi. "The Waratah Inn has become the kind of place people visit when they want luxury, beauty, exclusivity. The kind of people who come here now, are very different to the type Nan used to welcome. They're looking for the kind of destination they don't have to leave. We can't be a big resort, but we can offer some of the luxury that the bigger holiday places offer — like a spa, a swimming pool, that kind of thing. So that when our guests stay, they don't have to go anywhere else. Everything they need is on site."

"You make a good point," replied Reeda, her lips pursed. "If I were to stay somewhere like this, out of the way, secluded, I'd want them to offer a restaurant, and something to do during the daylight hours other than simply a beach and some horses. We do need more..."

"So, which do you think we should start with? A pool or

spa?" asked Kate.

Bindi shrugged. "I think the pool would be easier, and more appealing to a wider group."

"I agree," added Reeda.

"So, we're adding a swimming pool as well?" asked Kate.

"I suppose we are."

Mima lumbered into the sitting room. "Hello, my darlings... Bindi, there's someone on the phone for you."

Bindi followed Mima back to the kitchen. A swimming pool...she wasn't even sure where that idea had come from. Picturing a pool shimmering in the inn's back yard gave her a warm feeling inside. It was right. The perfect next step for the inn. But could they manage the construction of a pool as well as a new restaurant and commercial kitchen all at the same time?

She picked up the phone. "Hello, this is Bindi."

"Hi Bindi, it's Josh."

Her heart thudded. He'd said he would call, but she'd half expected not to hear from him. After all, he knew she was sick now, she wouldn't blame him if he kept his distance.

"Josh, how are you?"

"I'm great. How are you feeling?"

She inhaled a slow breath. "I'm okay today. Thanks for asking."

"Listen, I'm at the station and I'm famished. I was about to eat lunch with some of my mates, then I thought I'd chance it — are you free this morning?"

BINDI SAT IN FRONT OF HER DRESSING TABLE AND BRUSHED her hair. She sighed at her reflection in the mirror. Her face was even more pale than usual, and the smattering of freckles across her nose and cheeks more pronounced.

There was a knock at her door, then Kate stuck her head through the gap. "Can I come in?"

Bindi nodded, smiled.

"Are you going out?"

"Yeah, Josh called – he asked me to have lunch with him."

Kate sat beside her on the bed, grinning. "Oh? That sounds nice."

"Don't read anything into it," warned Bindi. "I told him about my illness, I'm sure he's just being nice. That's all." She didn't want Kate to make a big deal of it, better she downplayed their relationship since she wasn't even certain yet how to define it.

"You told him?" Kate's eyes widened. "Good for you. I didn't think you'd tell anyone but us. I think it's healthy to get it out in the open."

Bindi wasn't sure that was true. She felt exposed, vulnerable. Like telling other people somehow made it more real. And now she'd have to face it head-on.

Kate reached for her brush and began to slide it through Bindi's hair. Bindi's eyes filled with tears. So many times when she was a teenager, Kate had done her hair. They'd sat together in this very room at the inn, while Kate chatted to her about surfing, or boys, or whatever fight she was having with Reeda at the time.

"You okay, hon?"

"Memories..." replied Bindi, dabbing at her eyes with the back of one hand. "You always used to brush my hair this way."

Kate's eyes shimmered. "I remember. It was the only time I could get you to open up about anything."

"Is that true?" Bindi cocked her head to one side. "I didn't realise that's why you did it."

"Yep. I tried to keep an eye on you the best I could. I know Reeda did most of the work looking after us, but I was worried about you. You were the youngest, you suffered the most when Mum and Dad died..."

"I don't know about that. I think we all suffered."

"I wanted to take care of you," Kate continued. "So, I'd come in here, grab the brush and get to work. I'd talk and talk, and eventually you'd join in and tell me what was going on in your life."

Bindi huffed. "Wow, I never knew that. Good strategy, I guess. Is that what you're doing now?"

Kate winked. "Maybe."

"Well, as much as I enjoy it when you brush my hair, you can ask me anything — I'm happy to tell you about my life."

"Good to know." Kate continued brushing, her brow furrowed. "How are the treatments going?"

Bindi shrugged. "I don't know, to be honest. I think they're fine... I still have my hair. So, that's a positive. Right?"

Kate nodded. "That is very good."

"I'll find out more once the treatment round is finished and my doctor runs some tests."

"Be sure to let me know how it goes," replied Kate.

"Of course."

They sat in silence while Kate finished styling Bindi's hair and Bindi applied some powder and a little blush to her cheeks to try to combat their pallor.

"I guess you'll be going on your honeymoon soon?" asked Bindi.

"I can't wait," replied Kate, her eyes gleaming. "And I wanted to talk to you about Christmas... Alex and I will be coming back from the honeymoon and heading straight to Port Macquarie to spend Christmas with his family. I've already spoken to Mima about it, and she's happy to continue to fill in for me in the kitchen. Reeda and Duncan are going to Sydney for the holidays, so it will be just you, Mima and Jack holding down the fort here. Are you okay with that?"

Bindi shrugged. "I guess so. I'll miss you, but I'm sure we'll manage."

Kate hugged her from behind. "I'll miss you too. I can't imagine having Christmas without you and Reeda, but I promised Alex...he doesn't see his parents as much as he'd like to."

"Of course. You're married now, we have to share you." Bindi's throat tightened. She hadn't considered that her sisters might both be away for the holidays. Still, she wasn't up to travelling anywhere herself, and she'd have Mima and Jack to share Christmas with.

᎒᎒᎒

JOSH TOOK HER TO A SURF CLUB FOR LUNCH, THIS TIME IN Coolangatta. They sat at a small round table overlooking the beach from balcony seating. Josh had changed into a pair of shorts and a T-shirt. He was the picture of strength, vitality and health with his muscular arms, tanned skin, and almost glowing face. Bindi thought how much onlookers must think she contrasted with him — thin, pale, and sickly.

Still, he didn't seem to mind. He held her hand across the table while they waited for their food and regaled her with hilarious tales of mishaps and accidents he'd witnessed during his policing career.

She found herself stepping up to his level of energy, laughing until she cried, and telling him stories from her time in journalism.

"Did you always want to join the police force?" she asked.

He shrugged. "I thought I'd be in the army, actually. But then, my dad got sick."

"I'm sorry, I didn't know."

He smiled. "It was a long time ago now. When we were in high school, most people were thinking about surfing, dating and what to wear to the formal — you and I had other things on our minds."

"He was sick then?" she asked.

He nodded. "Died soon after I joined the force. I didn't want to be gone, needed to be close by. Then, I had to help Mum through her grief, and my little sister get through high school. It was a rough time for the family, but we got through it. Now, Mum's happy as Larry and my sister, Beatrice, is a hairdresser down in Banora Point. She's about to get married."

"Wow, that's amazing. You made a sacrifice for your family...kind of the way my sisters did for me. I was the youngest, they felt like they had to take care of me...still do sometimes. It can drive me a little crazy, but I know they do it because they love me."

He smiled. "Yeah, Bea says the same thing."

By the time they'd finished eating, Bindi had relaxed and stopped worrying about the reason for their lunch date. Everything was out in the open; she had nothing to hide. If Josh wanted to be friends, she could manage that. She hadn't made any friends since moving north, instead burying herself in work at the inn. It would be nice to have some local connections, people her own age to spend time with.

Josh drove her home in his police cruiser. When she climbed out of the car, he fell into step beside her.

"Want to sit on the verandah for a little while? Or do you have to get to bed?" she asked.

He grinned. "I can stay for a few more minutes. I'm used to operating on very little sleep when I'm on night shifts."

She shook her head. "I don't know how you do it."

He sat beside her, rocking the chair back and forth. Then his gaze locked onto her face. "I had a really nice time with you."

She smiled. "I did too. I'm glad we're friends."

"Friends?" He quirked an eyebrow.

"Yeah, friends. I don't have many around here."

"I'm grateful for you as well." He reached for her hand, pulled his chair closer to hers.

She stared at their linked fingers, her heart racing. This didn't feel like friendship. Warmth travelled through her fingers, up her arm and spread through her body. "I don't think we should be more than friends though," she continued, "I have a lot going on in my life right now. I'm sick, and I have to work at getting better. Besides, we're doing more construction at the inn, I'm going to be so busy managing all of that..."

His eyes narrowed and he closed the gap between them until she could feel his breath against her lips. He studied her lips, let his eyes wander up to meet her gaze, then licked his own. "That's too bad."

She frowned. "What do you mean?"

"You wanting to be friends...it's too bad."

"It is?"

"Yeah, I'm afraid friendship is off the table."

Her pulse skittered. "What...?"

"I don't want to be friends."

Josh moved onto his knees in front of her, cupped her cheeks with his hands and pressed his lips to hers. He tasted like salt and buttered bread. His hands were firm, but gentle against her skin, his lips soft and wet. Her pulse raced into overdrive and her breath stuck in her throat. This wasn't what she wanted, was it? She'd thought not, but now she couldn't be so sure. His kiss dragged her under, deeper and deeper until she couldn't think clearly, couldn't see, couldn't breathe. Her eyes drifted shut and her hands wove around the back of his neck, pulling him closer and deepening their kiss.

Perhaps he was right after all. It was far too late for friendship.

❦ 17 ❦

CASOLI, ITALY

Sweat beaded on Charlie's forehead. It trickled down his temples and formed a pathway down his spine beneath his shirt. He wiped his forehead dry with the back of his sleeve and climbed down from the house frame. He jumped the last bit, landing on his feet with a grunt.

"*Ci vediamo domani*," one of the carpenters called out that he'd see Charlie tomorrow as Charlie walked off the job site, his tool belt swinging over his shoulder.

Charlie waved in response, walked to where he'd left his things by his bicycle and found his canteen. He took a long swig of water, then packed up his tools and piled it all into his backpack. He climbed onto his bike and set off through the streets of Casoli.

He loved working with his hands and becoming a carpenter had been a natural progression for him. After the war ended, he and Maria had moved out of her uncle's place and into town. Charlie had found work almost immediately as a labourer, then did an apprenticeship as a carpenter under one of the local men who'd fought as part of the Italian resistance during the war.

It'd been hard to make ends meet, especially after their daughter, Marion, arrived. But they'd managed. By the time Stefano was born, they'd fallen into a pleasant rhythm of life. Charlie rode his bike to work each day, and Maria watched the neighbours' children for a small fee. They led a simple life, and sometimes it was hard to make his salary stretch to cover everything they needed, but after so many years of war they were used to doing without. Life seemed positively luxurious now, by comparison.

When the road became cobblestone and began to climb the hill towards the centre of town, Charlie stood on the pedals to push his way forward. He passed stone houses, pressed up against one another, through covered archways and climbed off to walk his bike up a staircase.

When he reached their doorway, set into a wall of stone, with two flowering pots outside it, he rested his bike against the wall and pushed inside.

"I'm home!" he called.

A squeal emanated from the small kitchen in the back of the unit and small footsteps pounded across the tile floor.

"Papa!" cried a little voice as Marion flung herself at his legs. Her rosebud lips pulled into a wide grin and her four-year-old arms stretched as far around him as she could reach.

He picked her up, setting her on his hip as he headed for the kitchen. "How are you my darling? Did you have a nice day with Mamma?"

She nodded, her light brown curls bouncing on her shoulders. "Sì, Papa."

"English, my love," he corrected. He and Maria had chosen to teach their children two languages, with him they spoke English, with Maria they communicated in Italian. It worked well enough, though caused some confusion at times.

The result was that at four years of age Marion could converse fluently in either language, though she generally preferred Italian, especially since beginning *scuola materna,* or pre-school as he called it.

Maria sat in front of a highchair, holding a spoon towards their son's mouth. He slapped the highchair with both hands, his face covered in orange-coloured mush.

"Well, hello there Stefano. You look as though you're enjoying your tea," said Charlie.

Maria sighed. "A little too much, I think. Most of it is on his face or the floor."

Charlie grunted. "Ah the life of a baby."

"What about poor Mamma?" she asked, guiding the spoon into Stefano's open mouth.

"Papa! Papa!" called Stefano.

Charlie kissed the top of Maria's head, then hurried upstairs to change out of his work clothes and wash up for the evening meal. Maria preferred to eat late, but he'd convinced her they should eat something with the children before putting them to bed each night, so they generally had a light dish now, then another before bedtime. It kept them both happy, and he'd grown to enjoy the Italian fare, though it'd been a little hard on his stomach those first few months with the array of rich sauces, olives, and fatty meats.

He stripped down to his undershorts and stood staring into the small closet he shared with his wife. Her clothes were hung neatly on wooden hangers, the rest folded in straight piles that squatted on two wooden shelves on one side of the closet. Something fell to the ground, startling him. It was a hat box, tired and creased from years of use. He swore beneath his breath, picked it up and looked up to find where it'd come from.

Above the hanging clothes, another shelf stretched from one side to the other. He stood on tiptoe to peer at what was stored there. Usually he ignored that shelf, hadn't looked at it in years. He set the box back in the space it'd vacated, then reached higher still on his toes to see what else was stored on the high shelf.

Beside the box, folded and sagging, was the dress Maria had worn on the day the priest married them at her uncle's farm. He fingered it with a smile on his face. Beside the dress was a smaller box. He pulled it from the shelf and looked through it. A series of keepsakes from their first years together. Some dried flowers, a pamphlet advertising a movie they'd seen together, a pair of knitted booties from when Marion was a baby.

He slid the box back into place but found it didn't quite fit where it'd been. He couldn't see what was blocking it, so fetched a chair from the other side of the room to stand on. There was a pile of drab clothing in the way. He took it out, pushed the box back into place and then examined what he held in his hands. It was his military uniform. He hadn't thought of it in years. Hadn't seen it, either. Maria must've shoved it into the back of the closet when they moved in.

Charlie stepped off the chair and sat down, laying the uniform in his lap. With narrowed eyes, he took the shirt and unfolded it, studied the faded, stained material. The place where the dark, rust colour of his blood still showed faint against the green woollen fabric. The insignia sewn in place over the shirt pocket. He opened the pocket and felt inside. There was something there.

His brow furrowed as his fingers explored the small opening. With a grunt he managed to get two fingers around a small piece of what felt like paper and tugged it free. He stared at it, eyes widening. It was a photograph of a woman and baby. The woman looked very young. Even in black and white he could tell she was blonde. The baby held a fist close to its mouth, chubby legs protruding from a plain suit.

He sat on the chair in his underwear, the photograph in his hand, back slouched, studying the woman.

Every line of her face, the curve of her lips, the way her hip jutted out to hold the baby in place. Her slender figure and the bounce in her blonde curls. Those eyes...*Edie*.

Edie. Her name was Edie.

He leapt to his feet, heart pounding. Edie...and Keith. He was their son. They were in love. He'd promised to return after the war and marry her.

Panic swept its way down his throat and seized his lungs, his breath coming in short bursts as memories washed over him. He was Charles Jackson from Bathurst, Australia. He was engaged to be married to Edith Watson. Or at least, he had been. What must she think? He didn't return home after the war, didn't send a letter to tell her where he was. She must have thought he was dead. And his parents too, they must be so worried about him. An image of their smiling faces flashed through his mind, along with a laughing Sylvia. His family.

He fell back onto the chair as memories returned, one after the other. It was as though a flood gate had been opened and every remembrance that'd been held beyond its border now returned with a rush of emotion and a flurry of images.

Tears pooled in the corners of his eyes, then spilled down his cheeks as grief welled up in his chest. A lump built in his throat and a wail grew there, though he held it back. Maria and the children were downstairs, he couldn't let them know, couldn't utter a sound. He bit on his fist, pain filling his soul.

Edie.

He'd left her without a husband, no father to their son. She must've been consumed with grief when his letters stopped coming.

He should write to her. His parents as well. He should let them know where he was, that he was fine.

He stood and paced across the room to Maria's small

writing desk, pushed up beneath a dormer window in the corner of their cramped bedroom. He took one look at her pile of correspondence, letters, bills, all notated in her neat script.

He couldn't do it. What about Maria and the kids? He couldn't return to Edie and Keith. He had a life in Casoli.

With a shake of his head, he slid into the chair and pulled a sheet of paper in front of him. He reached for a pen and began to write.

Dearest Edie,

I'm writing to tell you that I'm fine...

What else should he say? I'm married, I have two children, and am living a happy life in Italy without you. I forgot all about you and our son?

His eyes squeezed shut and he dropped the pen back onto the desk with a clatter. No, he couldn't do that. No doubt after he left, she'd built a life for herself. He couldn't disrupt whatever it was she'd built since there was no way for him to live up to the promise he'd made her. Not now. He was already married. Had a family of his own. He couldn't be the husband he'd said he would, couldn't love her the way he'd always planned to, the way he'd dreamed of for so many years of his young life.

He crossed his hands on the desk and let his head fall to rest on his arms, his tears dry on his cheeks. It was an impossible situation. Everything within him cried out for Edie, his soul longed to return to her. But he couldn't. It was too late.

And he loved Maria, Marion, and Stefano. They were his

heart, his life. Even if he reconnected with Edie, he wouldn't leave them to go to her. So it seemed cruel to write, only to tell her that.

He'd write to his parents instead. Let them know where he was and what had happened and ask them about Edie and Keith. It was the only way to find out what he desperately needed to know — that his family in Australia was fine, didn't need him, were happy without him.

He reached for a fresh sheet of paper and began to write, the words flying onto the page. What would Mother and Father think? He missed them so much, his chest ached with it. It was as though all the emotion he'd been suppressing for so many years welled up within him all at once.

When he finished the first page of the letter, he leaned back in his seat to read it through. The bedroom door flew open and Marion raced in, leapt into his lap.

"Papa, what are you doing?"

He embraced her, kissed the top of her head. "I'm writing a letter, my darling."

"Writing to who, Papa?"

"Some people you don't know, my dear." He set her feet back on the ground. "Now run downstairs and see Mamma, I'll be down shortly."

"Mamma wants you to come down with me," pouted Marion, crossing her arms over her thin chest.

He cocked his head to one side, studying her as the pain evaporated from his chest and a bubble of joy replaced it. He pulled her close to squeeze her tight. He'd never leave his family, he loved them too much. They were everything to him. No matter how much he missed Edie, he couldn't walk away from the life he'd built, the family who needed him.

"Papa, I can't breathe!" she muttered against his chest.

"I love you," he said.

"I love you the mostest, Papa," she boasted, her eyes gleaming.

He folded the letter and shoved it into a desk drawer, then strode to the closet to find something to wear.

"Are you coming down to eat with us?" called Maria up the stairs.

He slipped on a pair of pants and then pulled a shirt over his head, shouting through the fabric. "Yes, I'm coming. Just a minute."

❧ 18 ❧

CABARITA BEACH

Bindi tucked her legs up beneath the covers and linked her arms around them. Her head sank into the pillow and she stared at the wall. She'd moved into Kate's room, the suite on the ground floor of the inn, just before Christmas. It was hers now, not Kate's room any longer. Kate and Alex were back from their honeymoon and living in Alex's small brick house in Kingscliff. Bindi was getting used to the new state of affairs.

She sighed, her head pounding.

She'd been looking forward to this day for weeks. Her last day of chemotherapy. Reeda had driven her home after the treatment ended and tucked her into bed. She hadn't felt up to eating or drinking anything, though Reeda left a glass of water on the bedside table just in case. Since then, she'd slept fitfully, sweating through the sheets and her loose-fitting pyjamas.

What she really needed was a Panadol. Something to help with the headache. But she didn't feel like getting out of bed.

Outside her room she could hear the buzz of conversation as guests made their way down the hall to the dining room for tea. Waning sunlight filtered around the edges of the curtains that blocked her bedroom windows. The air-conditioning vents on the walls hummed, sending cool air into the room to beat back the oppressive summer heat.

It was strange to be holed up in bed with so much going on just outside her door. She should shower, get dressed, make an appearance. She highly doubted she'd manage to sleep through the night if she kept dozing the way she had all afternoon.

In one week's time she'd find out the results of her treatments.

Dread edged her stomach with nausea, making it tighten into a knot. What if it hadn't worked? What if the doctor told her nothing had changed? Panic worked its way up her spine.

She didn't feel well. If the treatment had worked, would she feel better than this? Would she know?

With a sharp intake of breath, she swung her feet to the ground, leaned forward, and stared hard at the floor while she worked at moderating her heart rate.

Breathe in, breathe out.

There was no sense in getting all worked up about something she couldn't control — that was what Nan would've told her if Nan were here. But she wasn't, and Bindi had to face whatever came alone. Well, not entirely alone. She had Kate, Reeda, Mima, Jack...and now Josh.

A smile tugged at the corners of her mouth.

Josh had been a surprise. Was still a surprise to her.

She hadn't expected their relationship to develop the way it had. Bindi had never experienced this kind of falling in deep, with a rush of passion, unable to stop the tumbling, laughing, joyful descent, not wanting to. When she and

Brendan had first begun to date, there'd been a spark, a warmth, a sensible attraction that had morphed into a companionable relationship. With Josh, everything was different. She felt out of control, but in a good way. The best way.

She padded to the bathroom and took a hot shower, washing away the stink of the hospital, the feel of the poison leeching cold through her veins. Then she stood in front of the mirror combing her wet hair until it hung lank and straight around her face.

Since Brendan returned to Melbourne, she hadn't heard from him. She shook her head, remembering how close she'd come to giving him another chance. It would've been a mistake to let him back into her life. He knew she was sick, yet all he'd done was run back to Melbourne, unable to stand with her. She'd expected him to call, check on her at the very least, but it seemed he'd only wanted to use her to get his job back and didn't care about her wellbeing at all. How had she been so deceived about his character for so many years?

She'd only just buttoned herself into a summer dress and slipped on a pair of sandals when there was a knock at the door.

"Come in," she said, her brow furrowed. The door had a privacy sign on it, which generally discouraged guests from knocking. It was most likely one of her sisters, or Mima, coming to check on her.

"How's the patient," asked Josh, pushing through the door with a smile. "I hope I didn't wake you."

He offered her a bunch of flowers, sylvan reds, pink ice proteas, dyandra, viburnum, privet berry, and banksias. Bindi loved Australian natives, the way they uniquely combined stylish beauty with strength.

She grinned and stood on tiptoe to kiss his soft lips. "No, I've been awake for a while. Just stepped out of the shower."

"I brought soup. I thought it might help," he replied as he held up a plastic bag with a round container in the bottom.

"Really? That sounds perfect, thank you." She smiled. "Let's go out onto the verandah."

They sat side by side in rocking chairs watching the last remnants of the sun reflect across the garden as it set behind the inn. Everything was bathed in a soft golden light. The chooks returned to their coop, the horses stood idle in the paddock, eyes blinking lazily, and a pair of plovers circled above a grassy clearing, their calls ringing out in the still air.

"We had a crazy case at the station today," said Josh, as he snapped the lid from the container of soup and set it on the table beside Bindi.

"Oh yeah?" Bindi reached for the plastic spoon and plunged it into the soup.

"We got a call from a couple who live out in the sticks. This guy was pacing around their yard, around the perimeter, in his birthday suit."

"What?"

He shrugged. "Yeah, completely sunburned from head to toe. He just kept pacing around their yard all afternoon, muttering under his breath. Poor guy, we had to bring him into the station, then they took him to the hospital."

"I hope he'll be okay."

"The couple were so wigged out. They didn't know what he was doing. They locked themselves in their house for hours, watching and waiting until they called us. When we got there, we couldn't get him into the cruiser, we tried everything. I didn't want to force him, not if we didn't have to. In the end, I found a half-melted Cherry Ripe in my pocket. I held it out to him and lured him into the back seat that way. He ate it on the way to the station, got chocolate everywhere. Seriously, we should use video of it as a public service announcement — don't do drugs."

Bindi giggled as she gulped down mouthfuls of soup. It was warm and good, and soothed her stomach.

"I guess you had to clean out the car," she said.

He grimaced. "No kidding. I hate it when people slide across the seat nude. I had to use gloves and bleach..."

Bindi giggled until her sides hurt as Josh regaled her with more stories from his time on the force. When she'd finished her soup, they took a walk along the beach together in the cove. The last glow of a pink sunset hovered on the horizon.

Josh took her hand in his, kissed the back of it. She nestled against his side, their strides matching as they walked. Her hand felt warm and safe in his, her arm tucked beneath his. A feeling of well-being trickled down her spine and spread through her stomach. She smiled, letting the peacefulness of the moment invade, pushing away the worry, the fear, the pain. For this moment, she was happy.

"You know, I had a huge crush on you in high school," he said.

She frowned. "What? No way."

He chuckled. "Yep. I did. You were so beautiful, sweet, kind and a little bit mysterious. Always off reading a book on your own. But whenever anyone spoke to you, you'd give them your whole attention. I noticed that."

He'd noticed her? She thought no one saw her in high school. She was the girl from Sydney, the one whose parents died in a horrible accident. Apart from a few other nerdy girls who accepted her into their group, she'd been anonymous in her years at school. She wasn't a surfer, wasn't tanned and athletic, wasn't outgoing or vivacious, didn't sleep around, didn't fit the mould the way so many of the locals did.

She'd glided through those years, under the radar and happy to be there. She didn't want attention, all she wanted was to disappear, to escape the pain, to get through the day. She'd made it through, left town, and never looked back. Not until recent years, when she'd begun to doubt that the path she'd chosen was bringing her the kind of satisfaction in life she longed for.

Then she'd lost her job, and the idea of moving to Cabarita began percolating in her mind. When Nan died, she knew it was time, past time. She wished with everything she had that she'd moved back six months earlier, that she'd had time to spend with Nan before it was too late.

"I had no idea..." she said.

He shrugged. "I was too shy to say anything."

"Okay, now I know you're lying. You weren't shy, you were the coolest guy in school, the one all the girls fawned over. You were the hot surfer... I couldn't even talk to you without getting death stares."

He shrugged. "What can I say? It wasn't really me. I might've seemed to fit in with that crowd, but you may remember I didn't actually date any of those girls. I wasn't interested in them. I was interested in you, but you didn't even give me a second look. You were smart, fun, sweet — way out of my league."

He stopped, faced her with the hint of a smile playing around his lips. "I never thought I'd get to be here, standing with you on the beach at sunset. Never thought I'd get to kiss you."

He stooped down and pressed his lips against hers, taking her breath away. Her eyes drifted shut and she inhaled his scent — aftershave mixed with salt and a masculine musk. It sent a tremor down her body and through her legs, making them wobble.

She linked her hands behind his neck, staring into his blue eyes with wonder. "If only I'd known."

"What would you have done?" he asked, one eyebrow quirked.

She frowned. "Absolutely nothing."

He chuckled. "That's what I thought."

"But it still would've been nice to know."

"Well, now you do."

She eyed him, still feeling the giddy aftereffects of that kiss. "I'm losing the fight to keep you at arm's length, Josh Owens."

He grunted. "My devious plan is working then."

"I don't know where this is going..."

"Neither do I. We don't always have to be in control, Bindi. Sometimes we simply have to catch the wave and ride it to shore. Do you trust me?"

"Yes."

"Then, trust that I won't hurt you," he said, brushing a strand of hair from her eyes with a gentle touch.

"And what happens if I hurt you? What if..." She couldn't finish the sentence. It hurt too much to think about what the future might hold for her, or what it might not. In this bitter-sweet moment, she couldn't imagine giving up on the life she'd built, the joy that hovered fragile in her heart.

He squeezed his arms tighter around her. "Whatever comes, we'll face it together. You and me against the world."

"Together," she echoed. She liked the sound of that. How long she'd waited to have family in her life. Now she was surrounded by it, and it might all be taken away in the blink of an eye. She sighed, rested her head against his chest and let her thoughts drift away to the rhythm of his heartbeat.

❦ 19 ❦

CASOLI, ITALY

Charlie tramped along the footpath, up the hill and stopped at the door to the unit. His breath formed a fog in front of his mouth and his eyes watered. He stamped both feet on the cobblestones while he rifled through his pocket for the key, then opened the door and stepped across the threshold.

A baby cried upstairs, and he could hear Maria's low voice shushing Stefano towards sleep. In the kitchen, there was a banging sound, likely Marion playing something on her own while she waited for Maria to return.

He hung his coat on the coat rack, grateful for the warmth from the fireplace in the living room that pushed the cold back out through the door as he shut it behind him.

With a sigh, he unwound the scarf from his neck and hung it up as well, then kicked off each boot and slid his feet into the slippers waiting for him beside the shoe rack.

He threw his keys into a small bowl on top of the credenza. A pile of unopened mail caught his eye. No doubt a series of bills. He shook his head. The bills were never-ending it seemed. No sooner did he bring home his paycheck, than the bills began arriving, one after the other. Keeping a family alive was a lot more work than he'd ever realised. His own parents had made it look so easy.

He picked up the mail and sifted through it. Gas bill, water bill...and an envelope addressed to him in a familiar hand. In one corner, an Australian stamp.

His breath caught in his throat. The bills went back onto the credenza and he carried the letter with him to sit by the fire. With one finger sliding beneath the envelope flap, he ripped it open and pulled the sheets of paper free.

His parents were alive and full of joy at receiving his letter. He stopped after the first paragraph and set the letter in his lap, his heart racing.

They'd thought he was dead. They'd even held a service. Everyone attended, it was the hardest day of their lives, his mother wrote. So, when they received his letter, she'd fainted on the kitchen floor. Thankfully, Father had been there to catch her, and everything was fine.

He shook his head as he read, almost hearing her voice through the words scratched out in what looked to be a flurry on the page. His mother usually wrote with such precision, each letter perfectly formed, each word well thought out. This was written all in a rush.

His sister, Sylvia, was well. She was enjoying living in Sydney with her carpenter husband. How funny, wrote his mother, that Charlie too had become a carpenter. She supposed there were plenty needed to rebuild the world after such a war.

She wrote then that she was overwhelmed with happiness to hear she was a grandmother again and couldn't wait to meet the children. She hoped she could persuade his father to allow them a trip to Italy to see Charlie and his family soon.

As for Edie...

As you requested, we have not mentioned your situation to Edie. You suspected that she would've moved on with her life, and you were right. She married Paul Summer, an American serviceman who we believe she treated when she was a nurse in Sydney during the war. She, Paul, and Keith have moved north, to Cabarita. A place we'd never heard of before, somewhere on the northern NSW coastline.

Edie and Keith seem happy, and Paul appears to be a fine husband and father. Edie was devastated at losing you, but as you know, she had to move on, for Keith's sake as well as her own. She waited for your return for as long as she could manage, but none of us believed you were alive. We all thought the worst.

We see Keith every now and then, when Edie and Paul visit her folks here in Bathurst. He's a wonderful boy, you would be proud of him. Your father has finally accepted that he is your child, so our time with him is enjoyable and I look forward to it for months before their visits. I will try to get your father to travel north with me to see them sometime, but don't think my chances of succeeding in that venture are particularly high. You know how he feels about travel. Only, I believe he will relent on this point for you, our dear son.

I'm sure you don't know, and I hate to be the one to have to tell you, but Bobby was killed in the war. He was a good friend to you, and we all miss his ready smile.

I'm so sorry, my darling boy, that you have been through so much and that we were unable to help you...

THE WORDS BLURRED ON THE PAGE AS COMPETING emotions fought to gain control inside Charlie's chest. Bobby was dead. He hadn't even realised his friend was gone, and he'd been dead for years now. Grief welled up within him and he choked back a sob.

He was happy that Edie and Keith were well, but that she'd married someone else filled him with another kind of grief. Of course, he'd done the same, so he couldn't blame her. For her to lose both him and Bobby must've been more than she could bear. He hated that she went through it all without him.

It made no sense to feel jealous of her husband. He knew it was crazy. But he couldn't seem to help himself.

He sighed. The relief he felt at knowing his family was well, safe, and still living in his childhood home, washed the other emotions aside for the moment. They were all well, happy and whole. It wasn't everything, but it was enough for now.

There was a creak on the staircase, and suddenly Maria was there. Her eyes narrowed, and she cocked her head to one side, resting a tender hand on his shoulder.

"What is the matter, my love?"

He shook his head, momentarily lost for words. He pushed the letter towards her. She took it in her hands and scanned the page, her eyes widening.

"I cannot read this. Is it from your home?"

He nodded. "My mother."

"Your mother?"

He hadn't told her yet that he'd recovered his memories. For months now he'd wrestled with the truth of what he'd recalled. Telling her would've opened him up to more pain and confusion than he was ready to bear. But it was time.

"I remembered everything a few months ago," he said.

She slumped into an armchair beside him, her hand fluttering over her mouth. "What? You didn't tell me?"

He shook his head, reached for her hand. "I'm sorry, I couldn't. I had to work things through in my head first. I wrote to my parents and told them I was fine and all about you and the kids."

He raised the letter. "And this is what she wrote back."

"What does it say?" asked Maria.

Marion ran into the room in a rush, a toy car held high in the air. "Zoom, brrrrooom..." she cried, racing around the outside of the living room.

"Papa!" she shouted, when she saw him. In a moment she was on his knee, kissing his cheek.

He laughed, his throat tight, and kissed her cheeks, then held her tight to his chest. "Hello, my love. I hope you've had a good day with Mamma."

She nodded. "We made biscotti."

"Mmmm, my favourite."

She grinned, then climbed from his knee and kept playing with the car, pushing it back and forth on the floorboards by his feet.

He sighed and faced Maria. "She and Dad thought I was dead. They held a funeral and everything."

Maria shook her head. "I'm so sorry."

"I was certain I didn't have a family, since I truly believed all these years I wouldn't have been able to forget them. I guess I was wrong." He scrubbed both hands over his face. "She wants to visit us, meet the kids."

Maria smiled. "That would be lovely."

"There's more," he said, his throat tightening. He cleared it with a cough, but the lump only grew. He inhaled a slow breath. "Before I left for the war, I was in love with a woman called Edie. We were childhood sweethearts and had promised each other we'd get married after university. Of course, the war got in the way and we were never able to make it to the altar."

Maria's eyes glistened with tears.

"After I left, she found out she was pregnant..."

Maria gasped, raising her hand to her mouth.

He swallowed around the lump in his throat and continued. "When Keith was born, I was so happy. Only I wished I could've been there, of course. But I made her another promise, that I'd be home soon, and we'd get married and be a family."

Tears fell from Maria's eyes, sliding down her cheeks in silence.

He reached for her hand, squeezed it. "When I didn't return after the war, she grieved and then married someone else. She and Keith are healthy, happy, and fine."

Maria slid from her seat and settled on the floor between Charlie's feet, resting her head on his leg. "I'm so sorry, my darling."

He smiled through the pain in his throat. "It's all for the best, because I have you and the children. So it helps me to know they're safe and happy. I can move on with my life."

"Yes, of course," she replied. "But it is a tragedy, no less."

He nodded. "It is and it isn't. I'm happy here." He cupped her cheek in his hand. "I love you and the kids, and this is where I belong."

She nestled her cheek against his hand, let her eyes drift shut. "You are happy here?"

He nodded. "I'm happy, this is my home."

He kissed her upturned lips and wrapped her up in his arms, even as his heart burned in his chest.

✻ 20 ✻

CABARITA BEACH

"Ready to go?" Bindi asked, slipping the purse strap over her shoulder.

Six loaves of bread sat rising beneath cloths on the bench in a rectangle of light from the window. The scent of yeast filled the air.

Kate dipped her head. "Just need to wash the bread dough from my hands." She ran them under the tap, then wiped them dry on a hand towel. "Let's go."

Bindi followed Kate out to the car. They climbed in and Kate started the engine, then sat still, staring out through the windscreen, her hands resting on the steering wheel.

"You okay?" asked Bindi, her brow furrowed.

Kate nodded, inhaled a sharp breath, but didn't otherwise move.

Bindi watched then pursed her lips. "Hey Katie, is there something you want to talk about?"

Kate faced her, eyes glimmering with unshed tears. "I'm scared."

"Okay." Bindi waited for more, her throat already tightening.

"Scared of losing you. I don't want to find out the test results. I want to sit here, with you, in the car, believing that you're going to be fine."

Bindi nodded, swallowing around the growing lump in her throat. "Yeah, me too."

"I know we have to go, but I want to live in this moment, right now, for a little longer." Kate brushed a tear from her cheek.

"I'm going to be okay, Katie."

"I know you are."

Bindi cocked her head and offered a wan smile. "Besides, you've got Alex and Reeda to help you through if anything goes wrong." Her stomach twisted with anxiety. She was nervous enough about finding out her test results, she didn't need Kate to make things worse.

Kate burst into tears. "I know I have them, and I'm grateful, but I need you as well," she wailed.

Tears spilled from Bindi's eyes. She couldn't let her sister cry without joining in. No matter what they were crying about, she'd never been able to manage holding in her own tears if Kate or Reeda were upset.

"I need you too," she reached for Kate's arm, rested her hand there. "I need you to be strong for me, right now. To help me through today. If the cancer hasn't gone completely, we still have options."

Kate sniffled and wiped her eyes with the back of one hand. "I know."

"So, pull it together woman!"

Kate saluted. "Yes ma'am." She wiped her eyes again.

"I'll tell you what, let's go get a croissant and a coffee first."

Kate nodded. "That sounds perfect."

Kate pulled the car out of the driveway and headed for the tiny hamlet of Cabarita. There was a small, rustic cafe in the centre of the village called *Joys*, and when they were kids it was where Mum and Dad used to take them for breakfast when they were staying at the inn and just needed to get out for a while on their own. The place held too many memories for Bindi to have visited much since, but today it drew her in like a warm blanket. She needed to be close to Mum and Dad, to be wrapped in memories.

Joys hadn't changed much in the past decade or so. When they walked through the glass door, a bell tinkled overhead. The scent of fresh baked pastries filled the small space. A teenaged girl stood behind an antique-looking register, chewing gum. Next to her, an array of simple, yet delicious-looking, pastries were laid out in a glass display box. The only addition to the space seemed to be the shiny new espresso machine. When they were kids, the coffee had come from a plunger.

They ordered coffee and croissants, then sat at the same table by the large square front window they'd always occupied as a family. It was the only table in the cafe large enough for a family of five. Bindi sat on one side, leaning her elbows on the square table, while Kate sat on the other.

Bindi blew out a breath of air between clenched teeth. "This place brings back memories."

"I know. I don't think I've been in here since..." Kate glanced around, taking it all in.

Square black and white tiled floor, rickety worn tables, and mismatching chairs. A sign on the wall with a hand pointing to the back of the space where the single toilet was located.

"Me either. But they do have the best pastries in the area."

"I remember them being divine, but I guess we'll see how I feel now," said Kate with a chuckle.

They talked about old times, about their parents and trips to the cafe.

"I realise now that Mum and Dad brought us here to get some respite from the craziness of the inn, but I didn't know that at the time," mused Bindi. "Funny how you see things when you're a kid."

"I don't blame them, Nan and Pop ran things so differently to us. They treated the guests like family, and looking back, I think it got a bit hectic. Do you remember the way Nan used to play piano and sing in the evenings, and the guests would sit around the living room listening, sometimes singing along?"

Bindi shook her head. "I do remember that. It's so strange... I can't imagine us breaking into song for the guests."

"Mum must've felt a bit overwhelmed, bringing three children into that chaos for weeks at a time."

"No doubt," replied Bindi.

The waitress set their croissants and coffees down on the table without a word, then returned to her place behind the register.

Bindi and Kate exchanged a look. Bindi bit down on her lip. The girl was so morose, every bit the teenager with her black Doc Marten boots, black jeans and black rock 'n roll T-shirt, with a flannel shirt tied around her waist. Black hair hung down her back in a ponytail and a black fringe obscured her heavily lined eyes.

"I wish there were gothic clothes when we were teenagers," said Kate, "I would've definitely been a goth."

Bindi hooted. "I would love to see that."

They ate while they talked. The warm croissants were almost as good as they remembered them to be, especially slathered with the fresh butter and jam that'd been included on their plates in small, round bowls. The coffee was hot and rich, and before long, Bindi's nerves had subsided. As she laughed and chattered with her sister, she wondered why they didn't do this more often. They'd have to make more of an effort, especially now that Kate didn't live at the inn any longer.

The drive to the doctor's office subdued them both, and Bindi sat in silence staring out the passenger window. They didn't have to wait long before Doctor Ash called them into his office. Kate took Bindi's hand and squeezed it as he returned to his seat, and steepled his hands on the desk.

"Well, Bindi, I have good news," he said, his eyes twinkling.

Her breath caught in her throat, eyes widening. "Oh?"

"I've got your test results here in front of me, and each result tells me that you're in full remission."

Bindi leapt to her feet, with Kate beside her. Eyes wide, Bindi threw her arms around Kate. They danced in a circle together, both hooting loudly. Doctor Ash beamed at them from behind the desk.

"Remission!" shouted Kate. "Woohoo!"

Bindi laughed, her laughter quickly turning to tears of joy and relief. "I can't believe it. I mean, I was hoping...but full remission? Are you sure?"

Doctor Ash nodded. "Full remission. You're free to go and live your life."

They took their seats, and Bindi inhaled a long, slow breath. Full remission. It was the best possible result. She hadn't dared to hope too much for it, instead preparing herself for the possibility of radiation treatment, but now that wouldn't be necessary.

"What are the chances she'll stay in remission?" asked Kate.

Doctor Ash's lips pursed. "Well, with everything we know about this type of lymphoma, the chances are very good. In almost every case where a patient goes into complete remission, they stay that way and live a long, healthy and full life."

Bindi sobbed, covering her mouth with one hand. She'd live a full, possibly even long, life. For months now she'd been preparing herself, even subconsciously, for death. She'd lost her parents when they were still so young, her diagnosis had brought all that rushing back to her. Life was short, you couldn't count on having long years on the earth. But now... now she had another chance. A chance to really live, to choose the kind of life she wanted. She wasn't going to waste it.

They left the doctor's office, Bindi's head spinning, her throat aching, and her heart full of joy. Beside her, Kate couldn't stop smiling.

In the car, Bindi sat without putting on her seatbelt. She stared ahead, a smile tugging at the corners of her mouth, tears of happiness filling her eyes.

"Back to the inn?" asked Kate.

Bindi shook her head. She had to see Josh. All this time, they'd been dating, but she hadn't been fully committed, one foot out the door. Now, she was well. She still couldn't fully wrap her head around the idea, but there was only one thing she wanted to do.

Kate dropped Bindi off outside the police station and waved goodbye as she pulled out of the parking lot. Bindi had assured her that Josh would drive her home, and if he couldn't, she'd get a taxi. Kate had to get back to the inn, but it wasn't where Bindi wanted to be right now. She needed to see Josh, to tell him the good news, to finally let go of everything that'd been holding her back from giving him her whole heart.

Inside, she wasn't sure where to go. A uniformed police

officer stood behind a counter. He was busy with something, and a few other officers milled about an office space behind him. People waited in a small room with chairs lining one wall. She wandered over to the counter and stood waiting for the man to give her his attention. Finally, he did.

"Hi, I'm here to see Josh Owens," she said.

"Do you have an appointment?"

She shook her head. "I'm a friend, Bindi Summer."

The man grunted, dialled a number on his phone and spoke in hushed tones to someone. Then, looked at her. "He'll be right out."

She leaned against a wall, unable to find an empty seat. After a few minutes, a door popped open and Josh pushed his head through the opening. "Bindi?"

She hurried to meet him, threw her arms around his neck. "Hey."

He ushered her through the door. "It's so nice to see you; I wasn't expecting you. Sorry you had to wait."

"It's fine," she said.

He led her to an open office space. Plain clothes staff clacked away on keyboards, phones rang, and the murmur of voices filled the air. They stopped at a desk, and he pulled out a rolling chair for her to sit on, then perched on the edge of the desk.

"You're lucky you caught me, I'm not in the office much, but we just brought someone in for booking. I've been filling in paperwork for about half an hour, and we were going to head back out again as soon as I finished."

She grinned, reached for his hands, and held them in hers. "I'm glad I caught you. There's something I want to talk to you about."

He smiled, setting her heart alight with the love in his eyes. "Okay, I'm all ears."

She stood, stepped closer until her leg brushed up against

his. "Ever since you asked me out the first time, I've been holding back a little part of my heart."

He arched an eyebrow. "I know."

"I was afraid."

"Afraid of what?" he asked.

She sighed. "Afraid of losing you, of you losing me. I was sick, scared... I wasn't ready to fall in love. I told you that, but you wouldn't listen."

He chuckled. "I'm stubborn that way."

She shook her head, smiling. "Anyway, I wanted to come here to let you know. I'm ready now."

"You are?" He pulled her closer, looping his arms around her waist.

"Yes, I'm ready to jump into this thing."

"Oh yeah, and what brought about this change, Miss Summer?" His eyes sparkled.

She inhaled a long slow breath. "I'm in remission."

"What? Really?"

He stood straight, pressed his hands to her waist and lifted her into the air, twirling her in a circle with a shout. When he brought her back down again, he pressed his lips to hers.

Relief flooded her, and she smiled as he pulled away, tears filling her eyes until her vision blurred.

Catcalls sailed through the room. Someone cleared their throat with a cough.

"Get a room, you two!" shouted one of Josh's workmates with a wide grin plastered on his face.

She leaned her head against his chest, letting herself be enveloped in his arms. His heartbeat pounded in her ears.

"I'm so happy for you."

She smiled. "Me too."

❧ 21 ❧

CASOLI, ITALY

Charlie cinched the tie tighter around his neck with a deep sigh that emanated from the depths of his gut. He stared at his reflection in the mirror that stood against one bedroom wall. The same mirror Maria had used to get ready each morning for the past twenty years, ever since they'd moved into the house.

At fifty-seven years of age, he had crow's feet around his eyes, grey in the scruff on his chin he was attempting to pass off as a beard, and silver running through his hair. He combed his fingers through it. It was no use. He hadn't slept well in days and it showed. He didn't care much what people thought of him today. It was his wife's funeral. She'd died far too young and left him alone in the big house they'd built as a home for their family so many years ago.

His heart ached. Both Marion and Stefano had left home when they were in their early twenties. Now the sound of his footsteps along the hallway echoed through a silence that only enlarged the lump in his throat and the pain in his soul.

Nothing would ever be the same again. Marion had married and moved to Paris to pursue her career as an art historian with a gallery there. Stefano was married as well. He and his wife had revealed their plans months earlier to move to Australia to start a new life.

Australia? Why Australia? That was what Charlie had asked as soon as his voice returned.

"Because that's where you're from," Stefano had answered. "I want to know more about my roots. See the country where you were raised. Besides, that's where the opportunities are. Places like Australia and America. We want to go there, build a life for ourselves. See what the future might hold for us."

His eyes had been wide, full of hope for a better life. Jobs in Casoli were scarce. Many of the younger generation had moved, were trying their luck in other parts of Europe or the world. Rebuilding after the war had taken everything the country could manage, and the younger generation, the ones born after the tragedy of those years were over, wanted to move on, put the past behind them, start afresh somewhere new. They wanted travel, adventure, excitement, and Charlie couldn't blame them. He wouldn't have minded a bit of excitement himself after so many years spent working long hours in the construction industry.

But then Maria had died. An aneurism, the doctors had told him after the fact. Another tragedy, another life cut too short. They hadn't even had a chance to retire together, to travel and see the world the way they'd been talking about ever since the children left the nest.

"Papa!" called a voice from the kitchen.

He inhaled a sharp breath. Marion was here from Paris, staying in the guest room with her husband. She must've been back from the local *mercato* where she'd gone to buy flowers for the service. He told her she didn't need to do that as he'd already ordered plenty for the church and the gravesite. But she wanted to have a small bunch to hold, she said.

He walked to the kitchen, working hard to buoy his spirits enough to be strong for his daughter. She'd taken her mother's death hard, which wasn't surprising. The two of them had always been especially close. After she moved to Paris, they'd spoken every chance they could on the telephone, but the calls were expensive, and they hadn't seen each other in months. Marion felt guilty about it, he could tell. She never was any good at hiding her true feelings from him.

"I'm here," he said.

Marion offered him a wan smile. "I found the flowers." She held up a thin bunch, white sprinkled with pink.

"They look nice."

"Come here, I'll fix your tie," she said.

He stepped closer and she worked on loosening the knot before retying it gently. "How are you, Papa? Coping okay?"

He nodded. "I'm fine."

"You don't have to be."

"I know, but I worry about you. You should eat something," he said.

She tried to laugh with her throat full of tears. "That's just what Mamma would say."

"I know."

She embraced him, resting her head on his chest the way she had ever since she was a small child. He cupped her head with his hands.

"We should get going," he said.

She nodded. Her husband emerged from the guest room, and the three of them walked to the church together. It wasn't far, and even though the weather was cold, it hadn't snowed yet in Casoli that year.

Marion walked with her hand in her husband's and her

arm looped through Charlie's. He patted it absently every now and then.

It felt strange to go to the church without Maria. She often attended mass there, more and more as the years flew by. He'd never been one for Catholic services, preferring the more casual approach taken by the Baptist church in Bathurst. But there were no Baptist churches nearby, and he accompanied her whenever he was able.

Not anymore though. She was gone. He still couldn't quite believe it. She'd been so strong, full of life. It wasn't right. The two of them had so many plans. Now none of them made any sense. He didn't want to face them on his own.

They met Stefano outside the cathedral's doors. Stefano kissed Marion and shook Charlie's hand. His wife stood beside him with eyes downcast. Together they walked into the sanctuary and sat in the front row.

The priest led a service that was sombre and beautiful. A choir sang some of Maria's favourite hymns and afterwards they all tramped to the gravesite. All the while, Charlie's throat ached. The service passed by in a blur. It didn't seem real. Only it was real, and now he was alone.

Afterwards, Stefano and his wife came back to the house to rest for a few minutes before the wake that was to be held at a neighbour's house. He sat in an armchair in the living room across from where Charlie hunched in a rocking chair.

Charlie had a sudden thought. He didn't want to stay in this house, not any longer. Not with memories of his wife around every corner, in every piece of furniture she'd thoughtfully selected. He needed to get away, be somewhere different, take some time to grieve without seeing her face in pictures on the walls around him.

"Are you still moving to Australia?" he asked his son.

Stefano sighed. "I'm sorry Papa, we don't have to talk about it right now. It's not fair for us to leave you alone."

Charlie leaned forward, his mind racing. "No, I don't want to stop you doing what you've dreamed of."

"We want to go...but we don't want to leave you. Not now."

He smiled. "You're a good son, Stefano. But I think you should go through with your plan. In fact, maybe I could come with you. I mean, I wouldn't stick to you like glue or anything, don't worry about that. But I could fly to Australia with you, and we could settle near each other, see each other when we wanted, that kind of thing."

Stefano's brow knitted. "Are you sure, Papa? Mamma only just passed. Now isn't the best time to be making big decisions."

"It's my home, Stefano. It's where I'm from. Your mother was the only reason I stayed here. Now she's gone... I want to go home." He sighed, releasing the emotion that'd built up inside him. He hadn't realised just how much he longed to set his feet on Australian soil until the words fell from his mouth. The feeling welled up inside him in desperation, like an itch that had to be scratched.

"Well, if that's how you feel..."

"It is."

"We were planning on leaving in February. I mean we still have to sell the house and our visas haven't arrived yet..." Stefano said.

"Great, that will give me time to get everything settled as well."

"What about Marion?" asked Stefano.

Charlie sighed. "I'll talk to her. She can come and visit sometime. I don't think she'll mind since she's got her own life to live these days."

"You're probably right." Stefano smiled with his eyes full of sadness. "I think Mamma would've wanted this for you."

"I think so too." And a pilot light of hope stuttered to life inside him.

FEBRUARY 1981

BATHURST

The main street of Bathurst looked the same as it always had, except for the vehicles. Cars hummed down the centre of the paved street, pulled into parking spaces, and accelerated away again. The carts and wagons were gone, along with the horses. And there were more people, as well.

It'd been four months since Maria's death and Charlie still felt as though something was missing no matter where he went, or what he did. A feeling of having forgotten something, or someone, plagued him at the most inopportune times. His conscious mind understood that she wasn't coming back, but his subconscious hadn't yet gotten the memo.

He was excited to be back at home. That was how Bathurst felt to him, like sliding his feet into an old pair of slippers. Excitement buzzed in his chest. Adrenaline raised his heart rate as he wandered along the footpath, peering into new shops he hadn't seen before, and stopping at the old ones to see if he recognised the shopkeepers.

He'd come to find Sylvia. The last he'd heard from her, a year or two earlier, she'd divorced her husband and moved back to Bathurst. At fifty-two years of age she was living on the outskirts of town in a big house on her own, with only a pair of Pomeranians for company.

Their parents had died years earlier, one after the other. His mother had gone first — cancer — then his father had followed several years later, the wind having left his sails after the death of his wife. Charlie was only grateful he'd had the chance to see his parents several times before they died. They'd met their grandchildren on one of the three trips they'd undertaken to Casoli and had formed a strong bond with them that lasted well beyond their death. Marion and Stefano both missed his parents almost as much as he did. It'd been an emotional experience for him, seeing them that first time after so long without them, but it hadn't taken more than a day for them to fall back into a comfortable rhythm with one another.

Still, he couldn't help wondering why his sister hadn't replied to the last two letters he'd sent or answered the phone when he rang her before he travelled to Australia. He'd left a message on her answering machine to let her know he'd be visiting, but he couldn't shake the feeling something was wrong, since she'd never called him back.

He recognised and chatted with several different people on his way back to his car, surprised at how many he knew instantly or after only a few moments of hesitation, from his childhood. Everyone was excited to see him although most were vague about the details of when they'd last seen or heard of him — seeming to forget that he'd been thought dead after the war. He was happy to let them believe he'd simply moved away after the armistice. It was easier that way.

He stopped in at a bakery and grabbed an iced bun to take to Sylvia's with him for morning tea. She'd always loved their mother's iced buns, and some things didn't change. He found he was nervous to see her. She hadn't been to Italy to visit him and the family, and he hadn't made it to Bathurst before now either. Which meant, they hadn't set eyes on each other in almost forty years.

The edges of a photograph slid out from inside the folded map on the passenger seat of his rental car as he climbed in and set the bun in the back on the seat behind him. He slammed the door shut, then tugged the photograph free. The woman who stared back at him, a smile pulling the corners of her mouth wide, looked like a stranger, and familiar all at the same time. Sylvia had been only fourteen years old when he'd left home to join the Royal Australian Air Force. Now she was fifty-two years old with greying curls. Her eyes still twinkled the same way they always had and there was a shadow of a dimple in one cheek where a deeper one had been in her youth.

He picked up the map and studied it, finding the place he'd circled with a fingertip. Just a few turns and he'd be at Sylvia's house. He started the car and pulled out of the parking space.

Stefano and his wife were travelling around Australia and planned to settle down in Brisbane when they were done. He'd decided to let them go backpacking on their own. He had no desire to sleep in bunks with strangers next to him any longer, he'd done enough of that in the war years. Besides, what he really wanted to do was visit his old neighbourhood. He'd meet up again with them in Brisbane when they were done.

Sylvia's house was a pale brick two story building set back from the street with a short driveway that led to a two-car garage. The garden looked as though it'd once been well taken care of, but now the hedges were overgrown, and the garden beds pockmarked with weeds.,

He climbed out of the car with one hand tented over his eyes against the glare of the sun. He'd missed the Australian sun and had forgotten how savage it could be. How bright it made everything, stealing away colours, and burning all it touched. Would Sylvia be here?

She finally answered the door after he'd stood in the heat

knocking for several long minutes. She threw her arms around him, almost bowling him over.

"Charlie!" she cried, her eyes immediately brimming with tears.

He smiled through his own blurred vision. She led him into the house, shutting the door behind him. It was cooler inside, if only slightly, and two small dogs yapped at his feet until he stooped to pet them.

"I'm glad you're home," he said. "I was afraid you wouldn't be. I've been calling...kept getting your answering machine."

Confusion flitted across her face and her eyes narrowed. "Oh?"

Then she smiled again, her familiar blue eyes sparkling. "It's so good to see you. I can't believe it's been so long."

She slid her arm through his and together they walked through a cosy living room into a spacious and bright kitchen.

He patted her hand where it rested on his arm. "It is very good to be home. I had no idea I'd be gone so long when I left for the war."

She fell silent a moment, her smile fading. "Me neither. I missed you more than I thought possible."

His throat ached. "Me too."

"I see you've brought me a bun," she said, voice brightening. "I love those buns, haven't had one in years. Come on, I'll put on the kettle."

She made tea and they sat together in the dining room, eating iced buns, and talking over the years apart. She was happy, it seemed, to be living in her hometown again.

"You must've made friendships in Sydney that were hard to give up," he suggested. "Wasn't it difficult to move away, back here, where you haven't lived since you were a girl?"

She nodded in agreement. "You're right, it was difficult. But I found Sydney a bit too much lately. The traffic, the people bustling everywhere. I caught the train a few times and forgot to get off at my station, found myself lost and alone in strange towns at the end of the track... I don't know. I think I'm getting too old for a city like Sydney. All the noise, the traffic. It's overwhelming."

Charlie's eyes narrowed. "But you're still young yet."

She snorted. "Doesn't feel that way, sometimes."

One of the dogs stood at the sliding glass door that led to the back porch, barking. She got up with a sigh and slid the door open. The dog raced out and she closed it again. The other dog lay on the floor by Charlie's feet, raised its head a moment, then settled back onto the floor.

"So, your son is travelling?" asked Sylvia, returning to her seat.

He nodded, sipping his tea. "We'll meet up in Brisbane."

"That sounds good. What was his name again?"

"Stefano," he replied.

She nodded. "Such a nice name."

"We named him after a boy who helped rescue me during the war."

"Well, how about that. What a wonderful idea." Her eyes shone.

They talked for a few more minutes about what had changed in Bathurst, who still lived there, and which businesses had closed. Then, the dog returned to scratch on the glass door with one paw.

Sylvia's brow furrowed. She lumbered to the door and slid it open. "Now how did you get outside, you naughty dog?"

"You let him out," said Charlie. "Don't you remember, only five minutes ago?"

Sylvia thought a moment, her eyes looking blank. "Well, I guess I must've." Then she settled back into her chair with a grunt. "And where will you go after you've seen everything you want in Bathurst?"

"I'm heading to Brisbane, to meet up with Stefano," he said.

"Oh, that sounds nice."

He studied his sister, a realisation dawning. She wasn't well. That was why she hadn't returned his phone calls or replied to his letters. She was struggling with her memory; it was clear enough to him now.

He pushed a smile onto his face. "So, tell me about what's been happening with our old house. I drove past it on the way here, and it looks like someone's tried to tack on a second story."

She sighed, rolled her eyes. "Can you believe it? I mean, really — if you want a double story house, buy one. Why would you buy a quaint old single story and build another level on top of it? I wish I had the money to buy it out from under them so I could keep it the way it is, but I suppose everything changes whether we want it to or not."

JANUARY 1997

CABARITA BEACH

Nyreeda Houston squinted at the large paper sheet spread out across her dining table. She smoothed out a wrinkle with one palm then pressed her hands to her hips.

The plans for the new restaurant at the inn were coming along nicely. She'd added a few touches here and there and was working closely with the architect to make sure it was everything she, Kate, and Bindi were hoping it would be. Kate was in charge of the kitchen plans, but the architect had asked Reeda to oversee the restaurant area and she was excited to take it on.

Ever since she and Duncan had left Sydney and moved to Cabarita, she'd been itching to get her hands on a juicy project, and this was it. As ideas flitted through her mind, she reached for a magazine, tore out a page, and set it on the table beside the plans. She wanted to decorate the restaurant with a Hamptons feel, in white with blue and silver accents.

Footsteps on the staircase outside their unit caught her attention. Then, a key turned in the lock. Duncan was home.

She flashed back to a memory of the dread she'd felt when they lived in Sydney the year before and she'd heard the garage door open to announce his arrival home. Back then, she hadn't been excited to see him, knowing that his presence would result in an argument, or him seated on the couch ignoring her. Now, everything was different. After her summer in Italy, they'd reconciled and changed their lives to rebuild the kind of marriage they both wanted.

When he walked in through the door, her heart leapt at the sight of him. She strode over to him and kissed him full on the mouth before he could set down his surgical bag.

"Welcome home," she whispered.

He grinned. "What was that for?"

"Because I love you."

"I love you too," he replied, dropping his surgical bag, and wrapping his arms around her waist to pull her closer to him.

"Did you have a good trip?" she asked.

His eyes sparked and he headed for the kitchen to pour himself a glass of water. "The Congo was amazing. We went into this village, and the hospital... I mean they called it that, but it wasn't like any hospital I've ever seen before... It was full of patients. All lined up waiting for us, *Doctor's Without Borders* — the only doctors they'll see in a long time."

She sat at the bench and rested her chin in her hands. "Were you able to help them?"

"Most of them," he replied with a shrug. "We did what we could. Some, we could only bandage up and wish them well, but a lot of them had treatable illnesses. We did surgeries for twelve hours a day... I'm absolutely exhausted." He grinned, looking more vitalised than she'd seen in a long time.

"You seem happy," she said.

He smiled. "I am. It was so good to be able to help those

people. They have nothing, no money to pay us with, nothing but their health. So, when that goes, it has a huge impact on their lives. I mean, that's true of everyone, really. But we have hospitals, doctors, surgeries, in-home nurses...they don't have any of that. I mean, we didn't even have enough pain relief or lighting for the surgeries we performed. It was challenging in a way I've never dealt with before."

"And you loved it!" chuckled Reeda.

He gulped a mouthful of water. "And I loved it."

"I'm so proud of you," she replied. "I wish I could've been there to see it."

"No, you don't," he quipped. "There was no air-conditioning."

She frowned. "I don't know what you think of me, Mr. Houston, but I'm not that kind of girl. I can rough it when I choose to."

He quirked an eyebrow. "You can? I'd like to see that."

She strode around the bench to him and rested her hands on his shoulders. "I'll prove it to you. One day..."

"Okay, one day you can show me just how tough you are, how outdoorsy and carefree."

"But not today."

"That's fine with me, because I could do with a shower and a nap." He winked.

"You go do that, and I'll make us some food."

Reeda buzzed around their small kitchen, throwing together a pair of turkey, tomato, and lettuce sandwiches with a generous slather of mayonnaise on the slices of fresh sourdough bread she'd bought from their local bakery that morning.

The sounds of the shower echoed down the hall, along with her husband's deep voice. He sang the chorus of a popular song, reaching for the high notes and not quite making it. She grinned at the sound. She couldn't remember the last time Duncan had sung in the shower. With everything that'd happened between them in the past few years, trying to get pregnant, going through IVF treatments, and almost losing each other in the process, she was grateful for every off-key note issuing from the bathroom.

She set the sandwiches on the dining table, along with two glasses of iced water, and then returned her attention to the architectural plans. The plans showed the entire inn along with the surrounding gardens. In the back, the outline of a lagoon-shaped pool caught her eye. She hadn't been keen on the idea of adding a swimming pool to the inn, but when she'd brought up her objections in a recent meeting with her sisters, Bindi had laid out a thoroughly researched and well thought-through justification for the addition. She couldn't fault her sister's logic, or the maturity of her approach.

Bindi was certainly not the young girl she remembered. She'd grown into a confident, thoughtful woman. Reeda's throat tightened. She hated what her sister had been through. Whenever anything went wrong — in the family, in her work — she was the one who leapt to the rescue. She'd dive in and do whatever she could to save the day. But this time, she hadn't been able to do that. Bindi's illness wasn't something she could overcome or bluster her way through. She could only be there for her sister, and that was something she struggled with. She wasn't one to show a lot of emotion, or to stand idly by offering platitudes and affection.

She slumped back on the sofa, rubbing her eyes with her fingertips. Tears stung her eyes. Why was she upset? The doctor had given Bindi good news, great news in fact. It made no sense. She'd held it together for most of Bindi's treatments. Now she was crying? She shook her head in an attempt to shake away the tears. Bindi was going to be okay. The relief of that thought only made her throat ache more.

Duncan strode into the room, whistling. His wet hair

clung to his head and his muscular arms bulged in a white T-shirt above a pair of soft, athletic shorts.

"Whatcha doing?" he asked.

He sat on the arm of the sofa to peer at the plans.

"Looking over the design for the new restaurant at the inn. Bindi thinks we should add a swimming pool as well, become a true luxury holiday destination. They're starting construction on it next week."

He nodded. "Great idea. How's she going, by the way?"

"She's good." Reeda swallowed around the lump in her throat. "Doctor Ash says she's in complete remission and could very well stay that way."

Duncan's eyes widened. "That's wonderful!"

Reeda's eyes filled with tears. He slid onto the couch beside her, wrapped an arm around her shoulders. "What's wrong, sweetheart?"

"I don't know," she sobbed. "I didn't cry while she was sick, but now she's well, and I'm crying...there's something wrong with me."

He kissed her forehead and held her tighter. "Nothing's wrong with you. I guess you've been holding it in a little too much, huh?"

She nodded, and her vision was blurred with tears. "It's been such an emotional rollercoaster ride. We tried to get pregnant for so many years and couldn't, then we almost lost each other. Nan died, and Bindi got sick. I don't know if I can take much more..." Her voice broke off into a wail.

Duncan rocked her a little as he held her close. "It's a lot to deal with. You've been so strong, but sometimes you have to let it out. Emotions need to be expressed, or else they'll burst out at the strangest times."

He winked and she couldn't help smiling even as the tears fell.

"Do you think we're going to be okay?" she asked.

His lips pursed. "I do."

"Even though we can't have a baby, and it's only going to be us two, possibly for the rest of our lives?" She blinked away the tears, studying his face.

He smiled. "Yes. I don't know if you've noticed, but I'm happy. And I think you are too, apart from Bindi's recent illness."

"I've noticed." She nodded, wiping her eyes dry with the back of her hand. "And I think you're right. I think we're going to be okay."

He squeezed her once.

"I've gotten used to the idea."

He arched an eyebrow.

"I mean, of no kids. For so long I wanted them, desperately needed them, in my life. I think it was because of the idea I had in my head of how my family should look. After we lost Mum and Dad, I drifted away from Nan and my sisters. I didn't have that kind of family. Even when I met you and we got married, it didn't feel like enough. But now... I've got you and my sisters back, along with Mima and Jack, and the inn... you're my family, and this whole thing is what I've been longing for without even realising it."

"Is this enough for you?" asked Duncan, sweeping a hand around above his head.

"You mean this apartment? Because I've got plans for a house near the beach..." she began.

He grunted. "No, I mean this life."

She snuggled against his side with a sniffle. "This life is perfect."

❄ 23 ❄

BRISBANE

The black conveyor belt sprang to life with a jerk, then smoothly slid in a snake-like curve away from him. Charlie crossed his arms over his chest and scanned the faces of the passengers emerging through the gates in dribs and drabs.

Then, Stefano and his wife Amara were there. They were thin, tanned, and smiling from ear to ear.

He embraced them both, kissing cheeks and slapping backs. Joy bubbled up within him at the sight of them.

"Did you have a good trip?" he asked.

"The best! We both learned to surf."

"I've always wanted to do that."

"Nothing stopping you now, Papa."

"Nothing but ageing bones," he countered with a wry smile.

They looked for the couple's backpacks, and Charlie helped carry everything to his waiting truck.

He'd moved to Brisbane two months earlier, found a unit

to rent and bought himself a Holden truck. It was strange to drive on the left side of the road, but he was getting the hang of it. At least, he hadn't had any accidents yet. He had managed to hit the curb a few times with his left front wheel, but otherwise, the change had been easy enough to make. At least people drove at a sensible speed in Australia, unlike on the highways of Italy.

They drove to Indooroopilly, where Charlie's unit was located. He helped them upstairs and into the guest room he'd prepared for them ahead of time. Then, he went to the kitchen to make coffee. He knew his son well enough to know that he'd be dying for a decent espresso after months spent travelling around Australia. He'd developed a taste for the thick, black brew himself during his time in Italy. So, one of his first purchases after he'd moved in, was an espresso machine.

He gazed out the window while he waited for the coffee to percolate. The dark red flowers of a poinciana tree blazed just beyond his small balcony. The hum of traffic was a constant reminder of the city beyond the sliding glass doors.

Freshly showered and dressed, Stefano and Amara wandered into the kitchen and sat at the small dining table he'd found at a nearby garage sale. He set a small cup in front of each of them, smiling as Stefano's gaze settled on his cup and his forehead creased.

"Espresso?"

"I knew you'd be dying for one."

Stefano's face shone. "There's no good coffee in this country."

Charlie filled his own cup with the brew and sat across from his son.

"Here's to being together again. Cheers," he said, raising his cup.

Stefano and Amara clinked their small, china cups against his, smiling.

"How was Aunty Sylvia?" asked Stefano, after taking a small swig of the coffee. He'd never met her, but he'd seen the photographs and heard the stories from Charlie's childhood.

"She was okay. Unfortunately, it seems she's got early onset dementia."

"What? Oh no." Stefano set down his coffee cup and leaned forward.

"Yeah, while I was there, I convinced her to see a doctor. He said she'd have to go into a home soon, when she isn't able to care for herself any longer. So, I'll have to go back to Bathurst to check on her every now and then and help her find a place to live."

"I'm sorry, Papa."

"Thanks." Charlie sighed. "After all this time, I was so looking forward to catching up with her. Still, she remembers everything from our childhood, just not what she did five minutes ago." He sighed. "Other than that, she was well — the same old Syl I remember. She was always a sweet, kind-hearted girl."

"Did you get to catch up with everyone you wanted to see?" asked Stefano.

Charlie's heart skipped a beat. There were two people he'd been longing to see ever since he remembered who he was, ever since he'd stared at their faces in a photograph, which had jogged his memories of the life he'd once had. Edie and Keith.

He swallowed, nodded. "I chewed the fat with a few people. Some had moved away, others passed on. It's strange to go home after so many years. You keep expecting everything and everyone to still be there, right where you left them. But of course, that doesn't happen."

"I see you're getting your Aussie accent and sayings back,

without any trouble," said Amara, with a laugh as she flicked her black hair over her shoulder.

Charlie chuckled. "I suppose I am."

She carried the empty cups to the kitchen. "I hope you don't mind, but I'd like to go for a walk. It's so beautiful outside."

"Don't get lost," replied Stefano with a smile.

"I'll try not to."

Once they were alone, Charlie leaned back in his chair and drummed his fingers on the table. "There are a couple of other people I'd really like to see...but I don't know if I have the nerve. I've been trying to work up my courage to visit ever since I arrived in Brisbane."

Stefano's brow furrowed. "Who?"

Charlie swallowed, linked his hands together on the table to still his fingers. "Edie and Keith."

"Who are they?"

"Edie was my first love, my high school girlfriend. We were going to be married."

"Oh. And then you went to war and lost your memory?"

Charlie dipped his head in acknowledgement.

"What happened to her?" asked Stefano.

"She married, raised our son with another man as his father." Charlie swallowed.

Stefano's eyes widened. "Your son?"

"Yes, Keith is our son."

"You mean, I have a brother?"

Charlie smiled. "Yes."

"Wow. That's... I don't know what to say. Have you ever seen him?"

"Only in photographs." The admission thickened the words in his throat, set his heart aching.

Stefano stared at the table, shook his head slowly. "Well,

you've got to go and see them. So much time has passed, you can't waste any more."

"But what about your mother?" asked Charlie with a sigh. "I don't want to disrespect her memory."

Stefano's brows knitted together. "What? It wouldn't disrespect her. You spent your life making Mamma happy. She'd want you to be happy now. And besides, it isn't fair on Keith — he should know you. If it were me, I'd want to meet my father."

"I'm not sure he knows I *am* his father... He was raised by someone else."

"Still, I'd want to know the truth," finished Stefano with a firm nod.

"I don't know... I could disrupt everything, their whole lives. Perhaps I could meet Edie in secret, talk to her before I blow everything apart." He inhaled a long, slow breath. It didn't seem right to show up after all this time and cause so much turmoil for Edie and her family. It wouldn't be fair on her, her husband, or their son.

"Do you know where they live?" asked Stefano, standing up suddenly.

Charlie shrugged. "Mum gave me an address years ago. I don't know if they're still there."

Stefano paced to the other side of the room. "They might be, and even if they're not, someone is sure to know where they went. It's worth a try, Papa."

Charlie chewed on his lower lip. Stefano was right, so much time had passed, they'd been robbed of an entire lifetime together. He couldn't give away more of it. But he wasn't certain Edie would even want to see him. He'd written letters to her over the years, poured out onto dozens of pages an account of his life, of what'd happened to him and why he'd disappeared the way he did. The letters sat in a dresser drawer in his bedroom, unsent. He couldn't decide if it would be better for her and Keith to continue believing he was dead, or to find that he'd been alive all this time and stayed away.

"She might not see me," he said. "I wouldn't blame her for being angry." He shook his head. "For many years I was angry enough with myself about it all."

Stefano slumped into the seat across from him. He combed fingers through his dark, wavy hair, setting it on end. "Papa, this is something you must do," he said, sighing. "Mamma is gone, she isn't coming back, and Edie, Keith, they deserve to know the truth, to see you again. If Edie loved you, she will want to know you are well. If Keith is your son, he would want to meet you."

"You think so?" Charlie knew the answer even as he said the words.

"Yes, of course." Stefano was so firm, so certain in his beliefs. It was one of the things he admired most about his son — that certainty, the belief that everything was either true or it was false. That there was nothing in between. And that he knew which it was, every time without having to question himself.

He'd carried that view of the world around on his shoulders since he was a young boy with wild hair and knobbly knees running through the streets of Casoli with a soccer ball permanently attached to one foot.

Stefano sighed at the look on Charlie's face.

"Papa, think of it this way — if you never visit them, you'll never know."

❧ 24 ❧

CABARITA BEACH

Bindi rested her feet on the lowest railing of the verandah and stared at the letter in her lap. She folded it slowly, her heart pounding and a smile forming at the corners of her mouth.

Charlie Jackson had returned to Australia after all. And he'd planned on visiting Nan. Had he come to the inn? Had Nan agreed to see him after so many years apart, so much heartbreak? She'd have to look through the stack of letters to see if there was one to follow the one in her lap. She could barely contain her excitement.

She giggled to herself. Fancy getting so worked up over something that'd happened when she was a little girl, and other things that'd passed before she was even born. But all this time she and her sisters had assumed Charlie had died in the war, then they'd believed he'd never returned to Australia. Now, it seemed none of those things were true.

What must've Nan thought when she received his letters so many years after he'd disappeared from her life and she'd married Pop? Had she been filled with joy? With grief? Regret?

And what about Dad? Had he discovered the truth about his parentage?

It was maddening not to be able to ask anyone. The only person who knew anything was staying virtually silent on the subject. Whenever she brought up the name, Charlie Jackson, with Mima, she acted as though she'd barely known the man, and didn't have anything further to add on the subject. Perhaps she didn't. Maybe Charlie hadn't come to the inn after all, or if he had, maybe Nan hadn't told Mima about his visit.

Bindi folded the letter, slid it into the envelope and stood to her feet with a yawn. Ever since she'd gotten the clean bill of health from Doctor Ash, she'd begun to feel better and better. She'd been eating normally again for weeks now, even her cheeks had begun to fill out again. She brushed fingers over her face, feeling the plumpness of her cheeks where before there'd been only angles and points.

She smiled and gazed out over the muddy back yard. There'd been just enough space between the inn's building and Nan's garden to fit a swimming pool. The pool sparkled, dazzlingly blue, under the summer sun. She smiled at the sight. It was still surrounded by upturned earth, the occasional rock, and clods of cement, but it looked beautiful anyway. The landscapers would be coming tomorrow to finish everything off, but she and her sisters had agreed to take the first swim that afternoon. Bindi couldn't wait. The water looked so inviting and she was excited about what was to come for their thriving business. The guests who'd seen the construction had been as enthusiastic as she was about it — promising to return for another stay when it was finished.

After a quick glance at her watch, Bindi hurried upstairs to put the letter away and get her purse. She was meeting

Mima at the retirement village. Mima had invited her over for lunch, and she was looking forward to spending some time at Mima's new home. She hadn't been there much since Mima moved in, since the former cook seemed to end up spending so much time at the inn instead.

When she reached the retirement community, she punched in the gate code and waited for the metal structure to swing open. She parked outside Mima's small cottage and grabbed the bee-sting pastry she'd bought at the cafe in Cabarita, before climbing out of the Land Rover with a grunt.

In the distance, a swimming pool glinted beside a large, rectangular building. The water looked inviting. A trail of sweat ran down Bindi's back between her shoulder blades, and beads formed on her forehead. Overhead, the sun blazed, warming her scalp in moments.

Narrow roads wove between rows of cottages. Mima's cottage was painted white with blue highlights and was surrounded by a pretty garden of green clipped hedges and colourful freesias, snap dragons and lavender bushes.

Bindi knocked on the front door, but there was no answer. She frowned. Mima knew she was coming. She peered in the front window but couldn't see any movement in the cosy living space.

She listened a moment. A voice that sounded like Mima's echoed from the cottage next door. Bindi wandered over to the next cottage, and along a narrow pathway to the back yard. She found Mima and Betty seated in rocking chairs sipping from cups of steaming hot tea.

"There you are," said Bindi.

Mima jumped to her feet. "Oh, I'm sorry, love. The time got away from me." She kissed Bindi's cheeks and took the offered pastry. "This looks delicious, thank you my dear."

"Hello, Bindi," said Betty, still rocking. "Pull up a chair and join us. We were just discussing the state of politics."

"Did you solve the country's problems yet?"

Mima winked. "We're getting close. If only the prime minister would ask us, he'd find we have all the answers."

Bindi settled into a chair beside Mima's with a grunt. Mima took the bee-sting inside and soon returned with it sliced up on a plate. She set it on a table in front of the three of them and handed Bindi a cup of tea.

"Thank you, Mima," she said.

Mima nodded. "So, my darling girl, what's new in your world? Tell us poor old biddies something exciting so we can remember what it was like to be young."

Bindi shrugged, reached for a piece of pastry, and took a bite. "I don't know... I don't really live a very exciting life. I prefer quiet, simple, drama-free."

Mima dipped her head in agreement.

"I hear you on that," added Betty. "Drama-free is the best kind of life to live."

"Especially after what you've been through," said Mima, reaching over to pat Bindi's arm. "You've had enough drama for a lifetime."

"Yes, I have," mumbled Bindi around a mouthful of custard and icing.

"Still... I can't help wondering about that handsome boyfriend of yours," continued Mima with a glint in her eye. "How are things going with your police officer?"

"You mean Josh?" asked Bindi.

"That's right...Josh. I like that name."

Bindi chuckled. "Josh is great...wonderful actually. He was by my side throughout my treatments, didn't let me push him away."

"Sounds like a keeper," piped up Betty before taking a huge bite out of a piece of bee-sting.

"He is a keeper." Bindi pondered her words as she spoke them. They'd been dating for several months now, more regularly in recent weeks than before. She saw him almost every day now, and each moment they spent together only drew her closer to him. With Brendan, she'd found that spending too much time together had only pushed them further away from each other, so she'd always moderated how often they'd seen each other. Although, as busy as each of them were with their jobs, that hadn't been hard.

But with Josh, time spent together seemed only to draw them closer. She never got sick of him. He didn't annoy or frustrate her, only drew her in with his charm, his charisma, his kind heart, and the humour that made her laugh out loud at the most unexpected times.

"Tell us about him," replied Mima.

"Well, he loves to surf. That's how we met, actually. I found out I was sick and went to the beach to look out over the waves. But when I went back to the car, I fell and scraped my knee. He helped me, got me a band aid..."

"A knight in shining armour then," replied Mima, her eyes gleaming.

Bindi nodded. "He really is. When I told him I was sick, he wouldn't let me push him away. He says he knew he wanted to marry me back in high school but couldn't work up the courage to ask me out on a date."

Betty pressed a hand to her heart. "Oh my word. That is truly beautiful."

Mima tut-tutted. "Ah. Reminds me of—" She didn't finish her sentence, instead wiping her eyes with a handkerchief pulled from a pocket in her dress.

"Reminds you of what, Mima?"

Bindi knew what Mima was referring to — Nan and Charlie. She wanted Mima to talk about them. Maybe she'd reveal a clue, some new information she hadn't spoken of yet. Or maybe she was hinting at her own romance all those years earlier with the American serviceman who'd died in battle soon after their engagement.

Mima only shook her head. "Never mind. He sounds like a wonderful young man. I can't wait to get to know him better."

"Do you feel the same way about him?" asked Betty.

Bindi sipped her tea, her eyes narrowing in thought. Then she set the tea back on the table beside her. "I think so...it's been such a whirlwind. I do know this, the more I get to know him, the more I like him."

"He's a catch," said Mima, the brightness returning to her voice.

❦

BINDI STOOD ON THE EDGE OF THE SWIMMING POOL IN HER green bikini, a droplet of sweat trickling down the side of her face. Next to her, Kate and Reeda looked at the pool, just as pensive, just as proud as she felt.

"I love it," declared Kate.

Reeda nodded. "This was a really great idea, Bindi. I'm glad we listened to you."

"There's a first time for everything."

Her sisters laughed.

"Alright, let's christen this thing," declared Kate, lowering one foot into the sparkling water.

Bindi shrugged. "We have to do it right."

She grabbed Reeda's hand and then Kate's and leapt forwards at the same time. Both sisters let out a shriek before all three of them plunged beneath the water's surface. The cold of the water hit Bindi's overheated body with a shock.

She burst through the surface with a smile. Beside her, Reeda and Kate groaned and spluttered.

"Give us fair warning before you do that!" cried Reeda, rushing her sister and dunking Bindi's head under the water.

Bindi emerged again, coughing, and rubbing the pool water from her eyes.

Every day she celebrated growing a little stronger, feeling more like herself. She hadn't realised how weak she'd gotten until she began to feel better. Simply jumping into a pool, splashing about with her sisters, the realisation of how much better she felt filled her thoughts. She thanked God for another chance at life, an awakening of sorts.

She might've gone through her whole life not appreciating these small moments, the beauty and poignancy of rollicking with her sisters in a brand-new swimming pool beneath the glare of the summer sun. But she did now. The beauty of the moment tightened her throat as she watched her sisters splash one another, laughing and squealing as Reeda pushed Kate's head beneath the surface.

They swam for half an hour before climbing out to lay on the narrow deck around the pool's edge. They didn't stay there long, anxious to get out of the sun's glaring rays. So they relocated to the verandah, lounging in rocking chairs and sipping fresh squeezed lemonade while they dried. Several guests from the inn had watched them play in the pool with smiles on their faces, but now they were alone.

"Did you ever think the three of us would end up back here?" asked Reeda.

Bindi shook her head. "Never. I hoped...but I didn't think it would happen."

"Definitely not," replied Kate. "I thought I'd be head chef in an amazing restaurant somewhere in the world by now."

"You're head chef at the Waratah Inn," interjected Bindi with a grin.

"That's true." Kate shrugged. "I guess part of my dream came true...but honestly, my dream changed and I'm fine with that. More than fine... I lived in the city and pursued that life and it didn't bring me any satisfaction. Well, not much anyway. It was exciting at first, but once that wore off, it was empty... I didn't have you guys. My family. I thought I could live without family, but I was wrong."

"Hear, hear," replied Bindi, raising her glass.

They all clinked their glasses together, then took a big swig of lemonade. Bindi's heart swelled. She inhaled a long, slow breath. This was exactly the life she was made to live.

❧ 25 ❧

CABARITA BEACH

Sunshine warmed the top of Charlie's head as he stood beside his truck, hands on hips, looking out across a dazzling, blue ocean. He'd never seen a beach like this before. Of course, he'd travelled to the Mediterranean with his family a number of times over the years, and it was beautiful. Stunning even, especially with a backdrop of lush cliffs and colourful villages. He'd been to Sydney Harbour and sailed from there to Africa. But nothing compared to the beaches at Cabarita.

Long, golden sand curved in an arch towards a horizon that faded to a point in the distance. Gulls hovered overhead, calling in a melody that overlaid the steady rhythm of the waves crashing against the shoreline.

He stood on a lookout that jutted from the beach, grass-covered and round. Below, black rocks held the ocean at bay, sending salt spray into the air that tickled the end of his nose like a light summer rainfall.

He inhaled a long, slow breath, let his eyes drift shut as the sounds and smells of the lazy, slow day enveloped him.

For so many years he'd worked hard to support his family, to build a life for him and Maria. He'd never taken time off, not more than a week or two for a family holiday. Since her death, he hadn't returned to work, and he'd finally begun to unwind. The tension had left his shoulders and he was less irritable, more able to enjoy the moment. Part of that might've been the shock of dealing with his wife's passing, but he knew it was also a result of rest. The kind of rest he'd needed for a long time. He wished he'd taken the time off with Maria. They could've travelled the world together. She would've loved Cabarita Beach.

He glanced at a small square of paper in his hand. Scratched with a pencil in an almost indecipherable hand, were the words, *The Waratah Inn.*

He'd stopped at a cafe in town called *Joys.* The girl behind the register had stopped smacking her mouthful of bubble gum long enough to write down the place where he could find the Summer family.

That was what Edie was now. A Summer. His mother had told him as much, and even though it'd been difficult to comprehend at the time, he was used to it now. Edie Summer. It had a nice ring to it. He hoped she'd been happy, that she still was. It would be almost unbearable if she hadn't.

The idea had kept him away from the inn at first. Instead, he'd stopped at the lookout to watch the waves curl to shore for half an hour, unable to step back into his truck. What if she'd led a miserable life? What if Keith's father had mistreated him? He didn't want to know, there wasn't anything he could do about it. He couldn't turn back time, and as much as it pained him to think of them suffering, he wouldn't change a thing because the path he'd taken had led him to a family he adored and a life full of joy.

He sighed and climbed into the truck, slamming the door shut behind him. It was time to take the step. Whatever he found when he reached the inn, he'd deal with it.

Butterflies jostled in his stomach as he drove down the long, narrow highway. The one thing he'd failed to consider, to let himself ponder, were his feelings for Edie. He'd pushed them down, denied they existed at all. He told himself he was checking on them, wanted to make sure she and Keith were okay. And if he could, get to know his son, at least a little. But the truth was, his love for Edie had never dimmed, it'd simply been locked away in a vault somewhere deep in his heart.

Pulling that love out and facing it felt like a betrayal to Maria. But Stefano was right — Maria was gone. She'd been dead for a year now; even the memory of her face was fading in his mind's eye and the pain he'd felt at every reminder of her life, had faded. Was it wrong for him to admit he still cared for the girl he'd loved all those years ago? He wouldn't act on it, she was married after all, but he could face it.

A driveway dipped away to the left of the road and he slowed to look down it. Beside an open gate hung a sign, painted dark pink, that read, *The Waratah Inn: Beachside Bed and Breakfast*.

He reversed the truck, then turned into the driveway with a brief grinding of gears. The tyres crackled on the gravel as he pulled slowly towards a three-story structure with pink walls, white gables, and a white wrap-around verandah. It looked like it hadn't seen a paintbrush in years, with bubbling and peeling in places and a few stained boards. Still, the garden that surrounded the inn was beautifully maintained, with vibrant pops of colour as flowers pushed through the greenery to smile at the sun.

That was Edie's touch for sure. She'd always loved gardening. Even when she was a teenager, one of her favourite chores had been to get down in the dirt beside her mother, digging in the large kitchen garden they'd kept behind the old farmhouse. That and feeding the horses of course. She'd loved her horse more than almost anything or anyone. Sometimes he wondered if she loved the feisty mare even more than she did him. Though she'd denied it of course and sealed her words with a kiss that had stolen his breath away.

A bubble of nerves burst free in his gut as the memory of her kisses washed over him. He found a parking lot beside the inn. A few cars were parked in haphazard fashion on its weed-covered surface. He pulled the truck onto the lot and climbed out to stare at the inn. Laughter bubbled from an open window, and several people lounged on the verandah talking.

He set off towards the inn, then veered around it. Perhaps he should look around first, then see if he could find Edie. He needed a moment to steel his nerves. Behind the building he found a narrow trail that wound through the yard and then down a short embankment to a beach that'd been hidden from view by a grove of pandanus.

The cove was breathtaking and untouched. There wasn't a single person in sight. At least, not at first. He'd walked for ten minutes along the shoreline, basking in the solitary beauty of the place, when he saw a family emerge from the trail he'd taken only minutes earlier.

Their laughter caught his ear first, then he swung his head to watch as a woman, a man, and three teenaged girls padded down the sand to the water. The girls ran towards the water. One scooped up a handful of seawater to throw at the others, who squealed and peeled off clothing to reveal swimsuits beneath. They dove into the water, beneath the waves, swimming like they were made for it.

His eyes narrowed, squinted in the bright sunshine. There was something about the woman that was familiar to him. He watched her. She held a hand over her eyes, shading them from the sun as she called to the girls. Her laughter floated back to him, and his heart skipped a beat. He'd recognise that sound anywhere. It was Edie. It had to be her. No one else laughed like that — her laughter was contagious, it bubbled up from within her and poured out like birdsong.

The man behind her folded his pants up until they were above his knees, then waded into the water. He shouted something that made Edie throw back her head. Then, he splashed the water in her direction. She pulled away with another laugh. He wished he could hear them, hear what they were saying. But if he drew closer, they'd notice, and he didn't want that. Could the man be his son? He certainly looked to be the right age. And if he was, if that was Keith, maybe the girls were his daughters. Perhaps they were Charlie's grand-daughters. His heart swelled and throat tightened. He had grandchildren. It didn't seem possible.

He was the only other person on the beach. They were bound to see him if he stayed where he was, and he couldn't return to the inn without passing them.

He'd come there to see Edie, to meet Keith. He didn't know what he'd hoped to achieve by doing that. He knew it could disrupt their lives. What would he say? How could he tell them the story of his life without causing them more pain than he already had? He'd brought the letters with him. The ones he'd addressed to Edie, that contained all the words he'd longed to say over the years but hadn't mailed. They were sitting on the front seat of his truck. A bunch of envelopes held together by a single elastic band. The story of his life since they'd last been together.

He spun on his heel, ducked his head, and strode away from them, towards the end of the beach. When he reached it, he stopped and sat himself down on an outcropping of black rocks. Just beyond the waves, a large black rock jutted skyward. He peered at it, studying the way the water swirled around it on the way back into the depths, then crashed and sprayed on its way to shore.

He should've taken off his shoes before he stepped onto the sand. Now there was sand in one of them. He tugged it off, still watching the waves, and poured the sand out. Then, repeated the procedure with the other shoe. He shoved both socks deep into his shoes and stood, shoes in hand, to return to the inn.

The family had moved now. He couldn't see them any longer. It should be safe to walk back to the truck and drive home. It'd been wrong to come. He couldn't bear to tell them the truth. It might make him feel better, to have them in his life in some way, but it would only bring them pain.

He marched back down the beach, then stopped where the family had stood, splashing each other at the edge of the shore. A pair of sandals sat there, alone, just out of reach of a rushing wave.

He stared at the sandals, then, stooped to pick them up. A voice startled him.

"Thanks, I was coming back for those."

He turned to see Edie, looking at him with those same blue eyes that'd stolen his heart all those years ago and never given it back. She was older than he'd remembered, of course, but looked much the same. Her hair was shorter, styled just above her shoulders. The curls were still there, along with the golden blonde hue. A few streaks of grey, much like his own, glistened in the sunlight. Her waist was thicker, there were wrinkles around her eyes as she smiled at him, but it was still her. The same Edie he'd fallen in love with.

He handed her the sandals.

"Thanks," she said. She turned to go, then faced him with one eyebrow arched. "You look familiar...like someone I once knew."

His eyes met hers.

She gaped. "What...?"

"Edie..." he said.

Her face crumpled. "No. It can't be." She stepped closer, threw her arms around his neck. "Charlie."

He found he couldn't speak at first. Instead, he embraced her and held her close as she trembled in his arms.

When she pulled back, tears had wet her cheeks. "I don't understand...where have you been all this time?"

His hands clenched into fists at his sides. "Can we sit...talk?"

She dipped her head in a nod and waved at the rocks on the edge of the beach. He followed her up the sand, and they sat side by side on a flat, dark rock, looking out towards the horizon.

Edie faced him, her damp cheeks flushed. "I'm listening. I'm trying to be patient, Charlie. But I have a lot of questions."

"I know you do...and I'll answer all of them."

He explained it all to her then. How he'd escaped the POW camp and lost his memory. Where he'd been living, with his family. And how he'd come to Australia after losing his wife, hoping for a new start, hoping to see her again.

She cried as he spoke, while she fidgeted with the sandals in her hands.

Finally, when he fell silent, she met his gaze. "I thought you were dead. I buried you, mourned you. It broke my heart to lose you."

"I'm sorry," he said. "If I'd remembered...I would've come back to you. I would've done anything...but by the time I regained my memory, I was married, had children. Then, when I wrote to my parents, they said you were married, that you and Keith had moved away with your new husband. I figured...it was best to leave things as they were."

"But you could've at least told me you were alive!" she

cried, wiping the tears from her eyes with the back of one hand.

He sighed. "I can see that now...but at the time, I thought it was best not to bother you. It was difficult for me, all those memories flooding back, going through the grief of losing you and Keith, and realising I couldn't do anything to change what'd already been done. Perhaps I made the wrong choice, but I can't fix it now. All I can do is to say that I'm sorry."

She grabbed his hand and squeezed it, new tears spilling from her eyes. "Thank you. I'm so glad you came to see me. I'm so glad you're alive. Even if we couldn't be together, the world is a better place for having you in it."

His throat tightened and he kissed the back of her hand. "I hope you're happy...that's all I can ask for, all I've wanted to know for so long."

She smiled through the tears. "Yes, I have a happy life. Paul Summer, that's the man I married, was a loving and kind husband, and a great father to our boy."

"Was?" Charlie couldn't help noticing she used the past tense.

She blinked, sighed. "Yes, Paul died three years ago. Heart attack, I'm afraid. I miss him."

"I'm so sorry, Edie."

"I'm sorry about your wife as well."

They stood in silence a moment. He shifted from one foot to the other. "I guess I'd better be going."

"I'll walk you back to your car," she said.

They walked side by side. His hand itched to hold hers. He glanced at her every now and then. It was hard to believe she was there that she was real.

She told him about the move from Bathurst to Cabarita to start a new life with Paul and Keith. That Mima had joined them to work as the cook at the inn.

She told him about her granddaughters, about how she

looked forward to their visits and missed them when they returned to Sydney.

He interrupted. "I'd like to meet Keith."

She sighed. "I figured you would. Let me think about how we can do that. He doesn't know about you."

"You didn't tell him?" he asked. The question caught in his throat.

"I did...I told him when he was very young. We used to spend time with your parents while they were still alive."

"They told me."

She smiled. "It was really lovely. But then, he grew up and we didn't talk about it so much. Paul was his father in every way that mattered to him, and then after a while I realised he didn't remember us telling him about you. I was going to bring it up again, to say something, but he and Paul had such a good relationship..."

His nostrils flared. He wanted to understand. He hadn't been there for them, Paul had. But still, not to tell his son about him?

"When Paul died, I thought it'd be unfair to his memory, and to Keith, if I said anything."

He swallowed the pain. "It's fine, Edie. You did your best, that's all I can ask for."

When they reached the truck, he opened the front door, leaned in, and retrieved the bundle of envelopes from the passenger seat. He handed them to her.

"I could tell you all about my life, but these letters will explain it better."

She took the bundle, turned it over, and read the addresses on the front. They were each addressed to her, in a variety of blue and black-coloured inks. Some envelopes were yellowed, some big and rectangular, others small and square.

She looked at him with a question on her face.

He shrugged. "I wanted to write to you so many times over the years. So, I did...I just couldn't send them."

Edie's eyes glistened. "Thank you. I'll read and treasure them."

He reached for her hand, held it a moment, turned it over and kissed her palm. She didn't pull it away, didn't say anything at all. His heart pounded in his chest.

He stepped closer.

Then she was in his arms, warm against his body. He kissed her with a passion he'd long since forgotten, had thought was dead within him. She returned the kiss, her lips strange, yet familiar all at the same time.

He wrapped her up in his arms, even as her hands curled around his neck, her fingers tracing lines through his hair. This was home for him, in Edie's arms with her in his. A strange sense of pain, sorrow mixed with joy and longing, swept over him until his throat ached with it.

❧ 26 ❧

CABARITA BEACH

The swell of a wave lifted Bindi, then lowered her back down again. Her legs rested in the water on either side of her surfboard. Ahead of her, the beach at the cove disappeared from view, blocked by another swell of water, then reappeared again as the wave journeyed to shore.

She wiped a strand of sodden hair from her eyes and squinted back over her shoulder at the horizon. Another swell was on its way. She lay on the surfboard and raised her arms to paddle. Beside her, Reeda and Kate did the same.

Kate grinned at her. "First in..."

"Best dressed," replied Bindi with a chuckle.

The three sisters paddled all at once, arms flailing, water flying as the swell rose up beneath them. Bindi managed to get ahead of the wave. Her arms stung with the effort, but she continued propelling herself forward. Finally, the wave broke as she leapt to her feet. She rode it until it was nothing but a whisper against the shoreline, then leapt from her surfboard.

With the board under her arm, she jogged up the beach and collapsed in the sand. Reeda and Kate had caught the wave behind hers and soon joined her, laughing, and gasping for air.

"That was amazing. The surf today is awesome," said Reeda, sagging onto the sand beside Bindi.

"Wow," added Kate. "What a great set."

"How are you feeling?" asked Reeda, her eyes squinting against the sun's glare.

Bindi shrugged. "I feel strong, good...really good."

Reeda grinned. "I'm so glad. It's amazing to see you out there. You look fantastic."

Bindi inhaled a slow breath, lifting her face towards the sunshine, eyes closed. "I'll never take it for granted again."

"This reminds me of that last time we surfed together as teenagers," said Kate suddenly.

Bindi opened her eyes, her heart falling. She remembered it too but didn't want to talk about it. They'd fought, argued over whose fault it was their parents had died. It was a moment in time she'd replayed over and over in her mind throughout the years that followed. A moment she'd wished time and time again she could take back.

She glanced at Reeda. Her sister's face had gone pale.

"You mean the day we fought," said Reeda, her voice thin.

Kate's cheeks pinked. "Yeah." She lifted a hand to rest on Reeda's back. "I mean that day. I'm sorry for what I said Reeda. That I hated you — it's not true. I never hated you."

Reeda offered a half smile, her eyes glistening. "Thanks."

"Me too," added Bindi, her throat tight. "I'm sorry for blaming you for the accident. It wasn't your fault. I know we've talked about it since, but sitting here, remembering that day...

I've regretted it ever since. I wished I could take it back so many times. We all lost Mum and Dad, and we all grieved that loss... I wish we'd been able to come together to comfort each other. But we were only kids, we didn't know how to manage that kind of grief, so we pushed apart instead. I'll always regret that."

She scooted closer in the sand until she could put her hand on Reeda's back as well, she and Kate both embracing their older sister together.

Reeda offered a tight smile. "I blamed myself as well. But I know now that wasn't fair."

"It wasn't," added Kate. "It was an accident."

"Thank you," said Reeda.

The three sisters embraced, a tangle of wet arms and sniffling noses.

Bindi's heart ached, but in a good way. It felt like the end of something. They'd finally put away the pain of the past, had mended the wounds they'd inflicted on one another in the process of their grief.

When they pulled apart, Reeda wiped her eyes with her fingertips. "If only Nan were here to see us."

Bindi chuckled. "She'd be so happy. She wanted us to reconcile, to remember that we're a family."

Kate sniffled. "She knew a thing or two about grief. Knowing what we know now about her life, she'd been through so much pain herself."

Bindi nodded. "I haven't kept you guys updated on the Charlie Jackson saga."

"Have you found something new?" asked Kate.

"Yes, he came to see Nan after the war."

"What?!" exclaimed Reeda, her eyes flying wide.

Bindi smiled. "I found some more letters from him, written to Nan. At first, I was confused, because none of the letters had stamps on the envelopes or were dated. I wondered what that meant. Now I know — he must've given her a bundle of letters when he came back."

"I can't believe he survived the war and came back to Australia all those years later." Reeda shook her head.

"It's amazing," admitted Kate. "What did the letters say?"

"All I've found so far is that he visited Cabarita, and saw us all with Mum and Dad, down at the beach. After we left, he saw Nan and talked to her. She was amazed to see him, obviously, after so many years away. But of course, she was already widowed, and a grandmother. He asked to meet Dad, wanted to talk to him." Bindi wrapped her arms around her bent knees, staring out at the ocean as she spoke.

"Did he? Did he meet Dad, do you think?" asked Kate.

Bindi shook her head. "I don't know. All I know is that he wanted to meet Dad, and Nan was pretty emotional about it. He mentions it in the letter. He must've written the letter after they saw each other, as a way to process everything somehow."

Kate shook her head. "Wow. Where is he now, I wonder? Is he still alive?"

"I don't know. But I do know one thing..."

"What's that?" asked Reeda, her brow furrowed.

"They kissed," replied Bindi.

"What?!" both sisters exclaimed in unison.

❦

THE WALKING TRAIL WAS NARROW AND WOUND ALONG THE edge of a steep incline. Bindi was surrounded by rain forest. Green fern leaves tickled her legs, a large fig tree reached skyward lower down the embankment, its thick root system winding and curving this way and that.

She puffed hard as she climbed the last of a series of steps, pressed her hands to her hips and turned to survey the way she'd come. Josh was behind her and he stopped as well, his breathing perfectly normal, and watched her with a slight smile.

"How can you be breathing normally?" she huffed.

He grinned. "It's not a hard walk, not really."

Bindi shook her head. "Show off."

She faced forwards and set off again. This time the sloping path took them downwards. All she could think was, if they descended, they'd have to climb back up again to get to the car. She sighed inwardly and kept going. She didn't want to give Josh the satisfaction of seeing her quit so early in their bushwalk.

He'd asked her to go bushwalking with him in the Gold Coast Hinterland, and she'd agreed, thinking it would be an easy stroll through some lush rainforest. Instead, it was more like mountain climbing, at least to her it was anyway. She wasn't exactly an avid bushwalker but liked to think of herself as fairly fit. That was before the lymphoma of course. Still, perhaps she should start back onto an exercise program now that she was feeling so much better.

"You okay?" asked Josh, his hand touching the small of her back.

"Fine," she replied.

They reached the base of the fig tree and she skirted around it. It was magnificent, so tall, regal. The root system formed a skirt around the tree, climbing and weaving its way into the dirt.

"Hey, let's stop for a moment," said Josh.

She sighed with relief. Thank goodness. She collapsed onto one of the roots, using it as a kind of seat.

He sat beside her and wrapped an arm around her. She nestled against his chest, resting her head on him.

"This is nice," he said.

She grunted in response.

"Come on, you're enjoying yourself. Aren't you?"

She nodded. "It's lovely. I'm not as fit as I used to be...but it's really pretty."

He lifted her chin with one fingertip until she was staring into his wide blue eyes. Her heart skipped a beat. She still couldn't get past the chemistry between them. He could raise her pulse rate just by a simple touch, or a look in his eyes.

"I love that we can do this together," he said.

She smiled. All her focus had been on getting enough oxygen into her lungs; she hadn't even considered how he might feel about their outing. It warmed her soul.

"Me too," she said.

"Do you think about our future?" he asked.

She nodded. "Sure, sometimes."

"I do, all the time," he confessed.

"Really?"

"Yeah, I know you're the one."

Her eyes widened. "I am?"

He grinned. "I want to spend the rest of my life with you."

"Oh." Bindi's thoughts raced. She should say something more than that. He was pouring his heart out to her, and all she'd said in response was "oh". Only, she couldn't think of anything else to say. She cared about Josh. He wasn't her usual type, but that was a good thing. No, a great thing. Her type hadn't been good for her, the experience with Brendan had made that clear enough. Still, was she ready to say forever? It was so soon. She'd only recently recovered from her illness.

His face clouded with confusion, then irritation. "You can tell me if you don't feel the same way. I want us to be open and honest with each other."

Bindi searched frantically for the words to say. Words that wouldn't hurt him but would convey her true feelings.

"I'm sorry."

His eyes narrowed. "What does that mean?"

Her cheeks burned. "It means... I'm sorry that I'm not in the same place as you. Not yet, anyway. I don't know how I feel exactly."

He stood to his feet, then paced back and forth in front of her, his hands on his hips. "I thought we were on the same page with our feelings. That we were headed in the same direction."

"We are..." she stepped towards him, but he brushed her away.

"I want to get married," he said.

She gaped. "I didn't know..."

"I want to spend the rest of my life with you."

Bindi couldn't gather words together in her mind to say what she wanted to express. She wasn't ready to make that commitment. Could she marry Josh? He was perfect. Seemed perfect at least. But she'd been wrong before about the man she'd thought she'd marry before him. So very wrong.

"Bindi! I love you."

Her breath caught in her throat. "Josh...I—"

He shook his head. "If you don't know by now, maybe you won't ever know."

"That's not true. I just need some more time. The past year has been confusing..." Her heart thudded against her ribcage and her throat ached.

"Forget it," he said. "Let's head back to the car."

Bindi plodded along the trail behind Josh. He strode ahead, his frustration evident in each step. She sighed inwardly, her heart heavy. She'd hurt him, the last thing she wanted to do. Still, she couldn't be dishonest with him. Saying forever, telling him she loved him, it wasn't something she was ready to do. Did that mean there was something wrong with her? After all, people she loved didn't stay. Forever wasn't something anyone could promise. No one could control their own destiny.

✻ 27 ✻

CABARITA BEACH

Bindi held a cup of tea in her hands and stared out across the inn's front yard. A set of long, wide stairs led from the verandah down to the perfectly trimmed grass beyond. At the side of the inn, workers were already busy, carrying timber, tools and whatever else they needed for the restaurant construction behind the building.

She missed Josh. Hadn't seen him since their disagreement while out bushwalking. He'd called a few times and they'd spoken on the phone, but he was distant and didn't seem to have much to say. In fact, when he hung up, she'd been left wondering why he'd called.

She'd messed up. He was the man of her dreams, and she'd pushed him away because her heart had too many fault lines in it. Now, he didn't want her.

She studied the long line of trucks, bulldozers, and other vehicles with a sigh. So much for a quiet cup of tea.

"You okay, love?"

Beside her Jack was positioning a ladder against the inn's wall. He smiled at her.

"I'm fine, but I can't believe we're doing the whole construction thing again. I'd forgotten how disruptive, noisy and dusty it is."

He chuckled and reached for a small can of paint and paintbrush. "That it is."

His wedding ring caught the sunlight and Bindi studied it and her brow furrowed. She'd never met Jack's wife.

He climbed the ladder and began painting over a cracked place on the wall. Bindi recalled the day the previous week when a guest had hit a cricket ball into the wall there. She'd only been glad they'd missed the window.

"You do a great job around here, keeping everything maintained," she said.

He shrugged. "Thanks, Bindi. You do too. You're a wonderful manager."

Heat rose to her face as her heart swelled. "Thanks Jack, that means a lot to me."

He continued painting, carefully covering the cracked paint with new. She couldn't help looking at the ring.

"Jack...we've never really spoken much about your wife. Do you mind if I ask...who was she?"

He faced her, ready to answer just as the ladder wobbled and he dropped the can of paint. It landed bottom down, splashing yellow paint over the sides and onto the verandah floor. Bindi gasped, set down her tea and hurried to help, as the ladder tipped. It landed with a crash, as Jack fell onto his side.

"Jack!"

She heard him groan as she knelt beside him. "Are you okay?"

He sat up, grunted. "I think so."

"Perhaps we should call an ambulance?"

He grunted. "I'm not *that* old, Bindi."

She shook her head, smiling. "Are you sure?"

He leaned on her arm as he stood.

"Any pain?" she asked.

He winced. "A little in my back. But it's not too bad."

She helped him to a long, cushioned bench seat against the wall. Then, sat beside him, still holding his hand.

"Can I get you anything?"

"Maybe some Panadol, and a glass of water?"

Bindi strode to the kitchen, filled a glass with water and found Panadol in the first aid kit. Then she rushed back to Jack's side to give it to him. He swallowed the tablets down, then leaned his head against the wall behind him.

"Still hurting?" asked Bindi.

He nodded. "Yeah, I think I'm going to have some bruises tomorrow."

"I could drive you to the hospital," she offered.

He shook his head. "No, but home would be good. I might have a lie down."

Bindi held Jack's arm as she helped him to her car. The Land Rover started with a growl and she followed Jack's directions along a track that wound past the garage, and away from the horse paddock. Bindi remembered running along the track as a teenager, but she'd never explored it to the end, since it came to a gate with a *No Trespassing* sign. They reached that gate soon after the inn had disappeared from her rearview mirror.

Bindi glanced at Jack with a frown. "Through here?"

He nodded.

She climbed out of the vehicle and opened the gate, setting it wide enough to drive through. Then, returned to make their way through it. Beyond the gate, the bush around them thickened until she couldn't see anything but the track ahead of and behind them.

Coastal gums and thick scrub crowded the car, as it slowly bounced along the potholed road. Finally, they emerged into a clearing. There was a house, with a wraparound verandah and long, rectangular windows. The timber house looked reasonably new and was painted a pale blue with white trim. Behind it, was a garage and matching set of stables.

"You have horses?" asked Bindi.

Jack nodded. "Just a couple."

"Can I see them?" she asked.

He shrugged. "If you like, I might head on inside and lie down on the couch though."

She helped him into the house, got him settled with a pillow behind his head and another glass of water by his side, then wandered out to the stables.

The stables were well maintained and neat. There were only two stalls, which were more like loose boxes than stables. They opened onto a small paddock where two horses grazed. She stood with both arms resting on the top rail of the fence to watch them.

They were magnificent creatures. Tall, majestic. Draft horses, she guessed. Both were solid, with feathered hooves. Long manes and forelocks covered their eyes as they cropped the short grass. A tail swished, chasing away a fly, a hoof stomped, and a shoulder shivered getting rid of another.

She shielded her eyes with one hand, smiling at the sight of them. They'd be a treat to ride, sitting so far from the earth on one of those wide, strong backs. Why did Jack have draft horses? She hadn't expected to see that.

When he returned to the house, Jack was right where she'd left him, one arm draped over his eyes. He glanced at her as she came into the room.

"Your horses are beautiful," she said.

He smiled. "Thanks. I think they are."

"Do you ever ride them?"

"Not so much anymore, but I used to. They're more pets now than anything."

"Should I make us some tea?" she asked.

He nodded. "If you like. Let me know if you can't find what you need."

She managed in the small, bright kitchen well enough and soon had two mugs of steaming hot tea in her hands. She carried them to where Jack lay, set one on the table beside him then settled into an armchair close by, one leg tucked up beneath her.

"How are you feeling?"

He shrugged. "I'm okay. You should head back to the inn, they need you."

She smiled. "Not until I know you're all right. Although, I might call Kate in a minute, if that's okay. I'd like to let her know where I am."

He nodded.

"Do you remember the time you drove me to my formal?" she asked.

Jack smiled. "Of course."

"Nan was sick, and there wasn't anyone else to take me. I was already pretty sad because Mum and Dad couldn't be there, and Reeda and Kate had left home. No one had asked me as their date, and I was meeting up with a group of girlfriends at the event. So, I'd decided that I'd stay home, since I had no one to take me. I didn't want to show up on my own. And then you spoke up, said you'd drive with me."

He chuckled. "You were the most beautiful girl there."

Tears pricked the back of her throat. "I don't know about that."

"Oh, definitely," he confirmed.

"If you hadn't driven me, I don't think I could've faced it. When we got there, you held my arm and we walked up the steps of the RSL club together. You stayed with me, chatting about heaven knows what, until my friends all arrived."

"I'm glad I could be there."

"It meant so much to me. I joined my group of girlfriends eventually, but I looked back every now and then to check, and you were still there. You stayed until we all went inside, and it helped me feel loved, just for a moment. Like I wasn't alone in the world."

"You weren't alone," he said.

She nodded, and her voice was thick with tears. "I know that, but I felt alone that night. Until you stepped in. I don't think you realised how much that meant to me, knowing you were watching over me. There if I needed you."

He didn't respond, simply sat up on the sofa and reached for his cup of tea with a grimace. "I think the Panadol is starting to work, but my back muscles are in revolt."

She smiled through the tears. "I'm glad you're feeling better."

He took a sip and she did the same.

"I miss Nan," she whispered.

"Me too."

"How long did you know her?"

He shrugged. "A long time."

"I can't remember when you first came to the inn."

He stared into his tea. "Um...I guess it was about fifteen or sixteen years ago."

They finished their tea, chatting about the past, and Bindi carried the cups back to the kitchen.

"I'm just going to call Kate, let her know what's going on..." she shouted over her shoulder, towards the living room.

Jack murmured a response as Bindi hunted through the kitchen for the telephone. She found it hanging on the wall by the back door and picked up the receiver to dial.

The dial tone rang in her ear, as her gaze rested on a

framed photograph hanging beside the telephone. The photograph was in black and white, and in it a young woman held a baby in her arms, smiling at the photographer.

Bindi set the receiver back in the cradle and stepped closer to peer at the image. There was something about it... something familiar.

Nan.

The woman in the photograph looked like Nan. She'd seen photographs of Nan from when she was younger, not many, maybe one or two, but still...the woman looked just like Nan. The same light curly hair, the same wide smile, and big eyes.

The photograph was creased in places and worn around the edges. The frame was newer.

Why would Jack have a photograph of a young Nan on his wall?

Bindi spun slowly in place, scanning the rest of the room, wondering what else she might find. There were more photos. A family: a man, a woman and two children, all with tanned skin, brown hair, and brown eyes. Another photograph, this time in a frame set on the kitchen bench, with a man and a woman in it. The woman had light brown hair, cut into a business-style bob, and was wearing a business suit. The man was dressed much the same. He had one arm around her shoulders, and they were both laughing.

Who were these people to Jack? Were they his family?

Another photograph, this time of her family — her parents, Reeda, Kate and Bindi, all sitting on the steps at the inn back when it was a dark shade of pink and all of them were young and carefree. A lump built in her throat.

She spun slowly in place, her eyes widening, as she took in the neat, clean house, the photographs on the walls, a painting of two draft horses pulling a plow over the dining room table.

The painting triggered a memory. Draft horses. Someone else had loved draft horses.

Who was it?

She strode towards the living room, passing another photograph, hung on the wall. She stopped a moment to study it: Nan again. This time she was much older. She held up her left hand. A golden ring sparkled on her ring finger. She was pointing at it with a wide grin, dressed in a pale blue gown, her hair curled, makeup done just right. Nan didn't dress up like that often. And why was she pointing at her wedding band that way?

Bindi's eyes narrowed as she sat on the table beside Jack. He met her gaze, confusion flitting across his face.

"What's up?"

"Tell me about your wife, Jack. Who did you marry?"

He glanced towards the kitchen and sighed. "You saw the photos?"

She nodded, crossing her arms over her chest. "What's going on?"

He hesitated. "Edie. I married Edie, your grandmother."

Bindi gasped.

She pressed one hand against the table, her head spinning.

He leaned back on the sofa and rested his hands in his lap. "We didn't want to tell you kids at first, because of everything that happened with your parents. We were going to, but we waited too long."

"And she died..." finished Bindi, her heart in her throat.

He dipped his head. "Yes."

"When did this happen?" How could they do this? Hide something so important? She thought she'd known everything about Nan, and now it turned out she hadn't known any of the things that mattered.

He shrugged. "A few years ago...six actually. At first, we weren't going to do it. We'd both been married, didn't really think we wanted to take that step again. But one day, we realised, we had to do it. We'd waited so long, been through so much."

That didn't make sense. How long? Why? She had so many questions to ask, she didn't know where to start. "So, the two of you were married for four years, and didn't tell us?"

He shrugged. "We wanted to, but we hardly saw you."

Bindi stood and paced across the room, then back again. "A phone call, that's all it would have taken."

"We didn't want to tell you over the phone."

"Why not?" She stopped her pacing to turn and face him with her hands on her hips.

He sighed. "Because there's more..."

She slumped into the armchair, her heart racing. "I'm listening."

"I don't know if this is the best time."

"Jack, you and Nan put off talking to us about your marriage until it was too late. No more secrets, okay?"

He combed fingers through his silver hair, nodded. "You're right."

She waited, her entire body tense.

"I've known Edie my whole life. We grew up together."

Bindi's eyes widened. What was he saying? Her mind struggled to comprehend his words.

He continued. "We were in love once, a long time ago. Then, the war took me away from her...her and your father."

My father?

Bindi's heart skipped a beat. Birdsong, the overhead fan drumming in circles and the sigh of the ocean — every sound faded away as all the blood drained from her face. Nan had been in love with Charlie Jackson, not Jack... What was Jack's last name?

Jackson and Jack.

This couldn't be happening. Sweat beaded on her forehead. Her hand went to her mouth, her breath stalled in her chest. "Wait...you're Charlie?"

He nodded, his face clouding with confusion. "She told you about me?"

"No, I've been reading your letters...and Nan's journals."

His eyebrows arched. "Ah...right. Okay."

Jack is Charlie Jackson.

She shook her head. It didn't make sense... "I never asked what your last name was. Why didn't I ask?"

"Charles Jackson is my full name. I grew up in Bathurst. Edie's brother, Bobby, was my childhood best friend."

"And he died in the war..." finished Bindi, her mind racing.

Jack nodded.

"This is crazy!" she whispered.

Bindi shook her head. "Unbelievable! But why the need for all the secrets? Why not just tell us?"

He shrugged. "Edie wanted to keep it quiet. I arrived at the inn a few years after your grandfather Paul died. We were planning to tell your father, all of you, about our history, and that we were in love. Then..."

"The accident," she finished, with a nod. "That makes sense."

He swallowed. "We never did get to talk to Keith about me being his father. I met him of course, but he thought I was a stranger." Jack scrubbed both hands over his face. "I'll always regret that."

Tears blinded Bindi's vision as she reached for Jack's hand and squeezed it. Then, she knelt on the floor to embrace him, her head resting against his shoulder.

"You're my grandfather," she whispered.

"Yes, sweet girl."

"You were always there for me, for us, after Mum and Dad died."

"I tried to be."

"You rescued us...more than once."

"The three of you were a handful, that's for sure." He chortled and squeezed her.

She stood to her feet, wiping tears from her eyes as she laughed along with him. "Very true. We have to tell Reeda and Kate."

He sighed, nodded, and stood as well. "Yes, I guess we do."

She studied him. "I can't believe it...and yet it all makes so much sense. The three of us have been dying to find out what happened to Charlie Jackson. If he survived the war, lived to write letters to Nan, where is he? And you've been here, under our noses, the whole time." Her eyes widened. "Mima knew! She knew all along, knew we were reading the journals and letters. We all asked her questions about you and she didn't say anything."

Jack shrugged. "I didn't think Mima could keep anything to herself. I guess I was wrong. And don't be too hard on her, she was only doing what Edie asked her to. Edie never wanted the three of you to have to deal with more grief than you already had. She sheltered you, probably too much in hindsight."

"Are you glad I found out?" asked Bindi.

He nodded. "Very glad. I've wanted to tell you for a long time."

Bindi inhaled a long breath. "And now we have to tell the others. Are you feeling okay? Do we need to take you to the hospital?"

"I'm fine. Just a little rest, and maybe a cold washer for my forehead and I'll be right as rain."

❦ 28 ❧

CABARITA BEACH

Edie studied her reflection in the mirror. When had she gotten so old? She grunted and swiped the end of her nose with the powder brush one more time, then set it on the dressing table.

Nerves fluttered in the pit of her stomach, like moths around a fluorescent light. She was going on a date. A real date. She hadn't been on a date with anyone other than Paul since her early twenties, and now she was fifty-six years old and felt like a teenager all over again.

She ran a brush through her hair, then set it down with a sigh. It was hard to believe he was real. Maybe he was only a figment of her imagination. She'd longed to see him so deeply that he'd appeared in her mind. Was she going crazy?

Mima knocked at the bedroom door. "You busy?"

Edie shook her head. "Come on in."

"I'm about to get busy with the tea service, but I thought I'd come and check on you. Ready for your date?"

Her lips pursed. "I don't know...it's crazy, right? Charlie is back, and I'm going on a date with him. I feel like I've stepped into an alternate universe."

Mima chuckled and settled down on the bed behind Edie. "It's crazy romantic."

"Now, you're going to stop cooking long enough to come out and see him, right?"

Mima nodded. "Wouldn't miss it. I loved him too, you know. Not in the same way of course, but we grew up together as well."

Edie inhaled a sharp breath. "Good, because I've begun to wonder if my imagination is playing tricks on me. You can tell me if it's all real or not." She giggled but was only half joking.

Mima laughed. "Okay, settle down. Everything's going to be okay."

"He wants to meet Keith..." Nan turned on her seat to face her friend.

Mima frowned. "I can understand that. But I'm not sure it's a good idea...for Keith's sake right now."

"Why not?"

Mima shook her head. "He lost his Dad a few years ago, and he has no idea that Charlie exists. It'll be a shock, that's all I'm saying. Maybe, break it to him slowly...they could meet, get to know each other, then find out that they're father and son."

"I don't know..."

"There's plenty of time, that's all I'm saying. Don't rush it."

Nan considered her friend's words. Then she stood to her feet and marched into the closet to find her purse. She slung it over her shoulder, stepped out.

"How do I look?"

"Beautiful," replied Mima with a wink. "I'm really happy for you, Edie."

"Thanks." Edie smoothed the front of her floral dress

with one hand. "I'm not sure where this is going... I feel like I'm on a rollercoaster ride and I didn't buy a ticket."

Mima stood to loop her arm around Edie's waist. "Those are the best kinds of rides."

THE PICNIC RUG BENEATH HER WAS SMOOTH, AND EDIE tucked both feet up under her as she reached for an olive and popped it into her mouth.

"This is delicious, thank you," she said.

In truth, the platter of cheeses, crusty bread, olives, and pastrami was a little rich for her. Not something she'd usually eat, but Charlie had put so much effort into the picnic, she hated to say anything.

It was certainly romantic. He'd taken her down a small, bush track on her own property, to a beach she'd never seen before. She'd lived at the inn for years and had never explored the farthest end of their property. It'd been too overgrown, and she'd been too busy. He'd found the path, when he'd visited the other day and been curious, he said. He'd taken a machete and cut through enough of the undergrowth to make a way for his truck. They'd emerged into a small clearing where he'd parked, then he'd led her by the hand, a picnic basket in the other, down a track to a small, private beach.

When he spread the blanket behind the dunes, and laid out the food and wine, she'd almost burst with joy. It reminded her so much of the times they'd spent on the banks of the creek at her parents' farm when she was just a girl.

Charlie lay on his side, across from her, eating olives and watching her with a lazy smile tugging at the corners of his mouth.

"I've been thinking about how we could talk to Keith," she said suddenly.

He arched an eyebrow. "Okay."

"It's a big thing to land on him, all at once. He was very close to Paul, and I think it would be a shock for him to learn you're his biological father."

"That's understandable." Charlie reached for another olive.

"So...I was thinking, perhaps we could wait."

He sat up his brow furrowed. "Wait?"

"Hear me out," she continued. "I could introduce you as a friend, and you could get to know Keith, Mary, and the girls a little before we drop the bombshell. That way, you won't be a stranger to them, they'll have had a chance to get to know you and love you—"

"I don't know..." he interrupted.

She continued. "Are you going back to Brisbane tonight?"

He shrugged. "I don't have to, if you'd like me to stay."

"I'd like you to stay."

He grinned. "Then I'll stay."

"And I had another idea."

He chuckled. "Here we go..."

"I need a handyman to help around the inn. Ever since Paul died, I've tried to find someone permanent, but haven't been able to get anyone who can do what I need them to do."

"Are you offering me a job?" asked Charlie.

She nodded. "If you want it. That way, you could live here, we can see each other more often. And you'll be close by when Keith and the family comes to visit, you'll be part of it all... What do you think?"

He sat silent a moment with his eyes trained on the picnic rug. Then, he met her gaze. "I'd like that."

"We could call you something other than Charlie Jackson, just to keep things under wraps."

"No one knows me around here," he objected.

"Just in case."

He rolled his eyes. "Fine. Some of the guys on the building site used to call me Jack. We can use that if you like."

"Jack," said Edie, rolling the name around on her tongue like wine. "Jack, yes I like it. It suits you."

He took her hand in his, threading his fingers through hers. A tingle ran up her arm and down her spine. He cupped her cheek with his other hand, then leaned close to kiss her lips.

His were soft against hers, gentle at first then more demanding. Something inside of her ached. The ache grew and spread throughout her body. She'd missed him. She'd mourned his death, and now he was here. How could it be possible? Mima had hugged him when he'd shown up at the inn to pick Edie up for their date. Tears had glistened in her friend's eyes when she'd stepped back and studied his face. She'd said, "Charlie Jackson, I never thought I'd see you again." And he'd smiled in that way that always melted Edie's heart.

She hadn't imagined him, he was real. His arms enveloped her, as their kisses grew more urgent and tears pricked her eyes. Charlie Jackson was real, he'd returned to her, and he wanted to be part of her life. They'd lost so many years, so many embraces, thousands of kisses. All lost, all snatched away from them. But they had a chance to start again, and this time she wouldn't let anything stand in their way.

❧ 29 ❧

CABARITA BEACH

A bulldozer dug its pronged shovel into the ground outside the breakfast nook and pulled, raking the earth away with a deafening roar.

Kate watched, her hands pressed to her hips, brow furrowed. She hated to see the garden destroyed that way, a garden planted with Nan's own hands, but they were making room for the restaurant. It would extend from the area currently used as the breakfast nook, out towards the cove, and would keep the nook's light, airy feel with long, rectangular glass windows along each wall. That was a feature Reeda had requested, and Kate had agreed would help retain the character of the place, even as they expanded its function.

She inhaled a long, slow breath. Were they doing the right thing? They were investing heavily in the restaurant, and it was because of her. A restaurant in a small beachside village — were they crazy?

A knot formed in her stomach. She swallowed down the

nausea that threatened to overwhelm her. They'd made the decision, it was underway, there was no turning back now.

With a shake of her head, she hurried back to the kitchen, past the dining room filling with diners ready for breakfast. The kitchen was being renovated as well, which meant the small eating area attached to the kitchen, usually reserved for family meals, had been turned into a makeshift kitchen, along with the attached laundry room. They'd be serving cold continental breakfast, along with baked goods purchased from *Joys* until Kate could get back into her kitchen again. Afterwards, the dishes would be washed in the laundry, much to the dismay of her kitchen staff.

"Let's go, the guests are getting hungry," she cried as she stepped into the bleak looking kitchen.

Staff looked up at her, seeming unsure of what to do.

"Let's fill up the buffet, keep everyone's plates full, get them drinks...whatever we can do to keep them happy," she said.

Servers sprang to action, and Kate reached for a pair of gloves, tugged them on and then found a tray of croissants that needed slicing. It would be a challenge to manage everything without their usual conveniences, but they'd do it, somehow. After all, challenge was the spice of life. Or was it variety? She couldn't remember, but it sounded right either way.

By the time breakfast was over, Kate had realised she'd have to cut her kitchen staff in half for the duration of the renovation. They simply couldn't afford to have waiters standing around twiddling their thumbs.

They'd noticed a downturn in bookings as well, since they'd asked travel agents to let guests know about the construction being done and the cold breakfasts. But the slower pace suited their needs, for now. As long as bookings picked up again after the restaurant was completed, it should all work out. Kate sat at the kitchen table and nibbled a fingernail.

The kitchen table was piled high with containers that'd contained croissants, muffins, and cereals, but were now mostly empty. Everything had been washed, dried, and stacked away. A large plastic sheet acted as a curtain between where she sat and the construction. The entire wall of the kitchen had been demolished and the inn exposed to the elements along one side as they extended the kitchen out onto where the verandah had been.

Just watching their progress had given her a tension headache. Bubbles of nerves and excitement competed in her gut.

"How'd it go?" asked Bindi, rounding the corner.

Kate shrugged. "Fine. I'm going to have to give some of the servers time off."

"That makes sense," replied Bindi, sitting beside Kate.

"I'll give them a call later."

"Okay."

Kate studied Bindi's face. Her eyes were red-rimmed, and her skin pale. Her sister sighed deeply, and it stirred Kate's already frazzled nerves. Something was wrong. Had the cancer returned?

"What's going on?" asked Kate.

Bindi met her gaze. "Do you know where Reeda is?"

"I think she's outside checking on the horses."

"I need to talk to both of you."

Kate's heart fell. "Okay."

"Let's go outside to sit, somewhere quiet."

"We might have to go to the cove to get some peace."

They found Reeda by the stables and the three of them

trudged through the sand and down to the cove. They found a long, smooth rock to sit on that looked out across the waves and perched on it, side by side.

Reeda and Kate exchanged a worried glance.

"There's something I have to tell you both," began Bindi, "but before I get any further, I can tell from the looks on your face you think it's my health — it's not."

Kate released the breath she'd been holding in her lungs. "Really?"

"No," said Bindi with a smile. "I'm fine, it's not about me."

"Thank heavens!" blurted Reeda. "You had me worried."

"Everything's still fine, I'm still in remission. But there's something else I need to talk to you about."

Kate leaned forward, tucking one foot beneath her.

"We've all been reading Nan's journals and Charlie's letters to her," Bindi began. "We've become invested in their story, their journey. All three of us have wondered, countless times, what happened to Charlie, how he got those letters to Nan and why we'd never heard about him before Nan died."

Kate nodded. "Yes, definitely. It's an intriguing and frustrating mystery."

Reeda sighed. "I even flew to Italy to find him...no luck there."

"But you came close," added Bindi.

Reeda shrugged. "I guess, I certainly found out more about him and where he'd been. It was fascinating."

"Well," continued Bindi, "I've found him."

"What?!" exclaimed both sisters at once.

"Where?" asked Reeda.

Bindi smiled. "Right here at the inn."

Kate's brow furrowed. "What do you mean?"

"It's Jack."

"It's Jack what?" asked Reeda, her head cocked to one side.

"Jack is Charlie Jackson," said Bindi.

Kate's heart rate accelerated; her head felt light. "What? Jack — our Jack — is Charlie?"

"Yes. I found out yesterday and have been looking for a time to tell you both. He confirmed it. And there's more..."

"More?" Reeda's eyes bulged.

"Yes, he and Nan were married for four years before she died."

Kate's gaze wandered to the horizon. A gull cawed, dipping its wings as it sailed over the water. Charlie was Jack, and Jack was Charlie. That didn't make sense. And yet it did all at the same time. That made Jack...her grandfather.

Her eyes narrowed. Why didn't he say anything? All these years he'd been living close by, working with all of them. He'd shared meals with them, laughed with them, cried with them. He'd had countless opportunities to bring it up.

Kate launched to her feet and headed for the stables. She'd seen Jack there, tending to the horses when they'd stopped to collect Reeda. If he was there still, she'd confront him, ask him all the questions that'd been swirling in her head from the first moment she'd read his name in Nan's journal.

"Kate! Kate! Where are you going?" Bindi called after her.

Kate didn't reply, kept on stomping through the sand, her hands clenched into fists at her sides. She could hear Reeda and Bindi murmuring together over something.

"We're coming too!" Reeda's voice echoed up the beach.

Kate didn't care. They could come if they wanted, but she was having a word with the man who'd walked her down the aisle at her wedding and yet hadn't thought to mention the fact that he was her grandfather.

He was in the stables, breaking up a bale of hay to scatter in the stalls. Jack glanced up and sent her a wide smile that slowed her pace a little. He was Jack. And he was Charlie.

She faced him, her throat already closing over before she'd

said a word. She cleared it with a cough. He crossed his arms over his chest, a quizzical look on his face. When Bindi came puffing up beside her, realisation dawned across his features like the sunrise.

"I see you've heard," he said.

Kate's entire body trembled and her words wobbled as they came out. "You...you are Charlie Jackson? Our grandfather?"

He inhaled a quick breath. "Yes, I am."

"And you never thought it might be something we'd like to know?" cried Kate.

Bindi slumped onto a bale of hay.

Jack's lips pursed. "I'm sorry, Kate. Sorry to you all. I should've said something...but things were complicated."

"You can say that again..." murmured Reeda.

Kate glared at her. "Not so complicated. 'Hey girls, I'm your long-lost grandfather.' Would that have been so hard?"

"I didn't know you had Edie's journals and letters. I thought it'd come as a complete surprise to discover Paul wasn't your kin, not by blood anyway. He'd been your grandfather, and he wasn't around any longer... Edie and I didn't want to ruin that for you girls. You'd lost so much already."

Kate's face crumpled and tears slid down her cheeks. "Ruin it? You couldn't ruin it. How can having another family member be a bad thing? We thought we had no one. Just the three of us. And now we find out we have another grandparent. And of all people, it's you — our Jack."

His face shone, he opened his arms and Kate ran into them. She cried against his chest as he patted her back.

"There, there," he said. "I wish...well, there are so many things I wish I'd done differently. So many regrets that I've learned not to dwell on them. You can't live your life holding onto a past that never was. You can't go around wishing your days away. So, I try not to hold onto the things I should've done. Instead, I live each day, enjoy the moment I'm in. And right now, I'm really glad you girls know the truth, that I've got my granddaughters here with me."

Reeda and Bindi joined in the embrace then. Arms tangled, tears fell, soon replaced by laughter as they all began to lose their balance in the mishmash of limbs.

"We're glad too," sniffled Reeda.

"I still can't believe it," added Bindi. "And yet, there's a part inside of me that feels as though I've always known."

Kate knew what she meant. She'd always had a close connection to Jack. He'd been a part of the family for years, and now they knew he was related by blood as well. The part she couldn't wrap her head around was the marriage. That Nan wouldn't tell them she'd gotten married made her heart hurt.

She pulled out of the embrace, wiped her eyes dry with the back of her hand. "Why didn't Nan tell us you were married?"

Jack shrugged. "She wanted to."

"I don't understand that part either," added Reeda.

"I can't pretend to know everything that ran through your grandmother's mind," said Jack with a chuckle. "But I do know this, she loved the three of you and would have done anything to protect you, to shield you from pain. She wanted the best for you. I know she wanted to tell you the truth, we'd discussed it a lot before she died."

"So why didn't you say something? Why didn't she talk to us? There were so many things she kept from us..." Kate's voice cracked, she sobbed.

He hesitated, inhaled a slow breath. "At first, she avoided it, after the accident she thought the three of you had enough to deal with. Then, time passed, and it seemed harder to her somehow. I think she was worried how you'd react. Finally, when we were married, we agreed you should know - but Edie was waiting to see you all in person, didn't want to do it over the phone. I guess she waited too long."

The truth tore at Kate's heart. It was her own fault Nan hadn't confided in her. All those years Nan asked her if she'd visit, when she'd be able to make the trip to Cabarita, and Kate had pushed back. She was busy. Had things to do in Brisbane. Soon. Not yet. If she'd made the trip, if all of them had agreed to come for a visit, perhaps Nan might've told them about Charlie Jackson.

30

CABARITA BEACH

The kitchen was clean, the cottage tidy. There was nothing more to be done. Charlie fidgeted, staring through the kitchen window over his new deck.

It hadn't taken him long to build the cottage, only a few months, while he worked as the maintenance man at the inn. They'd chosen the clearing where they'd parked for their first date, the picnic at the beach, as the site for his home. It seemed right, and the location was perfect. He had an outlook most people would die for, directly onto a small private beach.

The house was set back from the shore far enough not to be in any danger of king tides. The dunes and a steep bank separated him from the stretch of sand that curved around like a sliver of moon.

Excitement buzzed in his stomach.

Today was the day.

Keith, Mary, and the girls were visiting. They'd driven up from Sydney two days earlier and were camped out at the inn.

He'd gotten to know them a little over the Christmas period, when they'd stayed at the inn for two weeks. Still, they'd thought of him as the new handyman, not as part of their family.

They'd been warm, welcoming, friendly...but it wasn't the same. He'd spent Christmas day with Stefano and Amara in Brisbane. They'd had a lovely day, but he hadn't been able to stop thinking about the family he was missing. His daughter had called, the phone call brief. He hated that they were so far apart, but she seemed to be doing better than ever. She was thriving. She'd announced she and her husband were expecting a baby halfway through the next year. Could he come?

He'd told her he'd be there, of course he would. He wouldn't miss welcoming his grandchild into the world. He'd already missed so much.

But today things would change. Edie had promised they would talk to Keith and Mary. Mima was out for the day, having fun with friends somewhere or other, and there were no guests at the inn. It would be him, Edie, and the family. And they'd finally get to hear the truth about who he was, and who they were to him.

It'd be a shock for Keith at first, but Charlie hoped, in time, he'd come around. That maybe they'd be able to build a relationship. Go fishing together. Talk. Share their lives.

He'd missed out on so much of Keith's life. If he could only share in a little of it...

He pulled the door shut behind him, climbed into the truck, and headed down the long, winding track he called a driveway. He'd built a gate close to the inn, to discourage guests from heading that way. A sign accompanied the gate. So far, it'd worked to keep the track free of pedestrians.

Once he was through the gate, his heart crashed against his ribcage with every beat. His stomach churned. Nerves mingled with excitement as he parked the truck behind the garage and climbed out.

Edie was nervous too. He could tell. The last time they'd seen each other she'd barely spoken. She hated to hurt Keith and thought it might drive a rift between them. Charlie had embraced her then and told her she should trust that their love was stronger than that. After all, she was his mother and had raised him and cared for him every day of his young life. He wouldn't blame her for protecting his connection with Paul.

When he stepped into the kitchen, the first thing he noticed was the silence.

Why was it so quiet? Perhaps the family had gone for a walk along the beach. It was a cool day, a noon stroll along the cove would be a nice way to pass the time. Although, Edie had said she was putting together a special lunch for them all, so they could sit and eat together before the discussion began.

Yet, the kitchen was empty. Still. Every surface gleamed, and there was no food set out on the bench tops. No dirty dishes in the sink. It was as though there was no one around.

His brow furrowed and the pounding of his heart slowed. She'd changed her mind. Edie had decided they wouldn't have the talk today. She'd backed out of it. He sighed. He should've seen this coming. She hadn't wanted to do it at all, and he'd convinced her it was the right thing.

He leaned against the bench, crossed his arms, and stared out the kitchen window. From where he stood, he could see the edge of the garage. A taillight, orange and covered in dust poked from the enclosure.

He frowned. That was Edie's truck.

Charlie walked outside, peered around the end of the inn. That was definitely Edie's truck. But there was no sign of

Keith's vehicle. Perhaps they'd all ridden together in the minivan.

He walked back inside, his heart heavy. Then, he heard a thump, or a bang. It came from upstairs. He glanced up the staircase, perhaps it was nothing. That reminded him, he should check on the rat traps in the attic.

With a sigh, he decided to knock on Edie's door before he headed back to the cottage. It was possible she was in there, though he doubted she'd be hidden away with her grandchildren visiting. She loved her grandchildren more than anything. Whenever he'd seen her with the girls, she was always chattering, fixing hair, laughing at jokes, joining in with whatever they were doing. He imagined she would've been a good mother to their son. He wished he'd been around to see it.

When he raised his knuckles to rap on Edie's door, he was surprised to find it creaked open. Inside, it was completely dark. It wasn't like Edie to leave the draperies shut all day long. With a frown, he stepped inside and strode to the windows to pull the curtains wide, letting the light flood in.

When he did that, he noticed the covers on the bed were mussed. Then he saw her. Edie lay on the bed, the covers twisted around her, knees tucked up to her chest.

"Edie?"

He ran to the side of the bed and knelt next to her with his eyes wide. "What's wrong? Honey, what's going on? Why are you in bed? Are you hurt?"

Tears had streaked her cheeks but were now dry. The only relic of their presence the redness of her eyes, the flush of her cheeks. Her gaze was fixed on the bathroom door, her hands cradled beneath her pillow.

"Edie! Edie, talk to me." He was frustrated, afraid. He'd never seen her like that before. Adrenaline spiked as his breaths came in gasps. What had happened, something bad obviously. But if she didn't tell him, didn't open up to him, he couldn't help her, couldn't do anything to soothe whatever pain she was feeling.

He stroked the side of her face, tucked a strand of hair behind her ear. "Tell me what's wrong, love."

Her gaze travelled to his face, her eyes empty. "Keith and Mary..." she began, her face crumpling with the words. "They were killed in a car accident last night."

He fell onto his rear on the hardwood floor as though he'd been punched in the chest. His mouth opened but no sound emerged. It couldn't be true. That was too much, too ugly, too cruel. He'd only met his son for the first time six months earlier, was about to talk to him, embrace him for the first time today. And now he was gone.

No.

"No!" he cried.

On the bed, Edie began to wail. Her voice was filled with terror, sorrow, pain, and heartache. He couldn't bear the sound. He covered his ears with both hands as his back pressed to the wall. His throat closed over and he felt he couldn't breathe. It wasn't fair. This wasn't supposed to happen. He should've died, so many times. His son was young, with so much life ahead of him, and Mary too. In their brief time together, he'd learned to love her already. She was a wonderful mother to the three girls.

The girls.

His hands dropped to his sides and he stood with a grunt. Edie's wails had subsided, now she sobbed into her pillow.

"Edie, where are the girls?"

"I don't know," she mumbled, her voice muffled. "Reeda's in the hospital still... she's okay but they wanted to keep her a while longer."

He bent to kiss her forehead. "We'll get through this. We're going to be okay, my love."

She shook her head, still buried in the pillow. "No, we won't. I won't."

"I'll be back, but I have to check on the girls," he said.

He hurried from the room, leaving the door open so he could hear if she needed him. Taking the steps three at a time, he bounded up them, then stood in silence outside the door to the room where the family was staying. They always stayed in the same room Edie had told him as she cut fresh flowers to set in the vase there. It was the family room, big enough for all five of them, and she made sure it was vacant whenever they came to visit.

He raised a fist to knock, hesitated a moment, then turned the doorknob. The two girls were huddled in centre of the king-sized bed. They were quiet and eyed him with curiosity when he pushed the door open.

"G'day girls," he said. "Do you mind if I come in?"

Kate, the eldest one, shook her head. Bindi watched him, reddened eyes staring, bleary, unfocused.

Kate faced him with her legs crossed. "Is Reeda okay?"

He nodded. "She will be. She's still in hospital for now though..."

"What about Nan?" asked Kate.

His throat constricted. She'd lost her parents and her first question was about her sister, her second about her grandmother. He pushed a smile onto his face. "Nan is going to be okay. She's very sad, so it might take a while."

"We're all sad," spat Kate, then cried silently into her hands.

Bindi rested a palm on Kate's back, her own tears falling, punctuated by sobs.

"I know you are, and I am too. I wanted you to know that I'm here. If you need anything, I'll be downstairs with Nan. Just knock on her door and I'll come right out. Okay?"

Both girls nodded.

"I'm so sorry," he said. Tears choked him, preventing him from saying more.

He backed out of the room, pulled it shut behind him. The first thing he'd thought of when he'd heard the news was his own pain, his own mourning, but that was nothing compared with what those girls were experiencing. He had to be strong for them, and for Edie. They had no one else now.

When he returned to her room with a cup of tea, Edie hadn't moved, only now her eyes were shut. He set the tea on the bedside table, kicked off his shoes and climbed into bed with her. He wrapped his arms around her, pulled her close so that his chin rested on top of her head. He kissed her hair, his grief threatening to overwhelm him.

The girls had lost their parents. Edie had suffered another loss, after enduring so many in her lifetime. Mima wasn't there, but she'd find out soon enough and he knew how hard the news would hit her, after all she'd been through. She loved the family as her own, had helped Edie raise Keith while they lived at the inn together.

And now his son would never know him, never call him father. Never understand how much he loved him.

Tears fell from his eyes. The first he'd cried in a very long time. He held Edie tight and cried in silence, careful not to shake her in case she was sleeping. He was grateful for two things: that he'd met his son and found him to be a wonderful man, a loving husband and father, and that he was able to be with Edie, to comfort her as they mourned the loss of their son.

He squeezed his eyes shut, inhaled a long slow breath, and let memories dance across the screen in his head. Memories of times past, of the moments that'd shaped and driven the course of his life. A first kiss, a deepening love, the two of them skipping school to swim in a muddy river. Her agreeing to marry him as they lay on the shores of a creek, her face still streaked with tears at the idea that he'd be leaving. Him opening a letter and the photograph of her holding their son spilling out onto his lap.

The moments were precious to him now, like jewels that couldn't be stolen, reworked or damaged. He'd never have the chance to live through it all again, but he could remember it now in the midst of his pain and those memories brought a smile to his tear-streaked face.

❧ 31 ❧

CABARITA BEACH

It felt strange now, to read Charlie Jackson's letters, knowing he was Jack. Bindi let the piece of paper flutter into her lap. She stared at it, her eyes losing focus on the dark script that ran in lines across the page. There were still so many things she wanted to know, but she'd decided after his revelation that perhaps she should ask him questions in person instead of continuing with the letters. So she'd put them away... until today. Something had compelled her to pull them out and browse through them again.

With a grunt she clambered off the bed, straightened the quilt and folded the letter back into Nan's box.

Kate and Reeda were waiting for her at the bottom of the stairs. They were talking together, then smiled at her as she approached.

"Where are you headed?" asked Reeda.

"I'm looking for Jack... What's going on?" asked Bindi.

"They're finished," replied Kate, beaming.

"Completely?"

Reeda dipped her head. "Listen."

The chirp of morning birdsong, the distant crash of waves to shore. Her brow furrowed.

"I don't hear anything."

"Exactly," replied Reeda, with a smug grin.

Bindi waggled her eyebrows. "Well, let's take a look at our new kitchen and restaurant then."

The three sisters linked arms and walked together into the kitchen. It was twice as big as it had been. The bench, cupboards and appliances sparkled and shone. Everything was white and stainless steel with hardwood floors.

"Wow, it's beautiful," said Bindi, her eyes wide.

"I know," replied Kate. "I'm going to love cooking in here. And look, you go through this swinging door and here's the restaurant."

She let go of Bindi and Reeda's arms and pushed through the door, holding it open for them to walk through.

Tears gathered in Bindi's throat as she stepped into the restaurant. She'd seen it in progress many times throughout the build, but Kate hadn't allowed them to look over the past week while the cleaners moved in, then the tables, chairs and light fixtures were set up. It looked like a real restaurant now. Everything clean, neat and in its place. Chandeliers hung overhead, sparkling in the sunlight that issued through the many long, rectangular windows.

The view of the garden was spectacular. Coastal gums, pandanus, bushes and even Nan's waratahs could be seen.

"I love it," said Bindi.

"I can't wait to see it filled with diners," added Reeda.

"Me too." Kate surveyed it all with arms crossed over her chest.

"Is it what you wanted?" asked Bindi.

Kate nodded. "I always imagined I'd have my own restaurant one day. Then, when Nan died, I came back here and soon learned I didn't want to leave, but I thought my dreams of being a chef with my own place were over. Now..." She waved an arm, her voice choked over the words. "It's a dream come true."

The three sisters embraced. Bindi blinked back tears. Her stomach churned. This restaurant was amazing, but it was a huge responsibility. Would they be able to make it work?

Footsteps sounded on the timber floor behind them. Bindi wiped her eyes with the back of her hand and cleared her throat before turning to see who it was.

"Hi Bindi," said Josh.

She smiled. "Fancy seeing you here." She hadn't seen him since their argument two months earlier, and they'd only spoken on the phone a few times. She'd assumed he wasn't coming back, yet there he was, looking tanned and fit, in a pair of board shorts and a T-shirt that stretched across his thick chest.

The sight of him reminded her of how much she'd missed him, what he'd meant to her and how she hadn't been able to voice her feelings. He'd gifted her strength through the hardest time of her life. Stood by her side when she needed him. He was kind, thoughtful, funny, and steady. Exactly the kind of man she wanted to share her life with. Why hadn't she had the nerve to tell him so when it mattered?

"This looks amazing. Hi Kate, Reeda — I can't wait to eat here. Congratulations to all of you."

"Thanks Josh. Actually, I'm throwing a practice dinner for family and friends tonight, you're welcome to join us if you'd like."

He nodded. "That sounds great, I'd love to. Thanks."

Bindi headed for the kitchen, and Josh followed her. They left Kate and Reeda folding napkins. Through the kitchen and out the back door, Bindi kept walking, running through in her mind what she'd say to him. Why was he there? To break up with her officially? To reconcile? Nerves teased her gut and she crossed her arms over her chest in a kind of embrace.

She hesitated at the gate to the kitchen garden, rested her hands on it, and waited.

"Bindi, stop..." said Josh behind her.

She faced him with her head cocked to one side. "I thought you'd disappeared from the face of the earth."

He shook his head. "I'm sorry. I overreacted."

"Yes, you did."

"I pushed you away. After our last conversation, it seemed to me you didn't feel the same way about me, as I did about you. I told you I loved you..."

His nostrils flared.

Bindi swallowed. "I know. I understand why you were upset. I just...wasn't ready to say it back."

"But I've been thinking about it all, what we said, what we didn't, how I feel...and I don't care. If you're not ready to take our relationship to the next level, that's fine with me. I'm not going to push you away. If you want out, you're going to have to say so."

"I don't want out," Bindi said quickly. "It's been a difficult year, with my health and everything going on here at the inn. I was confused..."

His blue eyes softened. "I love you, and when you're ready to take the next step, I'll be right here with you."

She stepped closer, stood on her tiptoes and pressed a kiss to his lips. His arms moved to surround her, pulling her close.

She smiled, linking her hands around his neck. "I love you too."

He grinned. "You don't have to—"

"Shhh... I love you, you're just going to have to accept it," she interrupted.

"I guess I can live with that." His broad smile faded as he kissed her again.

WHEN SHE WALKED INTO THE RESTAURANT THAT NIGHT, her hand in Josh's, Bindi gasped. The chandeliers sparkled, sending dancing light around the room. White tablecloths were offset by the dark timber of the floorboards. Artwork on the walls and vases filled with fresh flowers added splashes of colour.

Kate waited for them by a long table, set with silverware and crystal stemware. She smiled with her hands linked in front of a white apron.

"Good evening, everyone," she said.

"This looks fantastic, Kate," replied Bindi, gazing around the restaurant.

"Thank you. Please take a seat, the food will be out soon. In the meantime, enjoy a drink."

Josh pulled out Bindi's chair and she sat. Reeda and Duncan followed them into the room. Then, Mima, Jack, and Alex strolled in behind them. Soon, the table was full, and everyone was talking, laughing, and enjoying themselves.

A waiter filled their glasses with water, then took drink orders. Kate had returned to the kitchen, and Bindi's stomach grumbled in anticipation of what was to come. She'd barely eaten a thing all day, hoping to save room for the feast.

Mima sat beside Kate with a grunt, her silver curls tamed to frame her face instead of pulled back the way she usually wore them. She'd donned a soft blue dress that shimmered beneath the glow of the chandeliers.

"You look lovely," said Bindi, hugging Mima's arm.

Mima beamed. "Thank you, love. You're adorable as always."

Mima greeted Josh, then returned her attention to Bindi. "How're things going between the two of you," she whispered, arching an eyebrow. "I thought he'd called things off... or was it you? I can't keep up with you young folk."

Bindi chuckled. "I thought he'd ended things as well, but he showed up this morning and told me he loved me."

Mima grinned. "And what did you say to that?"

"I told him I loved him as well."

Mima squeezed Bindi until all breath had been evacuated from her lungs. Bindi coughed, then laughed. "Mima, I can't breathe!"

Mima patted her on the back. "I'm so happy for you, my dear. He's a wonderful young man. I think the two of you will be very happy together."

Bindi's cheeks warmed. "We're not getting married or anything, Mima. We love each other, that's all."

"That's all? Listen to me, my love, when two people love each other the way you do, it won't be long before we hear those bells ringing."

"Which bells?" asked Bindi, her brow furrowed.

Mima waved a hand in the air. "Oh, you know, the metaphorical church bells."

Bindi giggled. "We'll see..."

"Is that what you want?" asked Mima, still whispering.

Bindi glanced at Josh, who was deep in conversation with Alex. She nodded at Mima. "I think so...how do you know?"

"Know what?" asked Mima, before taking a sip of water.

Bindi shrugged. "When you've found *the one*. I don't want to make a mistake."

Mima hugged her. "No one wants to make a mistake, my love. But when you find the man you're meant to spend the rest of your life with, you'll just know it. It'll be a calm kind of feeling, that sits down in your chest and doesn't move. A certainty, that if you lived your lives apart, they would never be what they could be if you were together."

Bindi nodded. "Is that how it was for you?"

Mima sighed. "Yes, love. That's how it was the day I met Ollie. We didn't take as long to figure it out as some people do. Of course, we didn't have the kind of time together that most get. He was leaving for the pacific theatre as soon as he was well enough, and I knew I'd have to say goodbye. It helps you keep perspective, having that kind of time pressure. We didn't want to waste a single moment, so we lived each moment as though it might be our last...and one of those moments was. When I got the letter from his family...I hadn't heard from him in a while. I knew deep down something was wrong, but I kept telling myself it was because the mail system was too busy, or disrupted somehow, that he'd write soon. Of course you know how that ended."

Bindi squeezed Mima's hand. "At least you made those moments count."

Mima nodded, her smile returning. "Yes, we sure did."

Kate pushed backwards through the kitchen's swinging door, carrying a large platter. She smiled as she set it on the table.

"Dinner is served," she said. "Roast lamb with figs, radicchio and chicory."

With the platter firmly on the table, she took a bow as the table applauded, a grin on her face. "Thank you, thank you. Now, Alex will carve, and the staff will bring the rest of the meal. Fill your plates and enjoy the feast!"

Alex stood to carve the roast, while the rest of the table exclaimed in delight over the dishes the waiters brought to the table. They set everything in matching white dishes and platters along the centre of the table. There was garlic and rosemary roasted vegetables, buffalo mozzarella and asparagus salad, buttered artichoke hearts, and potatoes au gratin. Bindi filled her plate to overflowing with the good food.

As she ate, she couldn't help smiling. The food smelled and tasted as good as it looked. The restaurant was going to be a success, she could sense it. It looked amazing, the food was the best she'd ever eaten, and the group of people seated at the table were all determined to do whatever they could to help.

"Everything good?" Kate stooped to ask Bindi once everyone had had a chance to taste the food.

Bindi nodded, swallowed. "It's fantastic. I love these potatoes, they're my favourite."

Kate smiled. "I think this is going to work."

"I think so too."

Bindi embraced her sister, who feigned losing balance. She fixed her skewed chef's hat back onto her head. "Careful, don't injure the chef."

"I'm really proud of you," said Bindi.

Kate's cheeks flushed pink. "Thanks."

"So am I," added Reeda from across the table.

"We all are," piped up Jack. "Well done, Katie."

Kate bit down on her lip, her eyes glistening. "I couldn't have done it without all your support."

Bindi watched as Kate returned to the kitchen, an extra bounce in her step. She smiled. The past eighteen months had dragged them through so much — grief, challenges, health issues, relationships stresses, and even had them questioning everything they knew about themselves and their family. It was time for some good things in her life, and she knew the Waratah Inn would be a big part of that.

SEPTEMBER 1982

COOLANGATTA

Waves curled along the shoreline and crashed against the sand. The water hissed and bubbled, sending froth swirling around Charlie's feet. He watched with interest. After an inland childhood, freezing his toes off, he didn't think he could ever grow tired of the beach. It was as if a part of his soul was made complete by standing there, letting the water wash around him, stripping away anxieties, worries, concerns and anything else on his mind.

Watching waves was a mindless activity. It helped him to focus, to forget, to simply *be* in the moment.

"Recruits! Are you ready to go? You're going to be life savers, that means you've got to be prepared to head into danger to save a life. But what we want to do is to mitigate the risk you're taking by making you strong, by helping you to understand the ocean and to give you the knowledge and skills you need to save people in trouble."

The trainer stood in front of the group, dressed in a yellow long-sleeved shirt and red shorts. His yellow cap was tied beneath his chin and his tanned skin stood in stark contrast to the whites of his eyes and the smear of white zinc across his nose and cheeks.

"I want suicide runs, right here in the sand. Run to those witches' hats over there, then back again. Go! Faster, faster!"

Charlie ran with the rest, struggling through the soft sand as much as the next person. It didn't take him long to find his stride though, and soon he was pulling out ahead of the crowd.

He'd been working at the inn as a handyman for three months but had decided that he needed something else to occupy his time. He'd never been much of a swimmer, so had joined the local swimming pool to do laps. While he was there, he'd met a surf life saver, swimming laps in the lane next to him. They'd struck up a conversation, and as he listened to the man talk about rescuing people from the surf, he couldn't help feeling a surge of excitement.

It hadn't taken him long to sign up for the next round of training. And even though he was struggling for breath, the muscles in his legs screaming for him to stop, he grinned as he ran. It felt good to push his body again; it reminded him of the training he'd done in the air force.

He might not be a strong swimmer yet, or know how to rescue himself from a rip, let alone anyone else, but he intended to work hard, harder than anyone else in the program. If his time in the military had taught him anything, it was that limitations were a state of mind, not a fact.

Finally, they struggled to the finish line and the trainer called out for them to do push-ups. He dropped to the sand, sweat giving the sand places to cling up and down his legs and on the front of his shirt.

When training was finished, Charlie washed off using the outdoor shower at the entrance to the beach. Sand slid from his legs under the cold water and he closed his eyes to let it cool his face. He walked back to his truck dripping wet and pulled a towel from the back to wipe down. It hadn't taken him long to figure out how the locals changed for the ride home, slipping shorts off beneath a towel wrapped around his waist, he exchanged them for a pair of dry ones and climbed into the truck shirtless.

A glance in the rearview mirror almost startled him at first. He barely recognised himself these days. His skin had darkened under the sun like it never had before. Bright blue eyes contrasted with the tan of his skin. His blond hair was streaked with grey, and he still wasn't used to seeing the wrinkles that'd gathered around his eyes.

He started the truck and his heart skipped a beat at the thought of who he was returning home to see. Home. It was a strange way to think of the small cottage he'd built by the ocean, but he liked it. Loved it, in fact. Loved that Edie was waiting for him.

After all these years, the sleepless nights lying in bed wondering where she was and what she was doing. All the moments he'd wondered what might've been if he hadn't lost his memory, met Maria, and stayed on the other side of the world. He didn't regret it, couldn't regret Maria and their children. Still, he'd missed knowing Keith, seeing him grow, holding Edie and building their family together. The feelings had built so much inner conflict, he'd found himself bleary eyed and irritable after nights of tossing and turning on the bed he shared with the wife he loved.

Sometimes he still felt that turmoil when he remembered Maria's smile, or the way she'd said his name, almost like a whisper.

But she was gone, and he had to move on. At least, that was what Stefano reminded him whenever the two of them talked it over together. He was proud of his son, the man he'd become. Stefano had taken on a carpenter's apprenticeship soon after arriving in Australia and would follow in his father's footsteps. The two of them had become the best of friends, sharing and confiding everything to one another.

Stefano was everything he'd always hoped for in a son, and together they shared everything he'd wished he could've had also with Keith. He wondered if the two men would've gotten along. Stefano had been excited to meet Keith, despondent when he died, but didn't talk about it often. He knew Charlie needed time to process everything that'd happened and seemed not to want to push him.

He pulled the truck into the inn's driveway, making a mental note to get some new gravel poured. The truck bounced and shuddered over potholes, before he pulled it into the almost empty parking lot.

Edie told him there used to be a lot more guests at the inn; back when Paul was alive, they'd been run off their feet. Still, she said she preferred the quiet now she was older. It gave her time to do some of the things she wanted in life. And besides, she said, she'd saved enough for retirement, so she didn't need the inn to be filled with guests anymore. Especially now the girls lived there. They needed her attention, and he was glad she'd pulled herself out of her grief in the past few weeks long enough to give them some.

Charlie couldn't help seeing the potential of the place. A little money invested, he'd said, would go a long way to restoring it to the type of holiday destination that people could love. But she'd been adamant, said she didn't want to do that. Wanted to keep the place exactly how it was for now. The girls could do what they liked with it once she was gone.

He considered driving to the cottage to change before visiting Edie, but didn't want to wait that long. Reeda, Kate and Bindi were out for the day, at the movies with friends, and from the parking lot he could tell there weren't many guests. Every chance he got, he wanted to be with her now they were reunited. He'd asked her to move into the cottage with him, but she'd told him she wasn't that kind of girl, grinning in the way that she'd done all those years ago and making his heart thud in the same way it had as well.

He found her in the garden, knees pressed to the soft ground, a trowel in her hand. Her face was obscured by a large straw hat and a pair of sunglasses that'd slid to the end of her nose. She pushed the glasses back into place and lurched to her feet with a grunt when she saw him. His heart swelled at the sight. She was out of bed after months of barely leaving her room. She was in the garden, something he'd been encouraging her to do. It'd been neglected, along with everything else after the accident. Finally, Edie was joining the world again, though her eyes still looked haunted and she was thinner than she had been.

"These carrots are going to be huge," she said.

"Hello to you as well." He kissed her lips.

"You taste salty," she said with a chuckle. "I see you've been out rescuing people again."

"Not yet, still training."

"I'm sure you'll be a natural. You always had a knack for saving people in trouble."

He shook his head. "I don't know about that…"

She wrapped her arms around him, staring up into his face with a smile. "You saved me many a time."

"I wish I could've…"

She shook her head. "You couldn't…you did the best you were able to do, and so did I. We talked about this, no more regrets. We're living in the moment, enjoying the time we have together now. We can't change the past, so there's no point in trying."

He nodded, then closed the gap to kiss her soft lips again. "You're right, my love. Of course you're right. Sometimes I can't seem to help it, I regret missing you and Keith, but then

I don't regret the life I lived, and get all tangled up inside not knowing how I should feel."

She laughed. "You should feel whatever it is you do feel. We've both been through enough, I think that we can let all that stuff go and simply love each other now. Dwelling on the past hurts too much. I can't..." She blinked, her smile fading.

"I do love you, you know," he said, his heart swelling.

Her eyes glimmered. "I know. And I love you too. Always have, always will."

He kissed her again, his soul warming with the feel of her body pressed to his. Even when he hadn't remembered who he was, or who he was missing, he'd felt the void inside that she'd left behind. Knew that some part of him wasn't there. Now, he was complete, whole. There was grief mixed in there as well, but grief was a feeling he'd held in his chest for so many years it'd become a familiar ache. Always there, waiting for a moment to be indulged.

"I think we should tell the girls," he said. "About me, who I am. They could use something positive in their lives."

Edie inhaled a sharp breath and pulled away. "I don't know."

She knelt again, picked up the trowel and kept digging. Weeds flew into a pile by his feet as she dug.

He'd avoided having this conversation since the accident. Didn't want to push Edie, since she'd barely survived the pain as it was. Still, the girls lived a quiet life at the inn, tiptoeing around their grandmother. He and Mima had done their best to help the girls feel at home at the Waratah, but he could see it in their eyes. They felt like visitors and didn't know how to cope with a grandmother who'd retreated so far into herself.

"They've been through so much," she muttered.

He raked a hand through his hair. It was almost dry now, and the heat of the day had chased away any cold he'd felt from the ocean and cool shower. Sweat beaded on his forehead and dampened his palm. "I know they have, but this could be a good thing for them. They have a grandfather, I could be there for them, be part of their lives."

"I don't want to cause them any more pain. They've got enough to contend with."

He wanted to say more but could tell from the curve of her back she was growing agitated.

"Okay, fine. We won't say anything for now."

"I've told Mima."

"What?"

She looked over her shoulder. "Told her not to say anything. She understands that it would rock them, it'd be too much for them right now. They need stability, a place to land that isn't moving beneath their feet."

He sighed. "Whatever you say, my love."

Back at the cottage, he pulled a shirt over his head then wandered out onto the small verandah to stare out across the ocean. White caps surged beneath a blowing north-easterly. The wind lifted the hair from his forehead as he slumped into a rocking chair and set his feet on a stool.

He didn't agree with Edie. The girls should know he was family; it might help them adjust to their lives at the inn. Especially since he was the one who drove them to dance lessons or after school activities. He was the one who met them when they stepped off the school bus, who helped Mima supervise their homework and encouraged them to keep going even when they wanted to give up and wallow in their grief.

He shook his head in frustration. Maybe if he gave her a little more time, she'd see things his way. He could go behind her back, but he didn't want to do that. She'd built this family on her own, without his help, he should respect her wishes when it came to what was best for them.

🎴 33 🎴

CABARITA BEACH

The ring glinted in the sunlight that glanced through the window and sliced the room with a narrow beam. Bindi turned it over between her fingers examining the tarnished silver. She slipped it onto her pinky finger. It fit perfectly. Nan's ring. The ring Charlie had given her. Jack, she corrected herself. The ring Jack had given her.

She shook her head. It was still hard to grasp the connection. Charlie was Jack, Jack was Charlie. What should she call him? She'd always called him Jack, should she switch back to Charlie, or perhaps Grandpa? No, that was too strange. She'd stick to Jack for now.

The wooden box closed with a soft thud, locking in Nan's journals. She slid it beneath her bed, the same place it'd sat for years. Different bed, same room. Her bed sat where Nan and Pop's had, with the box hidden beneath it.

The inn was full, it was a Saturday, and outside the room she could hear the sounds of staff buzzing around, tidying, serving, answering the occasional question from a guest, like

"Can we go horse riding today?", "Do you have beach towels?", and "Where can I buy a swimsuit?".

From what she could hear, the staff was doing well to manage everything without her. She'd taken the day off to meet Jack's family. His son's family were coming for a picnic. It felt strange to think about having a half-uncle and two cousins.

There was a knock at the door.

"Come in," she called, standing to smooth her shorts against her legs with both hands.

"There you are," said Kate. "I've been looking for you. They'll be arriving any moment. You can't stay hidden in here. Besides, Reeda and I are nervous enough, we need you out there with us."

She inhaled a slow breath. "I'm coming."

Out on the verandah, Alex and Duncan were deep in discussion over the fate of the cricket team after the last match with Sri Lanka. She kissed their cheeks, then hurried to the end of the verandah to peer around the front. She couldn't see the driveway from where she stood. She linked her fingers together, her heart pounding.

Why was she so nervous? After all, they were family.

The back door banged shut and she glanced up to see Josh striding towards her.

She smiled, stood on tiptoe to kiss him. He linked his arms around her waist and held her close.

"Hey baby," he said. "You smell amazing."

She grinned. "You too."

"I'm sure," he said. "I smell like a twelve-hour shift herding degenerates into the lock-up, with deodorant sprayed over the top to drown out the stench."

Her nose wrinkled. "Really?"

He smirked. "Just kidding, I showered. Most of the degenerate smell should be gone."

Just then, Jack walked through the back door, held it open and his family stepped outside. Bindi's heart skipped a beat. Then, she hurried towards them, hand outstretched.

"Hi, I'm Bindi. It's so nice to meet you," she said.

The man who faced her had brown eyes, brown hair and smiled at her, his eyes crinkling in a way that reminded her instantly of Jack. He ignored her hand and pulled her into an embrace.

"I'm your uncle, Stefano." He stepped back. "And this is my wife, Amara, and my girls, Sarah and Margaret."

She greeted them each with a hug. Reeda and Kate did the same, and soon the entire group were engrossed in happy conversation.

Next, they took the party down to the cove, and Bindi helped Kate and Reeda set up a picnic rug beneath a collapsible tent, some folding chairs and a table covered in delicious dishes and snacks. It wasn't long before Alex and Duncan had drawn everyone into a game of beach cricket.

Bindi caught out Duncan, much to his dismay. Then, it was her turn to bat. Josh was bowling and his eyes sparkled with mischief as he threw her the ball. She missed the first swing, but then connected on the second try. The ball went up into the air, even as she sprinted towards Josh for a run. He was looking up into the air where the ball had flown, then caught it as it came down, before she reached him.

He laughed, then grabbed for her as she careened past him. His arms tightened around her and her feet lifted off the ground and she squealed. He spun her around, before setting her feet on the ground and kissing her.

"Come on, we're in the middle of a game!" complained Alex.

Josh passed Alex the ball, then wrapped his arms around Bindi again, lifting her up for another kiss. Sparks ignited up and down her arms and all over her body. She smiled against his lips.

When he set her down again, she jogged over to where Sarah and Margaret had wandered off. They were at the end of the cove, studying the rock pools, ankle deep in the cool water.

"Did you find anything?" she asked.

Sarah peered at her, squinting against the glare of the sun. "There's a crab, right here." She pointed into a pool.

"And I found a crayfish," added Margaret.

"Wow, show me."

She meandered around the rock pools with the girls, examining the shellfish, crabs, and other creatures they found on the black rocks, nestled into crevices and cracks, waiting for the high tide to return.

"Where are you two going to school?" she asked.

"Indooroopilly State School," replied Sarah, without looking up.

"Do you like it?"

Sarah shrugged. "I guess so."

"I hate it," added Margaret. "I'd rather stay home and read books. Mum could teach us; I know she could. But she won't do it, says she needs us to go to school for her own sanity."

Bindi bit down on her lip to hold back a laugh. "I'm sure it'll get better. High school is more fun, at least I thought it was. You get more freedom and can choose which classes you want to take..."

"Yeah, but there's more homework too, I heard," added Sarah.

Bindi nodded. "That's true, there's definitely more homework. I'm sure, by the time you get to that stage though, you'll be ready for it."

"I want to be a professional netball player, anyway. So,

there's no point going to school at all," replied Margaret with pouted lips.

"There aren't any professional netball teams in Australia, you dope," sniffed Sarah.

"Not yet, but maybe there will be by the time Margaret is old enough to play," interjected Bindi, hoping to make peace between the sisters before things escalated.

Margaret glared at her sister. "Yeah, that's what Mum always says too. It's just a matter of time...and I'm going to be ready."

"Still, school is useful even if you are a netball player. You'll need to manage all that money they pay you," said Bindi.

Margaret studied her with eyes narrowed. "I guess that's true."

"Yeah, and school is a great place to make friends as well."

"I don't have any friends," replied Margaret.

Sarah rolled her eyes. "Here we go again."

"You don't?" asked Bindi.

"Nope."

"She does too, she's just saying that because they're being mean to her."

"Friends aren't mean to each other, that's what Dad says. So, they mustn't be my friends!" shouted Margaret.

Bindi sat on a round, black rock and faced Margaret with a smile. "I'll bet you and Sarah can say mean things to each other sometimes. I know my sisters and I had plenty of arguments over the years. Sometimes, I really didn't like them."

Margaret's eyes sought hers. "Is that true?"

Bindi nodded. "Oh yeah. Sisters can fight a lot."

"We fight all the time," sniffed Sarah, wading deeper into the pool.

"But..." interjected Bindi, "that doesn't mean you don't care about each other. You love each other, because you're sisters. Just the same way I love my sisters. And sometimes friends are a little bit like sisters. You care about each other, but you still fight. I remember primary school. It's a difficult time to be a girl. Everyone's trying to figure out how to be themselves, how to navigate friendships, how to manage peer pressure, there's a lot going on. You'll lose some friends and gain new ones. It's all completely normal."

"Really?" Margaret slumped onto the rock beside her.

"Yep. This is the time of life when you figure out how you'll let people treat you, and the kind of person you want to be."

Margaret sighed. "That sounds hard."

"It's really hard. But it's important to remember, if you want to become a kind person, then you should stay kind even when your friends aren't treating you with kindness. And if you want to be the kind of person who is treated well, then you don't put up with being treated badly. This is an important time in your life. You can set the standards to live by for the rest of your life."

"Wow, I didn't know that." Sarah shook her head. "This crab has a blue claw."

And just like that the subject changed. The girls forgot all about friendships and school and moved onto the colour of crabs and the transparency of small fish.

Bindi watched them with a smile. Her heart warmed as the girls drew closer and held things up for her to see, their laughter filling the air around her.

She glanced back to the cricket match, and saw Josh hit the ball into the air, with Jack chasing after it down the beach at a slow jog. Jack retrieved the ball, with a shout, then threw it back to Alex who was waiting with arms raised in the air. He tagged Josh who was mid-run, and Josh shouted in dismay, calling foul.

Their laughter and shouts rang out through the small

cove, over the sounds of the waves crashing to shore and the call of gulls circling overhead. The sun warmed the top of Bindi's head and she smiled at the sight of her family, some deep in conversation, others chasing each other across the sand, and her heart filled with joy.

❧ 34 ❧

OCTOBER 1982

GRAFTON

The truck hummed beneath him as the road slipped by. Charlie leaned one arm on the windowsill, the noise of the radio drowned out by the rush of wind through the cab.

He'd taken the turn from the highway and was making his way through the outskirts of Grafton. It'd been a four-hour drive from Cabarita, and the small city of Grafton rose sleepy from a landscape of dry gum forests and brown grass-covered hills.

Edie was doing so much better. She'd emerged from the darkness of her room at the inn to be the grandmother the girls needed and to manage the business she'd neglected. And her re-entry into life had given him the opportunity to do something he'd been wanting to since the first moment he'd set foot back in Australia — he was visiting Colin's family.

Colin and Henry had been his friends, his family, during their stint at Campo 78 and throughout the escape. When he recovered his memory, he hadn't been able to shake the thought that their families might not know how they'd died or when. It was his responsibility to talk to them, tell them how much their sons had meant to him, how they'd helped him through the hardest time of his life. How they'd died heroes. He'd written a letter to Henry's family but wanted to visit Colin's in person.

From the moment he arrived in Cabarita, however, Edie had needed him. Then, after the accident, the girls had as well. He couldn't get away until now. It was time, he wouldn't feel right until he'd done what he came to do.

He found Colin's parents living in a white clapboard structure set back from a narrow street, in the house that he presumed had been Colin's childhood home. He'd looked them up in the White Pages and given them a call to confirm who they were before making the trip.

A woman met him at the door, wearing a floral cotton dress. She looked about eighty years old and held onto the door as she opened it.

"Hi, I'm Charlie," he said, reaching out a hand to shake hers.

She smiled. "I'm Rose Statham, come on in."

He followed her into a dark living room and took a seat on a worn couch. A man was resting in an armchair, his feet raised, and eyes closed. She tapped him gently on the shoulder.

"Bill, Charlie Jackson is here to see us."

The man startled, then lowered the footrest to shake Charlie's hand, his eyes blurry. "Charlie Jackson, eh? Good to see you, son."

"Can I get you a cup of tea?" asked Rose.

Charlie nodded. "That would be lovely, thank you."

She tottered off to the kitchen and Charlie could see her from where he sat, filling a jug with water.

"I hope the drive wasn't too bad," said Bill.

Charlie smiled. "It wasn't bad at all. I've never been here before, it's a nice place. Got some great gum trees around here."

"It's okay. I always tell Rose we should've settled in Coffs Harbour instead. Less than an hour away and they've got some wonderful beaches. Still, the job was here, so here we stayed."

Charlie nodded. "I understand that."

"Jobs weren't always easy to come by, you know, back in my day. Then, once you have a family and build friendships, join a church...it's hard to move."

"We loved it here, don't listen to anything he says. I didn't want to live at the beach, everyone I care about is in this town," called Rose from the kitchen, over the sound of water bubbling in the kettle.

Charlie smiled to himself. "I know what that's like. After the war, I lived for years in Casoli, Italy. I built a life there, even though part of my heart was back here in Australia."

Bill dipped his head, lips pursed.

Rose returned to the living room carrying two steaming cups of tea. She set one down on a small coffee table in front of Charlie, the other on a side table next to Bill's chair.

Then, Rose lowered herself into the loveseat opposite Charlie.

"You said you knew Colin in the war?" she asked, hope flitting across her weathered face.

Charlie sipped his tea, nodded. "That's right, we were at Campo 78 together."

"Don't you remember?" interrupted Bill. "He wrote about a Charlie fellow in his letters. From Bathurst, weren't you?"

Charlie smiled. "That's right. I'm glad you were able to receive his letters, he worried about the two of you. Thought

295

you might not get the letters and wouldn't know where he was."

Rose's eyes glistened with tears. "We got the letters."

"That's good."

"I hope things weren't too bad for him, or for you, in that camp," added Bill.

"We were there for each other. Colin became like a brother during that time. It wasn't so bad, living in the camp. We had food, water, friendship...we even figured out ways to play games and have a bit of fun." He wasn't telling the entire truth, but they didn't need to know their son starved in a frigid prison camp over the last months of his life.

"That's nice to hear," replied Rose, with a quick nod of the head. "He said it in his letters, we weren't sure how much to believe. He always did want to make things seem better than they were for our sakes." She reached out a wrinkled hand and patted Bill's where it rested on the armchair. He offered her a wobbly smile in return.

"He was happy, as much as he could be," continued Charlie. "We had great times together. We talked about our lives, laughed, we even gave the guards a bit of trouble now and then."

Bill grunted. "That's my boy."

"And he died a hero," added Charlie, his voice catching in his throat. "I was with him...we'd escaped Campo 78. We'd made it to a small village called Pacentro, and we were on our way into the mountains when the Wehrmacht found us. He was shot, died pretty quickly. I...comforted him as best I could."

Bill and Rose held each other's hands, their eyes filled with tears.

"I'm glad you were with him. I'd hate for my boy to have to die alone," said Rose, her voice soft.

"He wasn't alone. I was there. He was brave and wasn't

afraid. He faced death as a hero." Charlie couldn't say more. He inhaled a slow breath around the lump in his throat.

Bill nodded with his eyes trained on the carpet. Rose squeezed her eyes shut.

"But I tell you what, he was a mischief when he chose to be," added Charlie. "There was this one guard at the camp..."

He told them about Colin's antics with Cabbage Hat, the guard who'd given them the most trouble in Campo 78, and consequently the one the men chose as the target for all of their mischief.

Bill and Rose's demeanour changed as he spoke, until they were laughing along with him as he regaled them with the things Colin had done to make Cabbage Hat's life miserable during his months at the prison camp.

By the time he left the Statham house, his heart fairly ached with memories. Nostalgia almost choked him. He missed them, Colin and Henry. He didn't miss the prison camp, or the war, but he missed his friends. Wished he'd been able to share a peacetime drink with each of them. He missed his parents, and his life in Bathurst. Missed Italy and the life he'd built in Casoli. There were so many people, so many things, so many lives he'd lived, built, and shared over the years that he couldn't get back, couldn't have again. People, places, and things he'd left behind and the loss of each had left a small hole in his heart.

But now he had Edie, along with their grandchildren. Thinking of Edie and the girls helped soothe away the sadness. Ever since he'd returned to Cabarita Beach, he and Edie had rebuilt their relationship stone by stone. Time had changed them both in little ways, but they were still the same two people who'd fallen in love before war tore them apart. He'd be forever grateful for a second chance to build a life with Edie.

He mourned the loss of his son, never getting the chance

to really know him, never being able to tell him the truth of who he was. But he'd learned something during the war that had helped him move forwards — no amount of wishing could bring a person back. All anyone could do was love well the people left behind.

❦ 35 ❧

CABARITA BEACH

The line of diners streamed out the door, down the front steps of the inn and across the yard. Cars were pulling into the almost full lot, and Bindi's pulse accelerated at the sight of headlights still turning into the inn's drive.

It was the official opening night for their new *Waratah Restaurant*. Construction had ended a week earlier, and they'd spent the past seven days rushing about getting everything ready for the opening. With a delay due to an issue with the wrong flooring being delivered, that'd pushed them back two weeks, they were in a rush to meet the opening deadline they'd been heavily promoting for the past month.

Bindi inhaled a deep breath, smoothed her hair back with one hand and stepped inside the inn. Conversations buzzed, and laughter filled the air, along with the warm scent of food that drifted in from the newly expanded kitchen. Roasted meats, vegetable soups, freshly baked bread: the night was heady with delicious smells that made Bindi's nerve-wracked stomach growl.

"I'll be right with you, ladies and gentlemen. Thank you for your patience. If people with a reservation could step to the front of the line, I'd appreciate it. Everyone else, I'm afraid we're booked out this evening, but you're welcome to sit at the bar for a drink."

There were groans of disappointment, and a few people left. Others came forward, smiling wide.

Bindi stood behind the small, reception desk, checking people in and then directing them towards a hostess who'd seat them at their reserved table in the restaurant. After she'd been doing it a while, she called one of the staff to take over. She wanted to take a look around the restaurant and see how things were progressing.

She strode into the restaurant. The hostess seated a couple to her left, then headed back to where the line of diners waited for her. Waiters were taking orders, and guests were smiling and pointing out the chandeliers, the wishbone timber flooring, the large windows that gazed out over a darkening garden.

Bindi stopped, hands clutching each other, to take it all in. It was beautiful. Everything they'd imagined had come together in the space. It was slowly filling up as the hostess returned with more diners.

She pushed through the swinging doors and the noise and scents of the kitchen greeted her. Kate, wearing a chef's hat, buzzed around, stirring this, tasting that. Mima was part of the action, seated on a chair slicing vegetables. Around her, staff fried, sautéed, and broiled, then filled plates with food. Everyone moved like they were part of an orchestrated routine.

Kate glanced up, caught sight of her. "We're somehow out of calamari," she shouted.

"What? Really?"

"I don't know what happened. I ordered plenty, but it's not there...I guess I didn't check the order."

"I'll run out and get some."

She checked with Kate exactly what they needed and how much and sprinted to the truck. In Tweed Heads, she had to drive around to several different suppliers before she found one that was open and had to beg them to keep from closing the door in front of her. By the time she'd returned with the order, things were well underway in the restaurant.

"Where have you been?" cried Reeda from the reception desk where a line of diners stood waiting to be seated.

"Buying supplies for Kate."

"A kid tripped on the front step, and cracked his lip open, there's still blood everywhere. I bandaged him up and sent him home but haven't been able to find anyone who's free to wipe up the mess."

"I'm on it!" shouted Bindi, handing the bags to Reeda and rushing for the broom closet.

She found gloves, a mop and bucket and carried it all to the laundry to fill with water and soap, then out to the front verandah. The blood had dried and was harder to remove than she'd thought it'd be. Guests stepped over or around her, and when they stood directly on the wet floorboards, she was cleaning, her frustration almost boiled over.

Finally, she was done and carried everything back to the laundry room. She left it there and returned to check on the restaurant. Diners were finishing up their meal, empty plates being carried back to the kitchen. She smiled when she saw most had been completely scraped clean. Then she frowned when she saw how many dirty plates remained on tables.

Bindi marched into the kitchen and confronted the first waiter she met.

"Please make sure to bus the tables quickly," she said.

He nodded and hurried out through the swinging doors.

She repeated the instructions to several other waiters, but realised she'd have to talk to the team about it after the shift was over if she was to make sure they all heard and received the instruction. As she pushed through the swinging doors and stepped back into the restaurant there was a shout from one of the tables.

Bindi's heart skipped a beat as a man near the front of the restaurant fell from his chair and onto the floor. The woman he was with screamed and ran to his side, kneeling on the floor beside him. Bindi sprinted through the restaurant, then squatted next to the woman.

"What's wrong?" she asked.

"I don't know," whimpered the woman. "He just turned red and collapsed."

The man's face was contorted in pain. "My chest," he grunted.

Bindi ran to the front of the restaurant where a telephone hung on the wall. She dialled triple zero, asked for an ambulance, then hurried back to where the guest lay.

"The ambulance is coming, just hang in there."

His face was pale now and had turned a shade of yellow. Bindi's throat tightened. She tried to run through the steps outlined in the first aid training she'd done months earlier. He was still breathing. She checked his pulse, it was erratic.

The woman sobbed beside her, clutching the man's hand in her own.

"It's going to be okay," soothed Bindi. "The ambulance is on its way, and you're going to be fine." She forced a smile onto her face.

Guests began to crowd around them, asking questions, offering support. Bindi stood and ushered them back to their tables.

When finally the ambulance arrived twenty minutes later, Bindi was bathed in sweat. Two paramedics rushed into the restaurant, carrying a stretcher between them. They attended to the man, even as a pair of police officers followed them in.

Josh.

Just the sight of him made her heart sigh with relief.

He squeezed her hand. "I heard the call come in and thought I might see if you need some help. Sounds like you're having an exciting night."

She shook her head. "This kind of excitement I could do without."

Josh and his partner helped the paramedics carry the man to the ambulance. His wife trotted in her stiletto heels along behind them.

Josh jogged back to where she stood, kissed her lightly on the lips. "My shift doesn't end for a while. I'll be back in a few hours. Okay?"

She nodded, then crossed her arms over her chest to watch as the ambulance and police cruiser left, one after the other, lights flashing.

᠅

BINDI SLUMPED INTO A ROCKING CHAIR. THE SONG OF A hundred cicadas swelled in the cool night air. Kate sat on one side, Reeda on the other. Each of the sisters looked as exhausted as Bindi felt.

"I hope it's not like this every night," moaned Reeda, her eyes wide.

"The first night is always the worst," said Kate, shaking her head. "And we had a doozy."

"I can't feel my feet," added Bindi. She reached down to massage one bare foot with her fingertips.

"You did so well, and so did you Kate." Reeda reached out a hand to squeeze Bindi's shoulder.

"Yeah, the food looked amazing. Smelled great too. And everyone cleaned their plates. I think the menu was a huge hit." Bindi grinned at Kate.

"Thanks, I'm glad to hear it." Kate grinned. "And you managed to keep everyone alive on the premises. That was no mean feat tonight."

Bindi rolled her eyes. "I'm so glad this night is over. I don't think I could take more."

Reeda grinned. "Let's hope things get much more boring from now on."

Kate sighed, leaned forwards and grunted as she stood to her feet. She stretched her arms over her head with a yawn. "I'm going home. I've got to get some sleep before we start all over again in the morning."

"Me too," replied Reeda.

Bindi kissed each sister goodbye then nestled back into her chair, tucking her legs up beneath her. A few minutes later, the back door opened again, and Josh walked through it, still wearing his uniform.

She offered him a weary smile. "There you are, I was wondering when you'd make it back."

"Sorry, things got crazy for us tonight."

"Ah...so you've had an evening like mine."

He chuckled, bent to kiss her lips then lowered himself into the chair beside her.

They talked together for a while about their day. Josh's stories made Bindi grateful she worked at an inn rather than on a police beat. One day of bedlam and emergencies was enough for her, she couldn't imagine dealing with worse every day of the week.

"I don't know how you do it," she said. "You're amazing."

He smiled, grabbed her chair, and turned it so she faced him. Then he picked up her feet, set them in his lap and began massaging them.

"Wow, that feels amazing."

He smiled. "You worked hard tonight, I'm really proud of you. You and your sisters did all this — it's something pretty special." He waved an arm towards the inn, the gardens.

Bindi glanced around with new eyes, seeing the Waratah as a guest might for the first time. Twinkle lights sparkled in the flourishing garden. The timber planks on the verandah floor gleamed, the pale yellow of the inn's walls contrasted with the dark light fixtures and complemented the light floral and wicker furniture.

"It really is beautiful, isn't it?" she murmured.

He nodded. "I visited this place years ago. It didn't look anything like it does now. You ladies have completely trans-formed it."

"The heart of the Waratah is still the same though," she mused. "Beneath the fancy decor, it's still Nan's inn. A place she built to give people somewhere to stay for their holidays to help them feel at home."

"And now it boasts the best restaurant on the coast," added Josh with a wink.

Bindi's heart flooded with warmth. "Yeah, it does." She grinned. "It's hard to believe, and I spent the night in such a tizzy over everything that was happening, I didn't get a chance to soak it all in. Thanks for reminding me."

He nodded. "My pleasure."

"I could get used to these foot massages," she said.

He cackled, winked. "It's all part of my devious plan. You know, the one I told you about months ago."

"Oh yeah?"

He nodded. "My plan to make myself completely irresistible. Before you know it, you won't be able to live without me."

Her cheeks flushed with warmth. "Well, it's working."

He set her feet on the floor, kneeled in front of her and kissed her hard on the lips. His arms wound around her waist, and when she pulled back his gaze fixed on hers. His eyes seemed to drink her in, making her heart pound against her ribs.

Josh took her hand in his, caressed it slowly. "Bindi, ever since I met you back in high school, you've held my heart. I didn't realise it fully at the time, but I loved you from that first moment. I never could get you out of my head, so when I saw you at the beach that day, I thought it was fate giving me a second chance."

Bindi's eyes brimmed with tears and she sniffled.

He smiled. "Ever since that day, the time we've spent together has confirmed it to me over and over. You're the one for me. I love you, and I want to spend the rest of my life with you."

A lump filled Bindi's throat and she blinked away the tears blurring her vision.

"So, what do you say — will you marry me?"

Josh's eyes fixed on hers, full of love, hope — expectant as he waited for her response.

When she was sick, she hadn't wanted this. Didn't want to saddle Josh with a sick wife, or with the pain of losing her. But now she was well. She'd never felt for anyone what she felt for him. He was the kind of man she wanted to spend her days with, to sit next to in these rocking chairs every evening. Whenever something happened in her life, he was the one she wanted to talk to about it. She couldn't imagine her life without him, not anymore.

"Yes, I'll marry you." She sniffled, then smiled wide.

He leapt to his feet, then cupped her face with both

hands to kiss her lips. She stood and their lips joined. His arms wrapped around her, pulling her close. Then, he lifted her from her feet and spun in a circle making her legs fly out, his lips pulled into a wide grin. She laughed, then he kissed her again as the world spun around her.

❧ 36 ❧

CABARITA BEACH

Mud had a way of travelling it seemed. Up her arms, all over her gloves. Her knees were covered in it too. Edie glanced at her pants with a wry smile and shook her head. No matter, the stains hadn't come out of those pants in years. They were her gardening pants for a reason.

She set the trowel down in the mud, staggered to her feet and waited for the feeling to return to her legs. She was getting too old to kneel in the garden for long. Though it was her happy place, so she hated to give it up. Still, perhaps she should cave and get one of those special kneeling pads she'd seen at the hardware shop.

Ugh. Getting old really was no fun at all. She paused, tipped her head to one side. Unless of course, the love of your life showed up unexpectedly. Then it became much more enjoyable.

As she gathered her gardening things together, she mused over the years she and Charlie had shared since his return.

Something she'd never thought possible. She'd lived with the grief of losing him for so long, it'd become a comfortable companion, something she returned to whenever she was feeling low or worried.

Then, he'd come back. She'd thought she was losing her mind at first. That day on the beach, when she saw him, she'd thought it was finally happening — she'd go crazy before she died and be a menace to her family and society. But then he'd touched her, brought her back to the moment, and she'd understood he was real. He was there. Her Charlie.

Her throat tightened at the memory. She'd been angry with him at first. How could he do that to her, to Keith? But after he'd explained, she'd fallen back into his arms. The letters were really the thing that'd turned her around. She'd recognised his handwriting immediately. Had read over his old letters in her box so many times she was afraid they'd fall to pieces.

He worried, regretted, even got angry at himself at times for what he'd put them through — her and Keith. But she'd assured him, there was no time left in their lives for regrets. They had to move forward, to enjoy every moment they had left. Regrets only shrivelled a heart, love expanded it to hold everything life now offered them — another chance at happiness, something she'd thought was behind her.

And she was happy. Happier than she'd believed possible. Mima teased her about it all the time. Told her she'd have to sell the inn and move into the cottage with Charlie full-time. But Edie didn't want that. She loved her inn, it held so many memories — Paul, Keith's childhood, the girls. Everything was wrapped up in its walls, her whole life. The shadows of it anyway.

The one thing that'd make her life complete was if the girls would come home more often. Call her more regularly. Losing their parents so young had changed them. Of course it had. No one could go through a thing like that without being changed.

They hardly called, and when they did the conversations were short, to the point. Their visits had slowed to a trickle, generally only Christmas and sometimes not even then. When they did all visit at the same time, their stay usually resulted in the three of them arguing, then not speaking to each other for days or storming out early to catch the first flight home.

She and Charlie wanted to talk to them about everything that'd happened, who he was, where he'd been — but each time they made a plan, the girls ruined it by either not making it home, or with some dramatic scene or angry outburst. In the end, she'd just about given up the idea. If she could only get them all together, have them visit the inn at the same time, and talk to them before things devolved into fighting or chaos. She'd have to call them again, see if she could manage it.

She sighed as she pulled off her gloves, shoving them into a her small, worn gardening bag.

"You seem lost in thought." Charlie's voice startled her.

She grunted. "Don't sneak up on me like that, I might have a heart attack."

He frowned. "Sneak...? I lumbered across the yard like an injured elephant. You're going senile in your old age."

She feigned exaggerated laughter, stepped out of the garden, and handed him her gardening bag. "You're such a romantic."

He grinned. "I work hard at it, practice my lines on the horses sometimes. They give feedback. It's a whole thing..."

Edie threw her head back and laughed, then looped her arms around his neck. "You make me happy, Charlie Jackson."

He kissed her soft on the lips, his familiar scent stirring a longing within her she'd grown accustomed to all over again.

"I'm glad to hear it. You know, I should really make an honest woman of you. After all, I did give you a promise..."

Edie's eyes narrowed. "Which promise exactly do you mean?"

"The one where I said I'd be back from the war soon, and I'd marry you and spend the rest of my life making you happy."

"Oh, that one," she replied.

"Yes, that one." He kissed her again. "So, Edith Watson, I apologise for the delay, but what do you say we finally do what we said we'd do all those years ago? Let's get married."

She inhaled a slow breath. "I'd love to."

❦

EDIE STARED OUT THE WINDOW AT THE OCEAN. SHE LOVED the beach, no matter where in the world she was. Fiji seemed like the perfect destination for a quiet wedding, and their cabin perched on the edge of the sand like a crab.

Charlie was already there, at the end of the beach waiting with the celebrant. Through a window she could see the sun setting over the water, shooting rays of pink, orange and yellow across the sea and highlighting the waves with a golden shimmer as they rolled to shore.

She smoothed the soft, blue gown against her legs, and glanced in the mirror one final time. She'd curled her hair, something she rarely did any more. She remembered a time when Mother had made her wear curls every day, the rags knotted and tangled against her head every night on her pillow.

With a soft brush, she added a last touch of blush to her cheeks, inhaled a sharp breath, then grabbed the bunch of frangipanis she was using as a bouquet.

Mima had been hurt and upset they hadn't invited her to

come, but Edie had explained they needed her to run the inn while they were gone. Besides, they'd have a party sometime, invite all their friends and family — they only had to talk to the girls first.

She and Charlie had wanted this moment to be just for them. They'd waited so long to commit their lives to one another, doing it alone seemed like the best thing. Besides, they could hardly invite Mima without also inviting Charlie's children and their granddaughters. And the latter was something she'd decided not to do. This was a special moment for her and Charlie to share together. So much heartache, grief, and pain had been replaced by happiness. She didn't want anything, or anyone else's confusion, to upset that.

She stepped onto the beach, the sand enveloping her bare feet as she walked. Charlie stood beneath an archway at the end of the beach, a man dressed in white beside him. Charlie wore white as well, an open-necked shirt, long pants, and bare feet to match her own.

His eyes gleamed as she took her place beside him. He reached for her hands, held them in his own as her throat closed up. She couldn't speak, just nodded. The thing she'd longed for in the still quiet of nights lying staring at the ceiling all those years ago, was hers. Charlie was alive, he was here, and they were saying vows that would tie them together for the rest of their lives.

Joy swelled in her heart. She held back a sob.

"I, Charles Jackson, do take you, Edith Watson, to be my lawfully wedded wife…"

He repeated the vows said by the celebrant, then it was her turn.

She swallowed around the lump in her throat. "I, Edith Watson, take you, Charles Jackson…"

When the vows were finished, Charlie dipped her with a

sparkle in his eyes, then kissed her gently. She kissed him back, the tears she'd held in check pouring down her cheeks.

"We did it," she whispered against his neck.

He set her back on her feet. "Yes, we did." With a thumb, he wiped away her tears.

"Let's never be apart again," she said.

He shook his head. "Never again."

"I love you, Charlie Jackson.

"I love you too."

"Let's party," she said, then took his hand.

They walked up the beach together. The restaurant was waiting with a table for them. Every other table held holiday makers, but Edie had eyes only for her new husband.

Her husband.

It felt strange to see him as her husband. When Paul died, she'd thought she'd never marry again. Had no desire to. Didn't want to date, had put that part of her life away in a closet and locked it. But then Charlie showed up and everything changed. He'd unlocked the door to her heart and thrown out the key. She couldn't shut it again if she tried.

They ordered a meal, then danced to music played by a live band until their meal arrived. Charlie's arms around her, his hand firm against her back, brought memories buzzing into her head. They were teenagers again, and he was whispering words of love, of promises, into her ear making her head spin with thoughts of the future, of lives woven together and adventures unfolding with him by her side.

Candlelight flickered over the walls, the scent of roasted meats and flowers filled the air. Conversation and laughter floated around them. But they were alone, everything else was background to the love that tied them together. She stared into Charlie's eyes and he held her gaze with an intensity that set her heart skittering in her chest.

Then, they ate together — fish wrapped in banana leaves,

scallops fried in garlic and butter, fresh salads with things in it Edie had never seen or tasted before.

"I know most of my life is behind me now," said Edie, "but I can't help this feeling I have that anything's possible."

He nodded, swallowing a bite of fish. "I know what you mean. It's like we've been given a second shot at life. We can be anyone we want to be, do anything we like."

"I know what I want," she replied.

He cocked his head to one side. "Oh?"

"I want to live out my days at the Waratah Inn, in that darling little cottage you've built by the water. I want to wake up in your arms and go to sleep there every night. I want to spend my time in my garden or walking in the cove."

"That sounds just about perfect to me," interjected Charlie.

"And I want my granddaughters around me." Her throat tightened and she choked on the words.

He reached for her hand and squeezed it. "It'll happen. They'll come around. In the meantime, we have each other."

"You're right." She cleared her throat with a cough and raised her wine glass in a toast. "To us."

"To us," he agreed.

They clinked their glasses together and drank.

❈ 37 ❈

CABARITA BEACH

Her eyes blinked open. She shut them, then opened them all over again and stared at the ceiling. The covers were bunched up beneath her chin, and she tugged them higher still with a shiver.

It was a cold morning. At least, cold for Cabarita Beach. Not that it ever got even close to the frigid temperatures she'd lived through in Melbourne. And it was her wedding day.

Her stomach churned and she ducked over the side of the bed, clutching one hand to her mouth.

What was going on?

Was she sick again? This couldn't be happening.

Her pulse spiked and she stared at the light blue rug beneath the bed. She was in remission; she wasn't supposed to get sick again. She'd convinced herself it was over, she was well, that the illness had been a blip on the road of her life, and it was behind her. She'd lunged for happiness and now it was all going to be stripped away again.

With a deep breath she climbed out of bed and padded to the bathroom. If she was going to throw up, she should at least try not to do it on the bedroom floor.

She stood at the sink, hands pressed to the bench, and stared at her reflection in the mirror. Her skin was pale. Was it more pale than usual? And were those smudges beneath her eyes the normal look she sported each morning, or something more sinister — like her body's way of telling her that something was very wrong.

This couldn't be happening today. She had a full day planned — fun with her sisters this morning, then preparations for an early afternoon wedding in the cove. Again, probably not her best idea, given it was winter. But it was always lovely in the cove, even in August. In fact, it was August that delivered the clearest skies, the bluest ocean and crisp air that took the sting out of the sun's harsh light.

August was her favourite time of year at the Waratah Inn.

It was meant to be the happiest day of her life, and now she was sick. Again.

She pressed both hands to her stomach and inhaled another slow breath. The nausea subsided as she exhaled.

By the time she'd showered and dressed, Kate and Reeda were sitting in her bedroom waiting for her to emerge from the bathroom.

"There's the bride!" cried Kate, throwing her arms around Bindi, and kissing her cheek. Kate's eyes glimmered. She swallowed. "I promised myself I wouldn't cry...at least not yet. Not until the ceremony, then I'm allowed to ball my eyes out."

Reeda patted Bindi's back. "How are you feeling this morning?"

Bindi's stomach lurched again. "I don't know... I feel a bit unwell, actually."

Both sisters looked at her. Reeda's eyes narrowed. "What kind of unwell?"

Bindi rubbed her stomach. "I feel sick... I don't know if the cancer is back but..."

Kate pressed both hands to her mouth, her eyes wide. "It couldn't...could it?"

"No, of course it's not that," stated Reeda with a firm shake of her head. "You've got nerves...wedding jitters. That's all it is. You're not sick, you're nervous, which is completely normal."

"You think so?"

"Absolutely." Reeda's chin jutted forward. "This is a special day for you. Some people say the happiest of your life, although that was never my experience. I threw up in the bathroom, then had my hair half pulled out at the hairdresser's before walking down the aisle in front of a bunch of people who stared at me. It was a special day, but not the happiest. The honeymoon however..." Reeda winked.

"You're probably right. I hope you're right. I don't want to have to go through all of that again. I don't think I could take it."

"Of course you could," interjected Kate. "But you won't have to, because Reeda is right, this is simply normal wedding jitters. Every bride gets nervous on the big day."

"Did you?" asked Bindi.

Kate grunted. "Of course I did. I tried to convince Alex we should elope."

"What did he say?" asked Bindi, her brow furrowed.

"He said he loved me and hung up the phone." Kate smirked. "In the end, it was a really lovely day. I'm glad we didn't elope and that our family and friends got to share in our wedding. That's what it's all about. You can marry the person you love anywhere but sharing the occasion with others makes it even more special."

"If it'll make you feel better, we could stop in to see Doctor Ash on our way to the hairdresser," Reeda suggested.

Bindi bit down on her lower lip. "Actually, I think it would help. If I could see him, I might be able to focus on the wedding instead of worrying."

"Fine, I'll make an appointment while you get ready to go," replied Reeda.

She left Kate and Bindi alone in the room. Kate sat on the bed and patted the space beside her. Bindi lowered herself next to Kate with a sigh. Kate encircled Bindi with one arm, pulled her close and Bindi rested her head on Kate's shoulder.

"Big day, Bindi-boo," said Kate, stroking her hair. "There was a time when I thought this day might never come..." She hesitated with her voice thick with tears. "I didn't know if we'd be able to celebrate you getting married or having a baby...but here we are. And I'm so happy."

"You haven't called me that in years," replied Bindi, her throat tightening.

Kate's face shone. "You've become a wonderful young woman, I'm so proud of you. I know the two of you will be happy, and I think Josh is the luckiest guy in the world. I've never met anyone who is so concerned about everyone else's feelings, and so intent on making sure everyone is happy the way you are. You've been a peacemaker since you were born, and you're still doing it today even after a career as a big-time television journalist. You haven't changed at all, and I love you so much."

Tears filled Bindi's eyes and her throat closed over. She couldn't speak, so she simply squeezed her sister tight.

After they got everything together they needed for the morning, they climbed into Reeda's car and drove to Doctor Ash's surgery. He greeted Bindi with a firm handshake and a wide smile, then sat on the edge of the desk.

"You're lucky you caught me. I only work the occasional

Saturday morning. I'm heading out to the golf course as soon as we're done. So, Bindi what can I do for you today?"

"Thank you for meeting with me so last minute. I'm getting married today..."

"Your sister mentioned that. Congratulations!"

Bindi smiled. "Thank you...anyway, I woke up this morning and felt nauseated, like I might throw up. It reminded me of how things were, when I was sick, and then I started to panic. Do you think it could return this quickly? I mean, I thought I was well, I'd moved on with my life. I can't believe..." Her voice broke, and she bit down on her lip to keep from crying.

Doctor Ash patted her hand, then walked around to sit behind his desk. He tapped on his computer for a few seconds, then faced her.

"I think perhaps you're nervous about the wedding."

"Could I be sick again?"

His lips pursed. "Of course anything is possible, but I doubt it. We'll run some tests to make sure, but I think you should forget all about this and enjoy your day. The most likely explanation is that you're worn out, nervous, excited... not that you're sick. It's completely normal to feel panicked at the idea that you might be sick again, but I'd encourage you to try not to do that. We're not going to panic without any confirmation that there's something wrong. Okay?"

"Okay." Her voice sounded small.

"Every time you feel unwell, if you let yourself get worked up about the idea of the cancer returning, you'll let this thing rule your life and your emotions. I want you to be vigilant, of course, and be aware of how your body feels, but I also want you to be confident in your health. Don't worry until there's something to worry about."

She pushed a smile onto her face. "I think I can do that."

"Good." He grinned. "Now, let's talk about the important

things... Is Kate catering the reception? Because I ate at the restaurant last weekend, and her crab dish was absolutely amazing."

⁂

"You look beautiful," said Jack, his eyes gleaming. He patted Bindi's hand where it rested on his arm.

"Thank you, Jack. You look pretty dapper yourself."

He was dressed in a white button-down shirt, navy dinner jacket and khaki pants. They both had bare feet, since walking through the sand in the cove was too difficult with shoes on. Besides, Bindi loved the feel of the sand between her toes. She had some stunning high-heeled white shoes for the reception at the inn, although she'd probably kick them off again as soon as the dancing started. She wasn't the stiletto type; bare feet had always been more her style.

The kitchen was abuzz with activity. The staff in the early stage of preparations for her reception. The restaurant was closed for the night, and as Kate had said, it was all about her and Josh. Bindi wasn't used to having fuss and attention, it all seemed a bit much and she'd objected at first, saying they could hold the reception in the garden, but Kate had been firm.

"You only get married once, and I want to do it right. We're celebrating," Kate had said.

Bindi smiled at the memory.

She rested her free hand on the skirt of her white dress. It was a simple dress, elegant, yet suited to the beach wedding. Lace trimmed the neckline, then it fell, straight, to the ground. It had long sleeves, and a hemline that brushed against her ankles when she walked. She fingered Nan's ring, still encircling her pinky. Then, held up the finger to examine it.

"What's that you've got there?" asked Jack.

She showed it to him, smiling. "It's the ring you gave Nan. I found it in her box. She must've had small fingers, because it only fits on my pinky."

Jack's eyes glowed. "That's the ring I made when we were still kids. Wow, I haven't seen it in years. She did have small fingers." His voice thickened in his throat. He patted Bindi's hand again.

" I feel like she's with me when I wear the ring, so now I never take it off."

"She'd have liked that," he replied. He shook his head. "I can't believe she kept it all these years. I thought for sure that thing was lost long ago."

Bindi held her hand to her chest. "No, it meant a lot to her, I can tell. She kept in the box with her journals and your letters...the box you whittled for her."

His blue eyes crinkled around the edges. "I wish...oh never mind. Wishing doesn't change a thing, does it?"

Bindi sighed. "No, it doesn't. But then if you changed anything, where would we be?"

"You're right," he replied. "Even if I could change things, I don't believe I would. Every single experience, every relationship, every broken heart and wound, every kind word and kiss, they all add up to a life. A life I don't regret. A life I wouldn't give up for anything, even if it didn't turn out the way I planned or hoped. It's imperfect and beautiful, a mess and yet so...I don't know...fulfilling."

"That's very poetic, Jack. I didn't know you had it in you." Bindi grinned, her vision blurred by tears. "And I understand what you mean. I think I'm beginning to feel the same way about everything that's happened in my life. Oh, don't get me wrong, I'd love for my parents and Nan to be here today, and if I could change that, I would in a heartbeat. But they're not, and instead I have a new grandfather, someone I've loved most of my life, here to give me away instead. There's something very special about the twists and turns of life."

Jack kissed her cheek. He blinked and inhaled a slow breath. "I'm glad I can be here for you, love. It doesn't get much better than this."

Bindi sniffled, shook her head. "I can't cry yet; I haven't even made it to the altar."

He nudged her. "Come on, I hear the music playing. It's time for your big entrance."

As they walked down the winding path to the cove, plovers called in the distance. The sound of the waves grew louder with each step. The afternoon sun was warm on her head, but the breeze over the water chilled her, goosebumps popping up across her bare legs beneath her dress.

The small crowd of family and friends congregated at the end of the cove turned to look when she and Jack stepped onto the beach. The sight of Josh, dressed in a white shirt and khaki pants, made her heart race. She still couldn't quite believe she was getting married. After everything that'd happened in Melbourne with Brendan, and then her illness, something inside her had accepted the idea that marriage wasn't going to be part of her journey. She'd missed her chance by wasting her heart on a man who didn't love her the way she loved him, and she'd never get another.

The nausea from that morning had passed, now excitement beat in her chest. She'd pushed away the panic and thoughts of illness returning, and focused instead on the wedding, just as Doctor Ash had recommended. It'd seemed to work. She felt vibrant, strong, and alive.

Her eyes brimmed with tears as she walked closer and saw the look on Josh's face. His mouth turned up at the ends and his eyes gleamed with joy. He'd given her another chance at love and happiness, even when she'd thought it couldn't happen. He'd stuck by her side when she was sick and tried to push him away.

He was the man she'd always dreamed of marrying without realising it. And he was waiting for her at the end of a short, sandy aisle.

She gulped in a short breath to keep from crying and forced a smile onto her face.

Kate and Reeda stood at the front of the group, wearing matching gowns in teal with faux fur shrugs. Both had tears in their eyes, both smiling wobbly smiles.

Mima and Betty stood on one side of the aisle. Mima nodded when Bindi caught her eye, then dabbed at her face with a handkerchief. Next to her, Alex and Duncan looked stoic and strong.

Kangaroo paw flowers were strung in bunches to the ends of the aisle. White plastic chairs were arranged in neat rows, their legs digging into the soft sand. Behind Josh stood an archway woven with fresh flowers from the garden. Jack had made the archway. He said it was worth the effort since he suspected they'd have many a wedding at the inn in the years to come and they might as well prepare for it.

Bindi was glad — he'd carved it and painted it with care. It was special because of who'd made it, and the love he'd built it with. She didn't want a big wedding, lots of fuss or expense. All she needed was her family and friends by her side, the sound of waves enveloping her and the outline of the inn that'd changed her life in the distance, hidden by a thicket of coastal gums.

On the other side of the aisle, Jack's son Stefano, standing with his wife and children, smiled at her. After losing so much of her family, it warmed her heart to gain so many new members. She'd felt alone when Nan died. Even her sisters hadn't been enough to fill the void, especially when they bickered and squabbled over what to do with the Waratah. But now, she knew she wasn't alone. She had a family who cared for her, was there when she needed them, and her heart was full.

Jack kissed her cheek. "I'm so happy for you, love," he whispered.

She smiled through a blur of tears. "Thank you, Jack."

Josh took her hands, kissed her cheek, then recited his vows as the pastor read them out. It was Bindi's turn next, and she kept her gaze firmly on Josh's blue eyes as she vowed to spend her life with him, through sickness and in health, until death.

The words brought a lump to her throat.

When finally the pastor encouraged Josh to kiss the bride, a wave of joy swept through her. They were married. Husband and wife.

He cupped her cheeks with his hands and kissed her tenderly. Sparks lit up her lips and travelled down the length of her spine. When he stepped back, she grinned, then moved forwards to kiss him again as the small crowd behind them cheered.

❧ 38 ❧

CABARITA BEACH

The pair of hooded plovers that circled overhead, calling their distinctive cry, were the same blighters who swooped him as soon as spring began, and they had little ones scurrying across the sand behind him. They'd settle in the sky with the sun behind them, so he had to strain his eyes, hand tented across his forehead, to see them. Then, they'd swoop as soon as he looked away, retinas burning.

Charlie's eyes narrowed as he poured the last of the water he'd saved from a bucket in his shower onto the small garden bed behind the cottage. It'd been a dry winter and he did his bit to save water whenever he could. Ever since Nan had moved in, she'd been planting flowers and bushes here and there around the place. Only made more work as far as he was concerned. The entire cottage was surrounded by natural scrub, brush, pandanus bushes and coastal gums, but she had to grow more. Of course.

He shook his head with a chuckle to himself and righted the now empty bucket, then carried it back to the house.

Inside, the small kitchen still smelled of the eggs Nan had scrambled for them both when they'd risen at dawn. He wiped the pan she'd used dry, then stowed it back in a cupboard along with the other pots and pans he'd accumulated over the years.

The cottage was more a home to him now than any place he'd ever lived, other than his childhood home of course. He still missed that, sometimes with an ache in his chest that couldn't be sated by anyone or anything. He figured that was something he had to live with until he died, that empty pain, the grief of losing a home too young, never to return again.

He'd visited the house when he was in Bathurst, but it wasn't the same now. The new owners had painted it, given it a rendered finish and a second story. The red bricks were gone, now it was a strange shade of grey. Bicycles had littered the yard, and children played beneath a sprinkler that showered the grass with drops of shimmering spray.

He was glad the place was still filled with joy, with children and laughter. Yet, he couldn't help the ache in his chest. It came and went. Usually showed up when he wasn't expecting it, then left again as soon as he managed to think about something else. But losing his parents, never being able to truly go home again, having to watch as his sister's memories faded and putting her in a home well before her time, those things stayed with him. He could go on in life, but the feeling of loss never went away.

Reeda, Kate, and Bindi had that to carry with them. They'd lost their parents at an age when they should've been carefree, living it up in Sydney with their friends. Instead, they'd had to give up their home as well, move north, and start again. He knew it'd been hard on them. It'd been almost unbearable for Edie, and for him as well. But that was behind them.

Now, if only they could get the girls to visit, to get along with one another long enough to enjoy some time at the inn with he and Edie, they could finally tell them the truth about their heritage. Not to mention the fact that he and Edie were married. They still hadn't broached the subject with the girls, much to his dismay. He'd reminded Edie that morning, in fact. She'd murmured something about doing it soon. As soon as she could get all her granddaughters together in one room. He'd shaken his head at that — when would that happen? Perhaps they should just do it over the phone, he wasn't getting any younger.

Charlie slid his feet into a pair of work boots by the back door, then tramped outside to get his tool belt from the small shed in the garden. He had a few things to fix at the stables this morning, then he'd promised Edie he'd look into getting some paint swatches. She hadn't agreed to paint the inn, not yet, but he was working on it. She'd gotten eccentric in her old age, didn't like anything in her life to change. But he couldn't blame her. Change hadn't been kind to her over the years.

Edie had left already. She liked to take an early morning walk along the beach at the cove, before she went into the inn to get started on the day. No doubt Mima was already there, preparing breakfast for the inn's guests.

Sometimes he wondered how they'd managed it. The three of them, living on the north coast of New South Wales, all running an inn together. He never would've imagined it back when they were scampering around Bathurst together as teenagers. Still, he couldn't complain. He'd dreamed of living somewhere warm, a place he could sink his toes into the sand, and here he was. He'd even become a surf life saver, had dragged befuddled tourists out of the ocean for ten years before he'd hung up his towel.

He was too old for all that now. At least, that was what Edie had told him. He'd been certain he could manage it for a while longer, although truth be told he could do without flinging himself into cold water, or having a wave smash him into the sand these days. Perhaps he was too old after all, though on days like today he didn't feel it. Felt on top of the world, in fact. He'd convinced Edie to take the afternoon off to spend it with him. Perhaps they'd go lawn bowling, isn't that what people their age did? Or maybe they'd see a movie, though he had no idea what was showing.

Whatever they did, they'd be together. And after four years of marriage, he found he still looked forward to spending time with his wife the way he had as a teenaged boy who longed to hold her hand for just a moment, if only she'd let him.

He grinned and shook his head. Mima called him an old softie, and she was right about that. He'd grown soft in his later years, and it didn't bother him one bit.

Charlie climbed into his truck and backed it up, then accelerated down the narrow, winding driveway towards the inn. The bush closed in on both sides of the trail, throwing dappled light across the hood that danced and flickered as he drove.

The Waratah Inn appeared through an opening at the end of the drive. He stopped and set the truck in park, then climbed out to open the gate. He hesitated a moment, the gate's lock in one hand, his other hand resting on the fence post it was attached to. The inn shimmered in the morning sunlight, its peeling pink paint seemed to recover in the golden light, and the inn looked almost new for a moment with the glare behind it.

He'd grown to love the place almost as much as Edie did.

He hated to admit it, because he'd often admonished her that she was too attached to the building for her own good. That she should sell up and move away with him, somewhere that didn't involve folding bedsheets all morning, and catering to the whims of a revolving door of guests.

But she'd never been willing to consider it. Thought of the inn as her legacy, the thing she'd hand over to the girls — the only thing she had left to give them of any worth. That was what she'd said, and the tears in her eyes had quieted his objections.

Now, he understood. He'd lived at the inn long enough to be drawn in by its charms. He couldn't sell it either, it was as much a part of he and Edie as anything else they'd experienced. And after leaving behind homes and loved ones so many times over the years, neither one of them could bear to do it again. The Waratah Inn was their home, and they'd stay there for as long as they could manage it.

He parked the truck by the carport behind the inn and strode to the stables to fix some broken palings.

He was hammering a nail into a fence post when he heard the scream. At first, he wasn't sure he'd heard right. He stopped hammering, one nail still held between his lips, and cocked his head to listen.

Another scream, this time more of a wail actually. He dropped the hammer, spat out the nail, and ran in the direction of the sound.

His heart thudded against his ribs as he ran, his breath even and steady. Something was wrong, very wrong. The sound had come from behind the inn, close to the chook coop. He rounded the coop, his pace accelerating.

Mima crouched on the ground by the trail that led down to the cove. She was bent over something, someone, and rocking back and forth on her heels.

His heart fell. No.

When he reached Edie's prone figure, he fell to the ground beside her, his knees stabbing with pain as they met the earth. Mima's tearstained face turned to look up at him, her eyes were slits, her mouth a circle.

"Edie, Edie!" he shouted.

He lifted Edie's head, to cradle in his lap. His throat closed over, as a lump built in the space behind his tongue.

"Edie! Wake up!"

He checked her pulse, her breathing. She had no pulse, no breath against his cheek as he leaned close. Her skin was cold. How long had she lain there?

After years of training as a life saver, he knew it was no use. She'd been there too long, was too cold. She was gone.

His eyes squeezed shut as he lifted his face to the sky. "No, no!"

Tears broke free and trailed down his cheeks, as he bent to kiss her lips. "Edie, don't leave me," he said. "Not now, not after we finally found each other again."

Mima shuddered beside him, her body wracked with sobs. She rested a hand on his back, and his gaze met hers.

He shook his head. "What do I do?"

Mima sobbed. "Oh, honey, there's nothing you can do now but hold her a little while. I'll call the ambulance."

Mima patted his back, then lumbered to her feet and headed to the inn. When she returned, he still held Edie, his arms around her as she lay, half in his lap, half on the earth. He was talking to her about the past, things they'd said and done, things he'd never said and wished he had. He felt a kind of peace come over him as he spoke.

She was gone. His beautiful girl. He'd never see her smile again, never feel her touch. Never know what it was to be kissed by those lips again. He needed time, more time. He wasn't ready to let go just yet. If only he could force his mind to remember every detail, the lines on her face, the curve of her lips, the way her lashes touched her cheeks and the stains of dirt on her fingertips from where she'd pushed so many flower bulbs and seeds into the earth.

They'd had a second chance together, he and Edie. He couldn't regret any moment of it. They'd formed a life, they'd lived together in the cottage he'd built with his own two hands, and they'd been happy. He looked at her again, saw that her lips were turned up at the edges. The hint of a smile had lifted her features before she passed. It was all he could ask for. There was nothing more to say.

EPILOGUE

CABARITA BEACH

The shelves of the refrigerator were backlit, and the appliance hummed steadily as Bindi scanned its contents.

"Do you think you have enough fruit?" she asked.

Kate peered over her shoulder. "Plenty. It's the same amount we always have."

"What about bread? Should we make more?"

"We? Don't you mean me?" Kate pushed the door shut then pressed her hands to her hips. "We've got everything we need. Stop worrying."

Bindi chewed on her lip. "Did I remind you about the electrician? He's coming Wednesday to check out the wiring—"

"I know, I know, you told me."

"And you've got to follow up on the linens. The laundry isn't always great at meeting our deadlines."

"Bindi! Enough! You've got to leave, or you'll miss your flight. We've got it all under control. Reeda's coming on full-time while you're away, she's across it all and will take care of the inn as if you were here yourself. Stop fretting."

She couldn't help worrying. Ever since they'd inherited the inn, she'd barely had a day off. And now she was taking an entire month to travel to Hawaii for their honeymoon. There had to be something she'd forgotten, something important. She should run through the list she'd written in her day planner in the office.

"I'm just going to check my day planner..."

Kate leapt in front of her. "No, you've checked it a dozen times. It won't say anything different than it did the last time you looked at it. You've thought of everything, and if you missed anything, we'll figure it out. We're not completely clueless you know."

Kate smiled, placed a hand on each of Bindi's arms. "Enjoy yourself. You deserve a break after the year you've had."

Bindi smiled back at her. She was looking forward to getting away with Josh, but everything she usually took care of at the inn kept flitting across her mind's eye, taunting her.

"You're right, I'm sorry. I'm sure you'll manage fine without me."

Kate nodded. "We'll miss you, but we all want you to enjoy yourself. It's your honeymoon, you'll have a blast."

Bindi inhaled a sharp breath. Truth be told, she was a little nervous. She'd never lived with a man before, except Dad and that was so many years ago she could barely remember what it was like. The only thing she could recall about what it was like to live with him in that moment was a picture of him rushing out the door for work in the morning, or Mum calling for him to take the rubbish out.

"What's wrong?" asked Kate.

Bindi sighed. "I'm nervous. I've never lived with a man, not since Dad, and what if I'm a complete slob and Josh can't stand me? What if I'm too much for him? I don't know how to do this... We've only been living together here at the inn for a few days and the whole time I've been anxious about making a good impression. I'm a wreck."

Kate chortled. "Ah, I see. Don't stress yourself out over things like that. He's new to marriage, just the same way you are. You'll find your way together. And trust me, you're not a slob, you're actually really easy to live with. I'm something of an expert on the subject."

"You think?"

"Absolutely." Kate gave a determined nod. "You're my favourite person in the whole world — don't tell Alex or Reeda. You're easy going, fun and of course disgustingly beautiful in the morning when you haven't even brushed your hair yet. Stop fixating on what could go wrong and relax. Things are looking up. You're healthy, the test results came back negative, you were just anxious about the wedding, everything's great, enjoy it. You've got to learn to chill."

"Okay, I'll try to relax."

"It'll be much easier to relax away from this place and all of us. Hawaii is the perfect place for the two of you to find your rhythm as a couple."

Bindi smiled. "I'm looking forward to Hawaii."

"I'm jealous," said Kate with a wink.

Jack hoisted Bindi and Josh's luggage into the back of the taxi. Bindi watched him, squinting against the setting sun. Josh could've carried out the luggage, but Bindi knew Jack would want to do it. He didn't like goodbyes, preferred to have something to do with his hands. He'd always been like that. Josh smiled at her over the taxi and climbed into the back seat.

Mima slipped her hand over Bindi's arm. "You have a wonderful time, my darling girl."

Bindi patted Mima's hand, then kissed her weathered cheek. "We will. Thanks for helping out so much around here. It's been crazy with the restaurant and all the guests, not to mention the wedding."

"Don't mention it," replied Mima. "I love being here and spending time with you girls. Although you're not girls anymore, are you? I always think of you that way, but of course you're women now. All three of you married — it's hard to believe."

"I'm so grateful you're in my life, Mima."

The older woman's eyes glistened with tears. "Me too, love, me too." She squeezed Bindi's arm. "The older you get the more time flies, and the more sentimental you get over how fast it's passing by." She inhaled a slow breath. "This is one of those moments in life, my darling girl. Take a hold of it, impress it on your heart, and never let go."

Bindi swallowed around the lump in her throat. She nodded at Mima, embraced her then gazed around the inn's front garden. The inn stood tall and majestic beside them. Yellow walls rose up high above with white trim gleaming in the winter sun's pale golden rays.

A kookaburra laughed in the distance, answered quickly by another. Their raucous calls echoed through the air, then ended as suddenly as they'd begun. The hush of the ocean as waves found the sand created a steady rhythm, a backdrop to the call of birds and the swelling chorus of cicadas who greeted the coming night with a steady hum.

On the white railing that ran around the verandah, Cocoa climbed like a trapeze on a tightrope. One foot in front of the other, she wobbled as she walked. Her young charge, now fully grown, emerged from the possum house that Bruno, their contractor, had built on a branch high up in the gum tree that caressed the inn with leafy fingertips. Bindi had named the youngster Ned, after Ned Kelly, the infamous Australian bush ranger, when the possum snuck into the kitchen and stole fruit night after night until they realised just how he was getting inside and plugged the hole in the fly screen.

The young possum circled down a post, tail curled to hold on tight, then followed Cocoa along the railing. Bindi jogged over to greet the two of them. She pulled an apple from each jacket pocket and handed the fruit to the possums. The creatures immediately sat on their hindquarters, grasped the apples in their front paws and bit into the fruit with a crunch of powerful teeth.

"I was hoping I'd run into the two of you before I left. Take care of the place while I'm gone, okay?"

She patted Cocoa's head, then tickled Ned beneath his furry chin, now damp with apple juice. Ned rested a paw on Bindi's hand and left it there while he continued to eat.

"Bindi, we've got to go. The plane will leave without us!" called Josh from the back seat of the taxi.

She gave the possums one last pat, then hurried over to where Kate, Reeda, Duncan, and Alex stood. She embraced each one in turn, murmuring goodbyes and promises to relax and enjoy herself. Apparently, they all knew her better than she'd realised.

Jack met her there, encircled her in his arms and rested his chin on her head. "Have a great time, love."

She nodded and pressed her chin to his chest. "I will. Take care of yourself."

"Of course."

"I'll miss you."

"Me too."

She stepped back, and he reached for her hand, holding it in his. His eyes misted and she frowned.

"What's wrong?"

He shook his head. "I'll be forever grateful to you, you know?"

"What for?" she asked.

"For discovering the truth about me. I missed knowing your Dad... I mean, I met him, but I never really got to spend time with him as his father." Jack swallowed, his eyes filling with tears. "And I didn't want to miss that with you three as well. I wanted to tell you about who I was, that Edie and I were married, so many times. But then, the opportunity didn't come up, and Edie made me promise not to say anything until she was ready. When she passed...it didn't seem right to say anything with her gone. I didn't even know if you'd believe me..."

Bindi shook her head, her throat aching. "I'm glad I figured it out as well. If I hadn't, we'd never get to spend this time with you as our family. I mean, we've always seen you as family, but now we know you really are. You're stuck with us... legally." She laughed around the lump in her throat.

He chuckled as well, before wiping his eyes with the back of his hand. "So, thanks for finding me out."

She nodded. "You're welcome."

"And you can call me something other than Jack now...if you want to."

"How about Grandad? I heard Margaret and Sarah calling you that, so I figured..."

"That would be perfect," he replied.

She smiled, the ache in her throat fading. "See you in a month."

"I'll be here," he said.

She climbed into the cab and rolled down the window to lean out through the opening. As the taxi pulled down the driveway, she waved furiously to the group, who waved back. Kate looped her arm around Jack, Reeda slid her hand into

Mima's and Bindi felt she might burst with happiness at the sight of it all. The vehicle accelerated onto the road, and the inn faded from view. The last thing she saw was the hanging sign that announced, The Waratah Inn, as it swung in the gentle evening breeze. Then it, too, was gone. She spun around in her seat to face the front, hugging herself with both arms.

Josh's hand found hers and pried it free from her waist, squeezing gently. "You okay?"

She smiled, scooted closer to him, and rested her head on his shoulder. "I'm fine. Just...well, happy actually."

"Good to hear," he replied.

"Did you ever think we'd be here? On our way to Hawaii, an old married couple?"

His eyes twinkled. "Married, yes, old no way! We've got years before you can pull that one out. And there are so many things we'll be doing before then."

He leaned in for a kiss and her heart skipped a beat at the intensity and passion in his eyes. "Mr Owens, you're making me blush."

He kissed her again. "Good. You need more blushing in your life. My goal for this trip is to make you blush every single day for an entire month."

She threw back her head and laughed, her body flooding with a sense of peace. Marriage to Josh would be fun. Then he kissed her again and her mind emptied of every thought but his lips.

THE END

ALSO BY LILLY MIRREN

Liz Cranwell is divorced and alone at Christmas. When her friends convince her to holiday at The Waratah Inn, she's dreading her first Christmas on her own. Instead she discovers that strangers can be the balm to heal the wounds of a lonely heart in this heartwarming Christmas story.

EMERALD COVE SERIES

Cottage on Oceanview Lane

When a renowned book editor returns to her roots, she rediscovers her strength & her passion in this heartwarming novel.

Seaside Manor Bed and Breakfast

The Seaside Manor Bed and Breakfast has been an institution in Emerald Cove for as long as anyone can remember. But things are changing and Diana is nervous about what the future might hold for her and her husband, not to mention the historic business.

GLOSSARY OF TERMS

Dear reader,

Since this book is set in Australia there may be some terms you're not familiar with. I've included them below to help you out! I hope they didn't trip you up too much.

Cheers, Lilly xo

Terms

Beesting - a pastry filled with custard.

Biscuit - cookie

Blighter - a person regarded with contempt

Chew the fat - chat in a leisurely and prolonged way.

Cupboard - Australians use this term to describe cabinets, pantries, closets and more.

Formal - a high school dance held in year 10, then again in year 12, similar to the prom.

Journo - slang for journalist.

'Love' - a term of endearment for anyone from your spouse to a perfect stranger

News-ohs - people in the news business

Panadol - paracetamol, a Tylenol equivalent

Washer - *wash cloth*

Right as rain - things will work out and be perfectly well

Ringtail possum - adorable, furry marsupial with a curling tail, grey-brown coat, big eyes and small pink nose

RSL Club - Returned Services League club, for returned war veterans.

Tea - used to describe either a hot beverage made from leaves, or the evening meal

DISCUSSION GUIDE

Book Club Questions

1. What were the things that most rocked Bindi's world at the beginning of the book?

2. Discuss the ways Bindi grew throughout the story.

3. Talk about the relationship between Edie and Charlie.

4. What was Mima's role in the book?

5. What did the renovations at the inn represent in the lives of the Summer Sisters?

6. Discuss the reasons the sisters had drawn apart over the years.

7. How did the sisters' relationship change over the course of the series?

8. Do you think Kate will be satisfied in her career working at the inn?

9. How do you feel about Reeda and Duncan's struggle with childlessness and how that was resolved, or not, in the story?

10. Did Charlie do the right thing by not contacting Edie when his memory returned?

ABOUT THE AUTHOR

Lilly Mirren lives in Brisbane, Australia with her husband and three children.

Lilly always dreamed of being a writer and is now living that dream. She is a graduate of both the University of Queensland, where she studied International Relations and Griffith University, where she completed a degree in Information Technology.

When she's not writing, she's chasing her children, doing housework or spending time with friends.

Sign up for her newsletter and stay up on all the latest Lilly book news.

And follow her on:

Website: lillymirren.com
Facebook: https://www.facebook.com/authorlillymirren/
Twitter: https://twitter.com/lilly_mirren
BookBub: https://www.bookbub.com/authors/lilly-mirren

Made in the USA
Monee, IL
13 June 2020

33554209R00197